Rose Wilkins had an idyllic childhood in the Welsh countryside before being sent to an all-girls' boarding school. She survived the experience and started writing while studying Classics at university, as an escape from all the gloom and gore on her reading list. She now lives and works in London.

I ♥ GENIE

Wishful Thinking

Rose Wilkins

MACMILLAN

First published 2007 by Macmillan Children's Books
a division of Macmillan Publishers Limited
20 New Wharf Road, London N1 9RR
Basingstoke and Oxford
www.panmacmillan.com

Associated companies throughout the world

ISBN: 978-0-330-43880-3

1 3 5 7 9 8 6 4 2

A CIP catalogue record for this book is available from
the British Library.

Typeset by Intype Libra Ltd
Printed and bound in Great Britain by Mackays of Chatham plc, Kent

To my mother and father –
for all those years of saying the right things
and always laughing in the right places.

It was 'Make a Wish for the World Day' at Conville Secondary and, after nearly an hour of debate, the Year Ten citizenship class had identified their three most burning ambitions:

1. Peace in the Middle East
2. An End to Global Warming
3. A Cure for Cancer

Of course, the unofficial version of this list was a little more modest – once you ticked off global stardom and a billionaire's bank balance, that is. As Francesca Goldsworthy explained to Fran Roper, the girls' priorities went something along the lines of:

1. Better Boobs/Bum/Legs/Nose
2. Snogging a Sex God
3. No More Bad Hair Days

And the male version was even simpler:

1. Naked Girls
2. Naked Girls
3. Naked Girls

Fran laughed but shook her head. 'Yeah, well, you're just a bitter old cynic. I still reckon the argument about child poverty or saving the polar ice caps was genuin – argh –'

Fran had become entangled with her PE kit. As usual, she was weighed down with a clutch of dog-eared folders and plastic bags spilling over various bits of locker-room debris. As usual, Francesca saun-tered along with just the one knitted bag swinging on her shoulder, a bag that never seemed to hold anything more than her mobile phone, cherry lip-balm and a Tate Modern notebook. As usual, she was magnificently indifferent to the chaos in Fran's wake.

'Don't forget the whales,' she said sardonically. 'Saving the Whales was popular too. Just five zillion points below getting the chance to cop off with Quinn Adams . . . C'mon, Fran, admit it: if you had the chance to wish for anything you wanted, you'd be just as selfish as everyone else.'

'And you wouldn't?'

'Wouldn't be selfish or wouldn't want to kiss Quinn?'

'Both.'

Francesca smiled. It was her new smile – an

amused, mysterious sort of smile, as if she knew things you didn't, thought Fran. Which was ridiculous, because best friends know everything about each other and the two Francescas had been best friends for ten years, ever since they were both five-and-a-quarter and chucking bits of Lego around the Milson Road Infant School. 'Yes to selfish,' Francesca said at last, 'but no to Quinn. Not my type.'

Hmm. Fran would have thought the desirability of Quinn Adams was something above and beyond personal taste. It wasn't just a matter of looks, though he was, everyone agreed, impossibly delectable: long and lean with dirty blond hair and eyes the colour of dark chocolate. His voice was dark and chocolatey too, and the star attraction of Firedog, the band he played in outside school. It was this that raised him above your average Year Twelve pin-up – 'Yes, but it's the music *I'm* interested in,' his groupies would proclaim, in spite of the fact that hardly anyone had actually heard Firedog perform.

'OK, so what is your type, at the moment I mean?' Francesca's last type had been an über-blond German-exchange student. The type before that had had spiky hair and a nose-ring and worked in a record shop. Francesca had never been especially gushing about either.

'I don't know,' she said after a while. 'Sexy but

smart, streetwise but sensitive . . . a bit different, I suppose.'

'Well, I'd have thought Quinn is all those things.'

'Maybe he is. But one thing's for sure, I wouldn't want to be just another one of his groupies. Because we're above all that, right?'

'We are?'

'Of course we are!' Francesca tossed her head. 'There's no point letting men have it too easy. I don't want to waste my time hanging breathlessly on some bloke's every word. I want him to hang breathlessly on *my* every word. You should remember that too.' She gave Fran's hair an affectionate tug, then turned right and walked away down the street.

Fran looked after her for a moment before trudging off in the opposite direction. It was nice to know that Francesca felt the two of them were 'above all that', united in their superiority to the rest of Quinn's groupies. It was even nicer to know that Francesca wasn't interested in Quinn anyway. Because although best friends should know everything about each other, there are some things that should be kept private, special, at least for a little while. Things like the exact moment thirty-five days, twenty-two hours and fifty-three minutes ago, when Fran realized that Quinn Adams was the only person in the world for whom she'd gladly break her heart.

It happened as she was coming out of the music suite late one Thursday after school. Fran used to be in the school choir, but everyone knew the choir was a bit of a joke, and it wasn't long before she decided she was better off doing her own thing. Last term she'd discovered a stack of songbooks in one of the practice rooms and she was steadily working her way through them. It was a rather odd collection – everything from Broadway show tunes to a Mozart aria – but Fran didn't mind. She didn't mind that there was no one to hear her either . . . well, not that much. One day, *someday*, she would show people what she could do. In the meantime, it was enough for her to know that the sound she made when she sang was supple and self-assured, and very different to her usual quiet, rather anxious self.

The song she was working on this particular afternoon was both melancholy and seductive, all about sleepless nights and hopeless love. So she couldn't help feeling that maybe fate had taken a hand when she walked out of the practice room and straight into the arms of Quinn Adams.

Well, 'straight into the arms' was perhaps a slight exaggeration – he was coming round the corner so fast that they went smack into each other and Fran would have fallen if he hadn't put out his hands to keep her balanced. For one glorious moment she stood there, swaying slightly, as the most desirable boy in the school held her steady and looked deeply into her eyes, his expression tender with concern.

'God, I'm so sorry! I didn't mean—'

'Don't worry,' Quinn said graciously, although he had been the one charging round the corner without looking. 'Just as long as you're all right.'

'Oh yes . . .' breathed Fran, who was having difficulty keeping upright now that Quinn had let her go. Her arms still tingled from where he'd held her. It was as if she'd been bewitched, just like in the song. 'I've been practising my singing, you see,' she blurted out, and then turned red. What an idiotic thing to say – it was as if she was some little kid, trying to impress a grown-up! It was all the more pathetic since Quinn was doubtless on his way to the big music room, the one with all the amplifiers and high-tech stuff, getting ready to work on Firedog's latest hit. But Quinn didn't laugh at her.

'So you're a musician too,' he said, as if they were equals. 'What's your name?'

'F-F-Fran. Francesca, I mean.' Might as well give her name its full three-syllable glory.

'Francesca? That's a pretty name.' Quinn pushed back a hank of tawny blond hair and gazed into her eyes again, smiling. Fran had never been looked at that way before. 'Take care now,' he said, and then he was gone.

That was six Thursdays ago. Now it was Friday, and with nothing to look forward to over the weekend but homework and chores and daydreaming. The hush of an audience . . . a spotlit stage . . . melting dark eyes meeting hers across a microphone . . .

'Fran! At last!' Her mother came clattering down the stairs the moment she heard Fran's key in the door. Mrs Roper's long, damp hair was falling down over her face, she was speaking through a mouthful of kirby grips and her new skirt was twisted round the wrong way. 'You haven't forgotten you're supposed to be babysitting Beth and Mickey, have you? We have to be out of that door by six thirty if we're ever going to make the restaurant on time! Halfway across the other side of London it is, and your father's going to be late back from work . . . damn it, there goes my mobile –' She twisted her head and shouted up the stairs, 'MICKEY, MICKEY, WILL YOU GET MY PHONE? Oh dear, he'll never find it – IN THE BATHROOM, MUNCHKIN! THE BATHROOM!'

The hallway was the usual muddle of discarded trainers, umbrellas, tennis rackets and plastic toys belonging to Fran's little brother and sister. Fran dropped her school bag on to a pile of shoes and made her way to the kitchen, where there was a distinct burning smell. Baked beans, she guessed, from the blackened remains smoking on the stove. Her mother hastened after her.

'Will you please wait a minute and listen to me? This is *important*, Fran. Right, Mickey and Beth have already had their tea and there's some quiche for you in the fridge. The number for the restaurant is on the pinboard. Or it was a minute ago. Hang on, it's by the bread-bin—'

'Where's Beth?' This was Fran's little sister, who, aged two and a half, was the youngest member of the family and had come as a bit of a surprise to all concerned.

'Sitting in front of a *Teletubbies* video. I'll put her to bed before we leave so she shouldn't be any trouble – oh, hell's bells –' Fran's mum had just trodden on a mutant robot toy with her bare foot. She began to hop around the kitchen, cursing. 'Will *nobody* in this wretched family ever tidy up after themselves?'

'Well, it's not my fault the kitchen's always such a tip—'

'I know, I know. Never mind. Just take that pan off the hob, will you? What an awful smell! And I only left it five minutes . . . Ow, my poor foot!'

The front door slammed shut, followed by a crashing sound and more curses, this time from Fran's dad.

'WHO'S THE IDIOT WHO LEFT THEIR BAG RIGHT WHERE I COULD TRIP OVER IT?'

'IN HERE, DARLING,' Fran's mum yelled back, still clutching her foot. The last strand of hair had escaped from its grip and was now tumbling over her hot pink face. As if on cue, the howls of a weeping toddler could be heard rising above Mr Roper's bellows. 'Fran, Fran, be an angel and go and see what Beth's crying about, OK? And then could you phone the Ridleys for me and say we're running late?' She began to put on her mascara, using a saucepan lid as a mirror.

Finally, just after seven, Mr and Mrs Roper whirled out of the house. Fran, meanwhile, was scraping at the baked-bean pan and mulling over Francesca's remark about blokes who hung on your every word. It was easy for *her* to say, of course. You looked at Francesca and straight away you could tell that she was interesting and sophisticated, a girl who was going places. Whereas Fran would probably turn into the kind of woman who goes out smelling of baked beans and with mascara down her cheeks. Hunched over the sink, she was uncomfortably aware of how like her mother she looked – the same long, fair, dishevelled hair, the same plump flushed face, the same anxious grey eyes.

She was still wrestling with self-pity and scouring pads when her brother wandered into the kitchen to fetch himself a glass of milk.

'Hello, Fran, would you like to play a game of Snap with me?' he enquired sweetly.

'Not particularly. And before you ask, not Tiddlywinks either.'

'OK.' He blinked at her owlishly over the rim of his glass. 'Please will you help me learn my lines then?'

Fran sighed. 'What's this one about?'

'A new kind of fish finger. I have to be a boy who doesn't like fish but then he discovers Captain Cod's Crumble Bites and sails away on a pirate ship.'

'Sounds gruesome.'

At eight years old, Mickey possessed a geeky charm that had made him the star of several successful advertising campaigns. A talent scout had spotted him in the supermarket and three weeks later he was the Face of Everfresh Toilet Spray. It wasn't something anyone had planned, and in fact little Mickey's burgeoning career – and the endless round of castings, call-backs, film shoots and promotional appearances involved – was one of the main reasons for the Roper's state of perpetual harassment. Nonetheless, Mickey wasn't the spoilt horror most people assumed he'd be. He was instead the kind of unnaturally wholesome child who genuinely believes that a glass of milk and a handful of dried raisins can be classed as a 'treat'. Fran – hapless binger on chocolate, hopeless counter of calories – thought this was yet another of life's great injustices.

She ended up spending Friday night yo-ho-ho-ing away in her role as Captain Cod. She could never resist Mickey for long and, besides, he *did* look rather adorable in his pirate hat.

Both Fran's parents had jobs (Jill worked part-time in a GP's practice and Harry worked at a bank) and so they invested a lot of time and energy in juggling office life with Beth's day-care and Mickey's career. They spent most of Saturday catching up on the appointments and chores they'd let slip during the week, and most of Sunday slumped in front of the television in an exhausted daze. The next weekend, they always promised each other, would be different . . .

As for Fran, it was more or less taken for granted that she would spend some of every weekend out and about with Francesca. In fact, when they were younger, Francesca was more likely to be found in the Roper's household than with her own parents. Mrs Goldsworthy was a TV producer and Mr Goldsworthy quite a well-known interior designer, and neither of them were particularly tolerant of secret dens under the stairs or mud-pie factories in their kitchen or Barbie fashion shows on the dining-room table.

Now that the two girls were older, however, Fran

often found herself wishing that her family would tidy up after themselves a bit more, or at least get rid of that hideous tartan sofa in the living room. Although Francesca's house had been made over countless times, the end result was unfailingly airy and uncluttered and highly polished. Her parents were highly polished-looking too, and were always very nice to Fran, in their graceful, distant way. So now whenever Fran and Francesca met up outside school it was either at Francesca's house or, more usually, in one of the chic little coffee bars Francesca liked so much. Francesca used to hate coffee, claiming it tasted of cat's pee, but she'd got in the habit of buying a double espresso macchiato on the way in to school, then sipping it languidly during morning registration.

This weekend, however, they hadn't made any plans to meet up. They hadn't done anything together last weekend either, and had really seen very little of each other outside lessons. Fran told herself that this was partly her fault for all the times she'd slipped off to the music suite to practise her singing and – might as well admit it – in the hope of bumping into Quinn again. So after wrestling with an especially gruesome section of her maths homework for most of Sunday afternoon, she decided she might as well ring Francesca and see if she was at a loose end.

'Hey, it's me.'

'Fran? Is that you?'

'Yeah, hi. I'm kind of drowning in quadratic equations over here and feel I could do with a break. So I thought maybe we –' Fran could hear voices in the background. 'Sorry, have you got visitors?'

'Just Zara and Sadie.'

'Oh.' She knew it was unreasonable, but Fran felt hurt that Francesca was hanging out with people from school and hadn't thought to include her. Zara and Sadie were two of the most popular girls in their year even though, to the casual observer, they were polar opposites. While Sadie was soft and blonde and dimply, Zara was dark and sharp-edged. Sadie played with her hair, Zara with her lighter. Sadie's trademark look was fluffy angora sweaters, Zara had piercings in mysterious places. Sadie was sugary, Zara was spiky, but both, in their own way, were equally intimidating. Until recently, neither Fran nor Francesca had had much to do with them, and Fran was quite happy to leave it that way.

'Yeah, they came round to listen to those new CDs I bought.' There was a pause. 'You should come over.'

'But if you're busy—'

'What, with this bunch of losers? No chance.' Zara, or maybe Sadie, shouted out something rude in the background and Francesca laughed. 'See you in a bit, OK?'

'Wait – Francesca?'

'What?'

'I don't want you to feel that, you know, you *have* to invite me. Because it's no big deal.'

'Don't be daft, Fran-flakes. Of course I want you to come. I was going to call you anyway.'

Fran caught up with the others in the Goldsworthy's huge drawing room. 'You know what,' Sadie was saying, 'this house would be a totally awesome place to throw a party.' (Sadie had spent the first eight years of her life in California and the next seven perfecting what she fondly imagined to be a US accent. It didn't convince everyone, but at Conville Secondary was considered wildly glamorous.)

'It's certainly very *Hello*!' drawled Zara, who was impressed and trying not to show it.

The Goldsworthys often had their home featured in lifestyle or design magazines and all the main rooms had been through several transformations over the years. At present the drawing room was painted a pale pistachio green with a chocolate-brown sofa and chairs in specially aged leather. There were no ornaments except for a very beautiful bowl made from a greenish, gold-flecked glass. All in all, it was the kind of place where you felt you left smudges just by sitting there.

However, Fran had been a regular visitor at this house for most of her life and so she plumped herself down on the sofa as if it had been the tatty tartan thing in her own sitting room. 'Hello, everyone,' she said.

'Oh . . . Fran . . .' said Zara, as if she couldn't quite figure out what Fran was doing there.

'All right?' said Sadie, with a super-cute, super-chummy smile.

'Have a biscuit,' said Francesca.

Silence fell.

'Well –' began Fran.

'Well –' started Francesca.

'So we were saying,' cut in Zara, tossing her head, 'that the way Anna Wilton has behaved to poor Rob Crawford is *so* not on.'

'Yeah,' continued Sadie, 'he treats her like a princess and then she turns round and comes out with all this crap about him pressuring her into *whatever* –'

'– when anyone can see she's the one who's been stringing him along just cos she's got a crush on his best mate,' Zara finished.

'Well, if Rob's too stupid to realize a girl's only going out with him because she's a Firedog groupie, then he probably deserves to get dumped,' said Francesca coolly. 'Right, Fran?'

Fran was about to say that Rob Crawford was a lecherous creep, and the fact that he was best friends with Quinn was one of life's great mysteries. Unfortunately Sadie got in first: 'Oh, but I think Rob's actually, like, totally caring? Deep down, I mean.' Soon they were embroiled in a long, complex discussion on the rights and wrongs of every failed relationship in school history. Fran joined in from time to time but her heart wasn't in it.

Afterwards, when Sadie and Zara had gone home and Fran was collecting their empty mugs and biscuit wrappers to take downstairs to the kitchen, Francesca asked her straight out what she thought of the other two.

'They're, um, good company,' said Fran cautiously.

'Yeah . . . Sadie's a bit of an airhead but she's rather sweet. And I think Zara can be quite amusing, don't you?'

Amusing? That wasn't how Fran would put it. Sadie was OK in small doses, she supposed, but everyone knew that it was a seriously bad idea to get on the wrong side of Zara Truman. Which was why it was so weird to see Zara cosying up to Francesca like she had this afternoon. Girls like her set higher standards of good looks and popularity for their mates than most boys would look for in a girlfriend.

Fran took a sidelong look at Francesca as she bent to straighten the magazines on the table. Francesca wasn't an obvious boy-beacon like Zara, with her dark, sulky face and bad-girl glamour, or Sadie, the professional cutie-pie. She didn't wear much make-up and she'd never gone in for short skirts or low-cut tops. But even so, she definitely had *something* . . . She was very slim, of course, and then there was her amazing dark reddish hair, which she used to get teased about so badly when they were little but which had somehow become part of her new, grown-up sophistication. Like her sudden fondness for espresso or all the black cashmere sweaters that had lately appeared in her wardrobe. Fran knew she was being ridiculous, but sometimes she wished she could see the old Francesca again – the freckle-faced, red-headed twiglet who thought that coffee tasted of cat's pee and that having parents who let you make mud pies in the kitchen sink was the coolest thing in the world.

'Hey, it's Francesca, isn't it?'

'H-hi, Quinn.'

'So I guess you're on the way to a lunchtime singing session.' Quinn Adams smiled at Fran as he pinned a poster to the music suite's noticeboard.

Oh my gosh, Fran swooned, he actually remembers me! She'd spent the past thirty-eight and a half days praying that she'd bump into Quinn in the music suite again, but now that she was face to face with the object of her every desire she was wondering if the stress was worth it.

'Aren't you going to tell me what you're working on?'

'I, well, you know, I like to sing lots of, uh, different stuff. I like to, sort of, um, experiment?'

'Do you now?' His voice was warm and teasing. 'So what are you experimenting with right now? Let me guess . . . could it be a love song?'

Fran blushed violently. Was Quinn Adams *flirting* with her? Get a grip, girl, she told herself. You wouldn't find Zara or Sadie reduced to quivering wrecks just because some cute guy dropped the L word into a conversation. She did a Zara-style head-toss and took a deep, steadying breath.

'Well, it's quite an old one – a Broadway classic.'

'Oh, but the old ones are always the best,' said Quinn. His face took on an intense, dreamy expression and he leaned in closer to her. 'All the great music in the world is about love, Francesca. It's the only real theme.' Their eyes met for a long moment. 'Catch you later,' he said, then he swung his bag over his shoulder and sauntered away.

'I just don't believe it. OK, girls – this is like *so* the most unbelievable thing, that could happen right now. I mean, can you *believe* it?' Sadie flung an A4 poster down on the table with a triumphant air.

Everyone dutifully leaned in to take a look. A group of girls from Fran's class had gone to Ronnie's cafe after school, but Fran was finding it hard to be sociable. It was the same day as her Quinn Adams Moment: Part II and she was still reeling. Right now, however, she could see that whatever Sadie had to tell them was going to monopolize all conversation for the next hour at least. So she leaned over Francesca's shoulder to see what the fuss was about.

It was just a plain sheet of paper, with a few lines of type:

FEMALE VOCALIST WANTED

Indie guitar band (bass, lead guitar, vocals, drums)
seeks girl singer.
Auditions Thursday, 5 p.m., School Hall

Please, no Pop Idol *wannabes*

There was a brief silence as everyone took in the significance of this announcement. Then the table erupted into a babble of excited exclamation. Quinn Adams's band was holding auditions! Well – it had to be Firedog, didn't it? Didn't it? Yes, and they wanted a *girl* singer! A girl to join the most prestigious, most exclusive and most eligible-male-packed club in school! Some lucky cow was about to spend most of her free time making sweet harmony with the Firedogs. Looking decorative with Rob Crawford. Singing duets with Quinn Adams . . .

'Who do you think is going to turn up to

audition?' asked Sarah Potock. 'You'd have to be ever so brave.'

Francesca wrinkled her nose. 'It'll be the usual love-crazed stalkers who spend their time making shrines out of Quinn's used chewing gum, I expect. Then there'll be a few leering blokes hoping to get their hands on the Firedog's leftovers. And no matter what that advert says about wannabes, *somebody's* going to arrive in gold hot pants.'

'I bet you anything Miss Duncan turns up to "supervise". She has *so* got a crush on Quinn,' put in Jessica Simmonds.

'Well, I reckon it's just a publicity stunt,' continued Francesca, 'or, more likely, a set-up so the likes of Rob Crawford get to drool over desperate girls jiggling their bits.'

'So does this mean you're not going to be auditioning?' asked Zara slyly.

'Let's just say I'm not in any rush to provide an ego-trip for a bunch of over-sexed boys with guitars. Right, Fran?'

'Er, right,' said Fran, caught unawares.

'Yes, but who cares if the auditions are a bit of a farce?' said Jessica impatiently. 'At least we'll get to see Firedog in action. There is no way I'm missing out on an event like this.'

'Whatever happens, Thursday is going to be *insane*,' said Sadie.

'Oh, I expect we'll all be there,' said Francesca, taking a thoughtful sip of her coffee.

In the end, Fran set off for home by herself, leaving Francesca with the others in the cafe. The more she thought about her encounter with Quinn at lunchtime, and the sensational news of the Firedog audition, the more unsettled she felt. Somehow she knew, just *knew*, that this was the beginning of something significant. A change, a transformation of some sort, was going to happen, and had perhaps already begun.

So you're a musician too. Could Fran's own voice be the instrument that would, finally, give her something special enough to stand out from the rest of Quinn's groupies? Of course, she knew that a two-minute exchange of pleasantries with the most popular boy in the school wasn't the start of true romance. She wasn't stupid. No, all Fran wanted for the moment was to be interesting enough, and self-possessed enough, to talk to Quinn face to face, eye to eye. To see him nod in agreement or smile in recognition or – perhaps – lean in to share some confidence with that same mix of tenderness and intensity she'd glimpsed before, when they'd been talking about music. Music about love.

And what an idiot she'd been this lunchtime! If only she hadn't been in such a flap and had paid proper attention to the notice Quinn was putting up she would have known about the auditions hours ago. She could have asked him about it then and there – he might have given her tips. He might have wished her luck! She remembered the way he'd taken her singing seriously, asked her what she was working on, listened to her with such absorption . . . The thing about Quinn was that he wasn't just so beautiful it hurt, he was intelligent and perceptive too.

As soon as Fran got home, she went straight up to her bedroom, locked the door and fetched out a small wooden soapbox from under her bed. When she was little it had been her treasure chest and the depository of such riches as a broken earring of Mrs Roper's, her lucky penny and a key which didn't fit any lock. Now it only held one: a half-completed song lyric from the hand of Quinn Adams that she had 'rescued' from the music suite's recycling bin. The lyrics were incomplete and there was the odd scribbled-out word or reordered line but all the same, it was easy to follow:

> *It's a looking-glass world*
> *For the looking-glass girl,*
> *Lost in a whirl*
> *Of smiles and champagne.*
> *It's her looking-glass world*
> *And she's having a ball,*

But I'll never fall
For her words again.

No, I'll never fall
For her words again.

Fran thought it was wonderful – as good as poetry. And weren't the lyrics a kind of warning that Quinn could see through girls who might look gorgeous but were actually shallow and self-obsessed? Perhaps poor Quinn had already had his heart broken by just such a girl. Fran had never heard Firedog perform and she didn't know what the tune was like, but she could imagine how well Quinn would sing something like this, accompanied by lots of dark, sexy looks and mournfully melodic chords.

Fran hadn't spent half as long as she would have liked on this particular daydream before she heard someone calling her from downstairs. Reluctantly she hauled herself to her feet and went out to the landing.

'Francesca's here to see you!' shouted up her mother, her voice muffled by the pile of washing in her arms. Mrs Roper was still in her smart office blouse but had exchanged her skirt and heels for her husband's tracksuit bottoms and a pair of fluorescent orange flip-flops. Beth, wearing nothing but a nappy, had both arms locked around one of Mrs Roper's legs and was whining to be picked up. 'Sorry I'm in such a state. Running late for my aromatherapy class as usual . . . no, no, darling, let mummy go . . .' At last she freed her leg from Beth's sticky clasp. Beth promptly began to wail. 'By the way, you haven't seen my Essence of Lavender, have you? It's in a little blue—'

But Fran was already halfway back to her bedroom, with Francesca close behind. As soon as she got through the door Fran went over to her desk and dumped a stack of magazines over Quinn's lyrics, in a pretence at making some space on the floor. In all honesty, she rather wished Francesca had chosen another evening to pop round. She needed more time to get used to the idea of the audition before she was ready to share her decision with anyone else.

Francesca flopped to the floor with a sigh. 'Why did you leave the cafe so early, Fran-flakes? If you'd given me a bit of warning, I'd have come along too.'

'Oh . . . sorry . . . I just wasn't feeling sociable, that's all.'

'You certainly kept very quiet.'

'Sometimes it's hard to get a word in edgeways with that lot.'

Francesca laughed. 'I know what you mean – this audition business seems to have got everyone's knickers in a right old twist. I wonder if Quinn and co. realize what they've started.'

'Mmm.'

'Fran?'

'Yes?'

'You're not annoyed with me about anything are you?'

'What?' Fran was startled. 'No, of course not. Why would I be?'

'I'm not sure. It's just that you've been a bit quiet recently, not only in the cafe this afternoon, but it was the same at the weekend, when Sadie and Zara came round. Almost like you didn't want to be hanging out with us. And then when you didn't wait for me at the cafe . . . I'm overreacting I guess, but it feels like ages since we've had a proper girly chat. I just wondered if I'd done something to upset you.'

Fran was embarrassed. It was true, she *had* been preoccupied lately and she should really try to make more of an effort when Zara and Sadie were around. If Francesca liked them, they were probably worth getting to know better.

'Of course you haven't done anything! God, I feel awful! I don't know why I've been so—'

Francesca flashed a smile. 'Oh good, I'm *so* relieved. I knew I was probably imagining things, but you know how I'd hate for anything to come between us. I don't know what I'd do without you, Fran-flakes.' She thought of something and started to laugh. 'Do you remember that time Mr Turner's class took a trip to the zoo? And I snuck off to

CORNWALL COLLEGE
LEARNING CENTRE

the gift shop and asked you to cover for me? And you—'

'Went up to a teacher and said you'd been fed to the lions,' finished Fran, and both girls dissolved into giggles.

Fran felt better than she had for days. Nobody could make her laugh like Francesca could, and that was because nobody knew her as well as Francesca did. She had been dithering about whether to tell her about going in for the audition or surprise her along with everybody else, but now she realized how stupid, not to mention unfair, it would be to keep this from her. Best friends share everything. And besides, Francesca would be full of practical as well as moral support.

'I'm going to audition for Firedog,' she blurted out.

Francesca was still wiping away her tears of laughter. 'What?'

'Quinn Adams's band. I'm going to try and be their new female singer.' Pause. 'So, um, what do you think?'

There was a long and uncertain silence. Francesca was looking at Fran with a slight frown. 'Oh, Fran-flakes, are you sure about this?' she said at last.

This wasn't the reaction Fran had been hoping for. 'OK, so I might not be the obvious choice,' she said defensively, 'and I don't expect I'm what he –

they are looking for. But I thought – I wanted – if I could just *try*. Have a go, at least, at getting up there and showing people I can sing. And I *can* sing, you know.'

'Of course I know,' said Francesca kindly. 'You've got a lovely voice. But – Fran – do you truly think this is the best way to show it off? What on earth are you going to sing, anyway?'

'I'll keep it low-key, but I want something different to the usual chart stuff . . . a classic, you know? Though I haven't decided yet.' Actually, she had. She was going to sing the love song she'd been practising when she'd met Quinn in the music suite. It didn't matter if other people went for the latest hits because at least this way she would be true to herself. Unique. And Quinn would understand why she'd chosen it.

'This isn't going to be like a proper music competition or a concert where people are nice and respectful and listen properly,' Francesca continued. 'It'll be Quinn's gang, and all their hangers-on, and lots of tarty little try-hards from the rest of the school . . . I mean, do you even know what Firedog sounds like?'

'Not exactly,' she admitted. 'But it's basically indie guitar pop, right? So it can't be that hard core – it's not as if I'm auditioning for a thrash metal or . . . or a trip-hop band.'

'I'm surprised you know what trip hop is.'

'Well, maybe it's time I surprised you,' Fran said a little sharply.

Now Francesca looked stricken. 'Look, I'm sorry, Fran-flakes. I do understand why you want to do this. And you know how fantastic I think your singing is. The thing is, I – well, I'm concerned . . . you . . . the others . . .' She sighed. 'Please don't think I'm being unsupportive. I want to make sure you know what you're letting yourself in for, that's all.'

'It's not something you need to worry about,' said Fran, and changed the subject. She was suddenly fed-up with the whole conversation.

Over the next three days of feverish speculation, Fran was surprised by her own sense of calm. She knew turning up on Thursday was probably going to be the most recklessly terrifying thing she'd ever done, but even so, she had a sense, deep down, that the whole business was out of her hands. Fran told herself it didn't matter if she actually got the place in the band or not – the important thing was to get up in front of Quinn and everyone else and show them what she could do, to make people shut up and listen for once. So it didn't matter that Francesca hadn't really understood.

Mid-afternoon Thursday and all this careful rationalization felt a lot less convincing. It didn't help that the last lesson of the day was Fran's worst subject: English with Mr Mayhew. Julian Mayhew was young-ish, trendy-ish and extremely embittered, having repeatedly failed to make it as an actor. His lesson plans were limited to devising 'dramatic improvisations' to help his students 'bring literature alive', and his speciality was matching the least capable person to the most wildly inappropriate role. Today, for example, poor lardy, lumbering Wayne Roberts was forced to flit around the classroom pretending to be an Airy Spirit:

'"... Where the bee sucks – puff – there suck I,"' Wayne panted, skipping down the aisle between the desks, '"In – puff – a cowslip's bell I lie – puff –"'

'That's right, Wayne,' called out Mr Mayhew. 'Light as a feather now. Try and spread a little magic through the air, yes?'

'"... Merrily, merrily shall I live now,"' wheezed Wayne, purple faced, and flapping his arms in a desperate attempt to spread a little magic, '"Under the – puff – blossom –"'

The rest of the class tittered dutifully. Fran, looking ahead to her own performance, felt particularly uncomfortable. She glanced over at Francesca who caught her eye and gave a reassuring smile, almost as if she knew what she was thinking.

As soon as the final bell went, Fran hastened off to the music suite to have one last run-through before the audition at five. But as she left the exit to the side of the main teaching block she heard Francesca calling after her.

'Wait, Fran –' She was struggling through a horde of Year Sevens.

'Sorry, I've got to go,' Fran yelled back through the end-of-day din.

'Look, I need to talk to you—'

'You're coming to the audition, right?'

'Of course, but that's—'

'I'll see you there then. I'm sorry, but I really have to go.'

When Fran arrived at the school hall at quarter to five, she found a queue had already gathered by the doors. These were guarded by Cath Watson, Jez-the-drummer's girlfriend and a leading member of the Firedog entourage. 'Sorry, guys,' she was telling the small crowd, 'but no one below Year Ten, OK? This isn't the Brownies, for Christ's sake.'

'Hi,' said Fran, raising her voice above the crowd's rebellious mutterings, 'I'm here to audition? My name's Fran Roper.'

Cath looked distinctly unimpressed. 'And what year are you?'

'Year Ten, obviously,' said Fran, annoyed.

'OK, Roper, go on in.' She looked at her clipboard. 'You'll be on sixth.'

Fran took a deep breath, then walked into the hall, which was already half-full of excitable girls.

She realized that if she was only the sixth person on the audition list, most of these people had come along just to see the show – which would account for the few sheepish-looking boys lurking on the sides. The rest of Firedog's entourage were easy to spot: a gaggle of older students with a self-consciously offhand air. And Jessica Simmonds had been right: there was Miss Duncan, hovering by the edge of the stage looking typically twitchy and ineffectual. There was no sign of Francesca.

Most of the rest of the girls from her class were there, however, and she made her way over to where Zara and Sadie were standing with a few others. They had gathered quite close to the stage, which was already set up with a microphone, percussion set and amplifiers. Sadie had changed out of her school uniform into a silver halter neck and matching miniskirt and was twinkling and dimpling away with a group of three other girls, all similarly dressed.

'Is Sadie auditioning for the band then?' Fran asked Zara.

Zara gave her a look of withering scorn. 'Oh no,' she said sarcastically, 'Sadie's dressed like that ready for the football-team try-outs.'

'Ready and waiting and all set to score,' said Sadie, with a flick of her ponytail. 'It's sweet of you to come and show your support, Fran.'

Fran gritted her teeth. Sweet and supportive was

all very well, but sometimes she thought it would be a lot more fun being bitter and obstructive.

'Actually,' she said, 'I thought I might have a go at singing myself.'

Silence fell.

'How very *brave*,' said Zara finally, and Fran felt her face go hot.

'You used to be in the choir, right?' asked Sadie chummily. 'I'm sure knowing all those old church songs and stuff must be *really* cool.'

'Have you talked about this to Francesca?' asked Zara, looking at her narrowly.

'She knows I'm auditioning – in fact, I was supposed to be meeting her here.'

'She was around earlier,' put in Jessica, 'before she had to go and—'

But at that point a thunderous boom echoed through the hall, as Miss Duncan had her first encounter with the microphone.

'Oh dear, I'm not sure this is working . . .' she began, through another crackle of static. 'Ah, there we go. Great.' She cleared her throat nervously. 'Welcome, everyone, welcome.' There was a pause as she waited for people to settle into an approximation of quiet. 'As you all know, our school is very proud of its musical achievements and so, although it's a little unusual, we were very happy to make the hall available for the, um, Firecats to hold their auditions.' More clearing of her throat. 'However, this is on the condition that people show respect for the school as well as the occasion. Rest assured, I will be keeping an *extremely* close eye on people's behaviour this evening.' Although Miss Duncan tried to look stern, her tone was pleading. 'Now, I understand we're going to be treated to a little sample from the Firefrogs' playlist and—' But the rest of her words were drowned out by cheers and whoops from the floor as the Firedogs sauntered on to the stage. The crowd had swelled considerably in the last five or ten minutes; it now looked as if most of the Upper School were in attendance.

Fran's stomach felt like she'd swallowed a whole swarm of butterflies. Up there on stage, and changed out of their school uniforms, the Firedogs looked older, leaner and edgier than she believed possible. They had all dressed down for the occasion, in baggy jeans or combats and old T-shirts, though Quinn was wearing what looked like a pinstriped blazer over his scruffy grey top.

'Hey guys,' said Quinn, coming up to the microphone. 'Glad you could make it.' Once more everyone broke out into applause and he had to wait for a minute or so before speaking again. 'Right, I'm going to keep this short – you all know why you're here. Basically, we think the band could benefit from the female touch and so we want a gorgeous gal to hang out with, have some fun and, hey, maybe even make some music along the way.' He ran his hands through his hair and grinned. 'Cath tells me we've got eight acts to look forward to this evening. Which is gonna be cool. But before we get on to all that, I guess I should tell you a little about who we are and what we do. As you've probably worked out by now, we're the Firedogs –' cue more cheers – 'and I'm the guy who mumbles at the microphone. Then there's my good mate Rob on guitar, Liam on bass, and the lovely Jez on the drums.' As their names were mentioned, each band member gave a salute and a grin. 'We're going to perform one of our new tracks for you now, and after that, if it's OK, it'll be the ladies' turn. Sound cool?'

The roar of approval from the crowd indicated that it would be very cool indeed. In a few minutes, the Firedogs had taken their positions, Cath had dimmed the lights and Quinn went over to switch the amplifiers on. A low, rich humming filled the hall and Fran felt a delicious tingle of expectation creep up her spine. Poor Francesca, to miss all this! But perhaps she'd arrived late and was standing at the back.

In the next moment, Fran heard the words she already knew by heart, sung by the voice of her most secret dreams. Quinn made each word sound low and dark and languid, just like she thought they should be, and the tune was every bit as seductive as she'd hoped.

It's a looking-glass world
For the looking-glass girl,
Lost in a whirl
Of smiles and champagne . . .

Firedog's audience might have been expecting something a little more rock 'n' roll, but if the low-key nature of the song had caught them unawares, it certainly didn't dim their enthusiasm. Perhaps the percussion overpowered the guitars at times, and it was true that Rob Crawford sounded a *little* off-key when he joined Quinn for the chorus. If you were going to be picky, you might complain that the bass was out of sync in at least two places . . . But there was no denying the sweet wistfulness of the melody or the smoothness of Quinn's delivery. Dark chocolate wrapped in silver foil. At the end of the song, Miss Duncan wasn't the only female to be practically swooning with excitement. Even the boys looked impressed.

'That was "Looking-Glass Girl,"' announced Quinn once the applause had started to die down, 'and we're the Firedogs.' Cue yet more stamping of feet and yells of approval. 'But that's enough of us for one evening – now it's your turn.'

An expectant hush descended on the hall. Quinn stepped back from the microphone and Jez, the lanky, dark-haired drummer, took his place.

'Right everyone, we're not looking for any fancy

routines, just a girl who can carry a tune, has got a bit of rhythm and looks like she's having fun on the stage. Then if someone takes our fancy – in a manner of speaking – we'll get back to her in the next day or two and take it from there. OK?'

'And first up is a group effort,' announced Miss Duncan, who had tottered up to join Jez at the microphone. Her cheeks were pink and her sensible brown cardigan had come undone at the top by several buttons. 'A big round of applause, please, for Sadie Smith, Emma Lane, Rachel Bertaut and Philippa Nokes!'

Sadie, Emma, Rachel and Philippa skipped on to the stage, dolled up to the nines in sparkly eyeshadow and short skirts, and immediately launched into a song and dance routine based around one of the latest girl-band hits, with a rousing chorus of, 'Don't make me cry, sweetie-pie/Let's have some fun, honeybun.' It was clear that this wasn't a serious audition, and in cheerful defiance of the 'No Pop Idol wannabes' stricture. They knew they could get away with it because they were all cuter than the proverbial button. Round the stage they strutted, wiggling their bottoms and batting their eyes as if their lives depended on it, while the Firedogs smirked appreciatively and the smattering of males in the audience whooped and whistled for all they were worth.

The next contestant was a very thin, very serious-looking girl from Year Thirteen, who was dressed all in black and had long, dyed-black hair that hung absolutely straight down on either side of her face. She'd brought a guitar and sat hunched down on the stage while she droned her way through what was clearly an original composition, all about Frozen Tears and Despair's Dark Kiss. After that was a girl who must have slipped past Cath in a moment of distraction, since she couldn't have been more than thirteen and had chosen to squeak her way through one of the big melodramatic numbers from *The Phantom of the Opera*. She was followed by an extremely pretty Japanese girl from Quinn's class, who performed a Beatles' medley in a light, attractive voice, but even with the microphone on she sang so softly that people were talking over her well before she'd reached the end.

After the last note of 'Yesterday' had faded into silence, Miss Duncan announced that there would be a short break. Fran would have preferred it if they'd gone straight on, as the longer she had to wait for her turn the more nervous she felt. So far, none of the acts she'd heard made her regret going in for the audition, but there was a world of difference between not making a fool of oneself and giving a memorable performance.

'Fran, I *really* need to talk to you.'

'Francesca! At last! I was beginning to think you weren't coming.' Then she noticed Francesca was wearing jeans and a white vest-top. 'Did you leave to change?' she asked, surprised.

'Yes, you see, er, that's what I want to talk to you about. I tried to tell you earlier but . . .' Francesca bit her lip nervously. 'Well, as a matter of fact . . . I . . .'

Fran stared at her. 'Oh no,' she said slowly, 'you're going to audition too.'

Francesca started speaking very quickly. 'Listen, Fran, I'm so sorry I didn't talk this over with you first. But you have to realize that it was a last-minute decision. I only decided to go for it this afternoon and then when I tried to tell you—'

'You didn't try very hard though, did you? And if it was a last-minute decision, how come you brought those clothes?' Fran felt as if the bottom had dropped out of her stomach.

'These? It's just the camisole I was wearing under my shirt and then Zara had a pair of jeans in her locker.'

Fran glanced over at Zara, who, along with the rest of their group, was openly listening in on their conversation. Francesca was now looking defensive. 'Look, there's no reason why I shouldn't have a go along with everyone else. It's just a bit of fun after all. It's not like anything's going to come of it.'

'But you went on and on about how it was all a set-up! For losers and wannabes! You even tried to talk me out of it –' To Fran's shame, she found her voice was starting to crack.

'Please, Fran-flakes, don't be angry. Please. You have to understand I didn't – well, anyway. We'll sort this out later. Look, I'm on next, I've got to go. Wish me luck, OK?'

And the next instant she was standing on the stage.

Francesca didn't start singing straight away. For about a minute she just stood there, supremely relaxed, as she looked out over the hall with that private smile of hers. Her dark red hair hung down in tousled waves around her face, the thin white cotton straps of her camisole were half slipping off her shoulders and her feet were bare. Her expression was thoughtful, amused, almost a little bored.

Finally she began to sing. Her voice was light and clear, if not very strong, and she'd chosen the right kind of song for it: a melancholy Bob Dylan ballad. Fran's own words echoed mockingly in her head. *Low-key . . . something different to the usual chart stuff . . . a classic.* This was something different all right: the audience had fallen quiet for the first time since Firedog had left the stage. Francesca didn't bother with any fancy moves, just swayed a little to the beat and occasionally shook out her hair. By the time she'd finished the final chorus, even Rob Crawford had stopped thinking about getting his sweaty hands under her top and was actually listening. Quinn was drinking in every note, word and sinuous inch of her. As for Fran, she thought she was going to be sick.

She knew there was no way on earth she could get up on that stage and follow on from Francesca's act. Now that she'd seen what a *real* performance was made of she knew that whatever she attempted, however hard she tried, all she could provide was the most humiliating of anticlimaxes. Whatever had she been thinking – to prance on stage in her school uniform and sensible plait, crooning about broken hearts! Better to admit defeat before she wasted everyone's time and patience. Better to keep her dignity while she still could.

Suddenly, she was overwhelmed by the misery and frustration and sheer unfairness of it all. Angry tears flooded her eyes and, before she could completely disgrace herself, she stumbled away through the crowd and out of the hall.

Once outside in the darkened schoolyard, she increased her jog to a run. The autumn drizzle cooled her hot cheeks and for a while she didn't slacken her pace, taking a grim satisfaction from every rasping breath and in the rub of her left shoe on her anklebone. Then the rub began to feel more like a stab, the drizzle turned to rain, and she was forced to stop. It was then that she realized that

1) she had fled the school without collecting her coat or bag, and 2) she didn't have a clue where she was.

Fran wasn't immediately worried. She still had her travelcard and some change in her skirt pocket; all she needed to do was find a homeward-bound bus or stop a passer-by and ask for directions. The residential street she found herself in was, however, deserted, and so she decided to try her luck at the small corner shop at the far end. By the time she limped through the door of 'Oronames – Local Convenience' she was soaking wet. Distant thunder rumbled in the air.

The shop was small and dimly lit, and had the usual array of magazines, snacks and a grocery section that mainly consisted of overpriced tins of cat food and instant noodles. There were no other customers, only the shopkeeper, who was seated behind the counter flicking his way through a DIY magazine. He was wearing a vast turban in purple silk, his belly strained against a Guns n' Roses T-shirt that was several sizes too small for him, and he had a carefully waxed goatee.

'Er, hello,' said Fran. 'I wonder if you could help me? I've got a bit lost, you see, and I was hoping you could tell me where—'

'This is a convenience store, dearie. Not a tourist-information office.' He tore his eyes from a double-page spread of power drills long enough to look her up and down. He didn't seem impressed with what he saw.

'I only want *directions*.'

'That so? Then you can bleeding well buy something first.' He waved a pudgy hand towards the rest of the shop. 'Think of it as supporting the local economy.'

Fran sighed. 'OK . . . but I've only got about fifty pence.'

'Have a ring, they're on sale.' He rattled a box full of bits of glittery plastic. 'Top-class fashion accessories!' Now that he had the prospect of a deal, an entrepreneurial gleam had come into his eyes.

'So if I buy a ring you'll give me directions to Milson Road?'

'Certainly!' All of a sudden, the man was beaming at her.

'Fine . . . whatever.' She handed over her fifty pence and was rewarded with one of the novelty rings, still in its cellophane wrapper. It looked as if the 'top-class fashion accessories' had been culled from some particularly cheap Christmas crackers. 'And now will you tell me what's the quickest way to—'

'Bus two-eight-nine from the end of the street. It's on diversion,' he said abruptly and, with a parting scowl, plunged back into his magazine.

During the slow bus ride home, Fran had time to

regret not spending her fifty pence on something useful. Like a newspaper. Or, even better, some chocolate. As for the ring . . . Fran was surprised to find that it wasn't plastic but made of a dull kind of metal, inscribed with strange markings, and set with a spectacularly fake purple jewel. The ring was stuck to a card with 'Oronames Enterprises Ltd' on the back and a picture of a belly dancer on the front, overwritten with curly Arabic script. The translation provided was only slightly less mystifying: 'Welcome to Old Time Entrancing Jewl! Employ Suitably for Hart Desiring!'

If only it were that simple, thought Fran as she wearily put her key into the lock. Right now, her heart's desire was for a hot bath and a dose of painkillers. She'd got thoroughly wet again during the walk from the bus stop and her blister felt like someone was rubbing it with a rusty cheese-grater.

This time it was her father who met her as she came through the door. His hair was sticking up in little anxious tufts, his glasses were slipping off his nose and he was wearing one of Mrs Roper's frilly aprons. 'About time! What on earth happened to you? Why haven't you been answering your mobile? It's nearly half past eight! I was getting seriously worried, young lady.'

'I'm fine.' Fran tried to move past him and get up to her room. 'I was at a school, er, concert, remember? I caught a bus back cos of the rain. The traffic was awful.'

'Humph. I thought this concert was supposed to be over by six.'

'I told Mum this morning that it would probably run late.'

'Typical! Typical! I'm always the last person to know *anything* in this house.'

'So where's Mum?'

'It's her Russian class tonight.' Mr Roper ran his hand through his hair distractedly. 'She left instructions for how to get dinner ready but then Mickey's agent phoned about an audition on Saturday and Beth started crying and all the pans boiled over . . . I don't suppose you'd like to give me a hand would you, love?'

'Oh, Dad, not now. Please. I'm wrecked. And I've got tons of homework to do.'

Her father pushed his glasses back up his nose and took another look at her. 'Hmm. You are looking a bit peaky. I suppose I'll have to let you off . . . By the way, Francesca left a couple of messages on the answer machine.'

Fran didn't say anything, just slowly limped up the stairs.

'It sounded quite important,' he called up after her. But there was no reply except the slam of Fran's bedroom door.

*

Now that Fran was finally by herself the wretchedness of the evening came flooding back. So Francesca had tried to phone had she? Was it to commiserate? Apologize? Or share the news that she'd just become Firedog's new singing starlet?

Fran slumped on her bed, listening to the rain drum against the window, and staring at her reflection in the mirror on the wall. Long damp strands of hair had come out of her plait and straggled around her pale face. Her school shirt was rumpled and grubby looking and her legs speckled with muddy water from the puddles. What's more, she'd somehow managed to slip that ridiculous ring on to her left hand, and now it wouldn't come off. There it was, stuck fast, the gemstone glinting at her in a malevolent sort of way. Fantastic. The day had already deteriorated into a disaster-strewn epic – maybe she should grow some hair on her feet and call herself a hobbit.

Fran pulled at the ring first irritably, then frantically, as it refused to budge. Swearing at it didn't have any effect either. As her efforts only made her finger grow pink and puffy, she began to sob. It was absolutely the last straw. Crying in earnest now, she began to twist the ring back and forth, in a desperate attempt to loosen it.

What happened next takes time to describe, but in reality was over in a matter of seconds, so quickly, in fact, that Fran barely had time to react. It began when the purple jewel in the ring began to glow, not consistently, but with a slightly unsteady flicker. The air in front of Fran began to flicker too, and increase in brightness, as if the light in the jewel was projecting some kind of image before it. Then the brightness, still rippling, began to fade into a purplish haze, amorphous at first, but soon gathering shape. For a second, a one-dimensional image floated in the air before her, before – with a final flicker – condensing into solid form.

A young man was standing in front of her; a dark, hawk-nosed youth wearing voluminous black silk trousers, a supercilious expression and very little else. He took one look at her blotchy, miserable, tear-stained face and heaved an immensely long-suffering sigh.

'Oh no,' he said, rolling his eyes in disgust, 'not *another* one.'

For the next few moments, Fran did nothing but sit on her bed and gibber.

'Wh – wh – what – whaaa – wh – who – whooo – hooo – oooh – oooh –'

Then her mouth went so dry she couldn't even gibber, just open and close it witlessly.

She screwed her eyes tight shut, said a little prayer, and opened them again. The young man was still there, examining his nails.

Fran began to whimper. Oh hell oh help oh hell.

She must be having a manic delusion. Or . . . could she have been *drugged* without knowing it? Was this what a bad acid trip was like?

She opened her mouth to scream.

'Before you start screaming,' said the manic delusion, 'I should perhaps reassure you that as the Slave of the Ring, I am bound by the Most Great Name engraved upon the Seal of Solomon to do no injury, mischief or slight to the ring's possessor.' He walked over to her window and peered out. 'Joy of joys. From the weather, I'm guessing I'm back in England again.'

'L-L-London actually.'

The Slave of the Ring frowned. 'I was hoping for New York. I hear it's improved immensely – last time I was there, of course, it was a few muddy fields and a donkey cart . . . Ah well, I guess London's not too bad. On my last visit,' he continued chattily as he wandered around her room, looking over her things with an appraising sort of air, 'everyone was going crazy over a group of singing boys – the Weevils? Centipedes? – and they'd just invented something called the miniskirt. Do British girls still wear them?'

Fran nodded dumbly. Her visitor brightened considerably. 'Now *that's* progress for you,' he said. 'Over the centuries, female emancipation has been a joy to behold.'

'So, er, you've, um, been here before?' she quavered.

'Didn't I just say so?' The young man plumped himself down on her chair and stretched out his legs, hands clasped behind his head. He looked, and sounded, very solid for a hallucination, though Fran noticed a tendril of purple smoke escape from under the hem of one trouser leg before fading into air. 'Ah yes, it's a wonderful life us genies have. Foreign travel, immortal youth, godlike powers . . . as far as eternal servitude goes, it's not too bad.'

'Genie? *Genie?*'

He gave her a look. 'Have you been listening to *anything* I've said? Or did you think my whole Slave of the Ring speech and reading your rights about the sacred seal was just for dramatic effect?'

'I was in *shock* at the time. I haven't ever met a, er, genie before,' said Fran defensively. For an enslaved spirit she thought he was very condescending.

'Then you've a treat in store, haven't you?' he said, and grinned. 'I'm Ashazrahim, by the way. Ashazrahim the Resplendent, Dispenser of Enchantments, Indulger of Desires, the Jewel of Arabia and Lion of Baghdad. Otherwise known as Ash.'

'I'm, uh, Francesca. Otherwise known as Fran.'

For the first time since her strange visitor had arrived, Fran dared to take a proper look at him. Apart from his exotic attire and the wisp of purple smoke (all trace of which had now vanished), there was nothing extraordinary about him – certainly nothing to suggest he was an ancient mythical being who'd popped out of a magic ring. He was wearing embroidered slippers, loose-fitting trousers made of black silk shot through with purple and a flimsy kind of waistcoat in the same material. The waistcoat was unbuttoned and Fran suspected this had been done for deliberate effect – there was something just a little bit preening about the way Mr Resplendent was lounging on his chair. His only ornament was a metal bracelet that encircled his upper left arm. As far as the immortal youth went, he looked no older than seventeen or eighteen. He had a head of thick, wavy black hair, an arched nose and cool dark eyes. They were now examining her with a faintly sceptical expression.

'You *are* another one of them, aren't you?' he asked.

'Another one of what?'

'Lovesick snivelling females, that's what.' The Lion of Baghdad sighed. 'That's all I ever seem to get. It's like I attract them or something.' He brooded for a while. 'You know, I wouldn't be surprised if the spiteful cow who put me in the damn ring had arranged it specially. It's the kind of thing that would appeal to her warped sense of humour.'

'Someone made you a genie on *purpose*?' Fran had been going to protest about being called a snivelling female but her curiosity had got the better of her. She was also trying to recall what she'd read about genies in the *Arabian Nights* – as she remembered, they tended to be very large dust clouds with homicidal intentions. She sincerely hoped Ash wasn't about to start throwing thunderbolts or whatever. 'Do you mean you used to be human?'

'It's a dark, tragic tale,' said Ash sorrowfully. 'One day I may tell you the full story. First, however, we should get down to business –'

But at that point there was a knock on the door.

'Fran? Are you all right in there?' It was her father.

Fran shot up from the bed, scarlet faced.

'Wait – don't come in – I'm not wearing –' Then she thought of Ash listening in and went even redder. Never mind the whole genie angle; how on earth was she going to hide a strange half-dressed foreigner – a strange half-dressed foreign *male* – from her immediate family? She began to sweat.

Ash, however, was unconcerned. 'It's all right,' he assured her. 'You're the only one who can see or hear me.'

Fran wasn't taking any chances. She sidled out of her door, shutting it immediately behind her, and stood protectively in front of the handle.

'Sorry about that, Dad. I thought I'd take a bath.'

'Can't it wait? I came to tell you that supper's ready.'

'Great. Fantastic. Er . . . do you mind if I don't join you? It's just that I had something to eat after the concert and I'm not very hungry.'

'Well, all right. Though, honestly, I don't know why I bother trying to get food on the table in time . . .' He turned to go, still grumbling, and Fran heaved a sigh of relief. Her mum would never have let her off so easily. 'By the way, did Francesca want anything important?'

'Francesca?'

'That's who I heard you talking on the phone to just now, wasn't it?'

'Oh . . . no . . . I was . . . um . . .' Fran searched frantically for inspiration. 'I was practising for my multicultural social-studies assignment. We have to create a dramatic monologue on the theme of, er, the *Arabian Nights*.'

'Multicultural social studies? Goodness me.' He shook his head in bafflement. 'Right then, I'd better leave you in peace.'

Fran went back to her bedroom and locked the door behind her, just in case. 'Sorry about that,' she said to Ash, who had moved to her wardrobe and was flicking through her clothes with interest.

'That's all right,' he said graciously. 'As a matter of fact, I think you're handling the situation quite well. Mild hysterics I can cope with, it's when clients – sorry, Commanders of the Ring – start throwing crucifixes around and threatening me with exorcists and crusaders and what have you that I start to get annoyed. Ungrateful, I call it . . . Now then, where were we?'

'Something about business,' said Fran, closing her wardrobe door firmly. There couldn't possibly be anything of historical or cultural interest in her outgrown 'I Love Kylie' T-shirt.

'Ah yes. OK, so I'm supposed to grant you seven wishes –' Fran opened her mouth – 'and don't even *think* about trying the old "my first wish is to have another hundred" trick,' he said sternly. 'The Powers-that-Be who set the rules for this sort of thing weren't born yesterday.'

Fran didn't mind. How could she? She'd just been granted seven whole wishes! It was as good as being in a fairy tale! Or – better – like having super-powers. She could do *anything*, be anybody! Her thoughts went back to the class debate last Friday, and Francesca's contention that every girl in the school would prioritize designer boobs over polar ice caps. Well, she'd show *her*! Fran Roper wasn't about to waste a chance like this on shallow self-indulgence! No, every wish would be a noble deed, a fantastic, grandiose gesture in the face of world suffering! She'd go down in history books – Fran the champion of the oppressed; Fran the benefactor of mankind; Fran the toast of London, New York, Paris;

a saviour of the world turned superstar! She opened her mouth to speak again, but once more Ash got in first. 'And you needn't bother wishing for World Peace either,' he added. 'Because one, the effects of each wish don't last for more than seven hours, and two, it's out of my league.'

Only seven hours? This was a blow. 'But I thought you said you had godlike powers!'

Ash looked huffy. 'From my experience of history – which is a lot more comprehensive than yours, by the way – World Peace appears to be beyond the means of all the gods *I've* ever heard of.'

'Oh . . . but . . . can't you even, I dunno . . . Save the Whale?'

'I'm a *genie*, not a marine biologist!' He glared at her. 'Honestly! Can't you just be grateful that you've got seven opportunities to be recklessly selfish?'

'I'm sorry, Ash,' said Fran penitently. 'I didn't mean to sound ungrateful. It's just it's all so fantastically, amazingly, unbelievably . . . well, unbelievable. I guess I'm still coming to terms with everything.' She rubbed her eyes. She was suddenly overwhelmed by tiredness. 'Part of me thinks I'll wake up tomorrow morning and find it's all a dream.'

'Well, I'm not going anywhere,' he said. 'Worse luck.'

That was a point. Before she got to grips with her wishing strategy she needed some serious thinking time . . . on her own.

'OK,' she said brightly, 'I'll think I'll call it a night then. We can sort out my first wish in the morning.'

'OK.' But Ash didn't look as if he was planning to vanish in a puff of purple smoke anytime soon. In fact, he settled himself more comfortably in his chair.

'So . . .'

He raised an enquiring eyebrow. 'So?'

'So I need to get ready for bed and go to sleep.' She blushed. 'In *private*.' He was grinning now, arms folded across his chest, and she could see that he was enjoying her embarrassment. 'Can you get back in your ring, please?' Fran asked, trying to sound stern.

'Well, if you *insist*.' He yawned, stretched, and got to his feet. 'Though, in fairness to the whole thy-wish-is-my-command set-up, I should probably tell you that you have the power to dismiss me the same way as you summon me. Night-night.'

But his last words were almost lost as, having touched the metal bracelet on his left arm, his figure flickered, blurred and faded as rapidly as it had first appeared. Fran was once more alone in her bedroom, a cheap little novelty ring on her hand.

It only took a moment or two before Fran relapsed into the state of shock she'd been in when the genie first arrived. Except this time her predominate emotion was elation, not terror. She had to bite her lip and wrap her arms around her chest to stop herself from laughing and screaming at the top of her lungs, or rushing into an all-singing, all-dancing lap of victory around the house. After bouncing on her bed until she was breathless, pinching her arm until it was red, and pulling a variety of hideous faces at the mirror, she finally managed to calm down to the point where she could sit still, without gibbering, for more than thirty seconds at a time.

Seven wishes! Seven chances for her heart's desire! Seven daydreams to be lived! Seven-times-seven hours of selfishness to be indulged! She could take tea with the Queen or drink cocktails with Madonna. Spend an afternoon at the Taj Mahal and the evening in Las Vegas. Any time she liked, she could attend a Hollywood premiere – swim with dolphins – orbit the earth in a space shuttle – fly to the moon! Whatever, whenever, whoever she wanted.

Whoever she wanted . . . OK, so how would it feel to be irresistible for seven hours? What then? Perhaps it was cheating, but if Quinn had the opportunity to get to know her better . . . well, who knows. This was magic, and with magic anything could happen! She could –

But the next thing she knew, daylight was spilling through the window, there was drool on her pillow, and her mum was hammering on the door.

Crap, was Fran's first thought, I've overslept. Her second was, Oh God, please let it be real. Her heart twisted at the thought that both ring and genie had been figments of her imagination after all. And yet the moment she was properly awake she knew this was ridiculous. Whatever had happened last night, however improbable, was living, breathing, hard-edged reality. She *knew*.

In the cold light of day, the ring didn't look any more impressive than she'd remembered it, though at least she was now able to slip it on and off with ease. Remembering how it had all started, she slid the ring on to her finger and twisted it experiment-ally: first left, then right. A tiny spark flashed within the gem and she pulled the ring off hurriedly. Could the genie see her? Was he squinting up at her through the plasticky depths of the jewel right now? Caught up in her dreams of moonwalking and Hollywood premieres, Fran hadn't had much time to think about Ashazra-whatsit himself. The sudden acquisition of a slave would take almost as much getting used to as the ownership of a magic ring – in some ways, she thought, a disembodied voice or an animated dust-cloud might be easier to deal with. He was so *very* condescending.

As her mum yelled for her to get a move on and her dad thundered up and down the stairs looking for his keys, Fran scrabbled around in her jewellery box for a gold locket her godmother had given her.

She slipped the locket off the end of its chain, which she used to loop through the ring and then fastened around her neck so that the ring was concealed by her school shirt. She felt much better now her treasure was safe from prying eyes and, just as importantly, it couldn't slip off her finger. Finally, she clattered downstairs, grabbed an apple from the kitchen in lieu of breakfast, and raced out of the front door.

Fran's headlong rush came to an abrupt halt as she saw that Francesca was waiting for her on the pavement. Post-genie, she had barely thought of the audition, but standing there in the very unmagical environs of Milson Road, the preoccupations of ordinary life came surging back. She supposed that she must still be angry with Francesca, but since the wondrous events of last night surely everything had changed?

'Hey.'

'Hey.'

Both girls stood looking at each other for a while.

'Are you still talking to me?' Francesca asked in a small voice. 'Because I wouldn't blame you if you weren't.'

Fran shrugged, uncomfortable. 'We're not little kids any more,' she said at last. 'I'm not sending you to Coventry, if that's what you mean. And . . . I suppose . . . well, it was only a stupid audition for a stupid school band. I don't want to make it into a big deal.'

They began to walk along the road together.

'Maybe it shouldn't be a big deal,' said Francesca, 'but I still feel bad about it. I should have found a way to tell you earlier. I –' She hesitated – 'I should have handled it better.'

'I don't want "handling". Just honesty,' said Fran, and immediately realized how self-righteous that sounded. Francesca raised her eyebrows.

'I never deliberately *lied* to you, Fran-flakes. Like I said before, I only decided to audition at the last minute, on impulse . . . There was no reason you couldn't have taken part as well. It's not my fault you got stage fright.'

Stage fright? Fran began to regret her 'no big deal' remark. She knew there was no way she would have bottled out like that if she hadn't just had been terminally upstaged and outclassed by her best friend's show-stealing performance. For a moment, she was tempted to have it out with Francesca right then and there, but she realized how ridiculously petty that would be. After all, she had her very own Slave of the Ring now, and seven wishes! What would Francesca say to that? But although Fran was burning to tell somebody her news, something stopped her from sharing it. Perhaps there was an aspect of the ring's magic that prevented you from revealing its powers. Perhaps she was afraid of what

Francesca's reaction might be, that she would be disbelieved and laughed at. Or perhaps she didn't quite trust her enough.

The first people Fran saw as the two of them arrived at the entrance to the Upper School were Sadie and Zara, who'd taken possession of the fire escape at the end of the block. The fire escape was established in-crowd territory and was always surrounded by a little sprinkling of cigarette butts to prove it. Sadie was sitting on one of the lower steps blowing bubblegum (pink) and playing with her hair (blonde) while Zara lounged against the rail, smoking a cigarette with the air of someone auditioning for a Quentin Tarantino film.

'Hello, girlies,' drawled Zara. 'And how are you both this glorious morning? Do I detect a hint of frost in the air?'

'The only thing in the air right now is a toxic cloud of carcinogens,' said Francesca drily.

'And let me tell you, they taste *great*,' said Zara, exhaling another stream of smoke. Right on cue, Sadie popped another candy-coloured bubble. 'Congratulations on your performance last night, by the way. You really blew us away.'

'Thanks . . . though I think I could have benefited from some of Sadie's dance moves,' said Francesca, settling down on the bottom step of the fire escape.

'So whatever happened to your debut?' Zara asked Fran. 'A frog in your throat . . . or was it a knife in your back?'

'You looked totally freaked out. Like, in *major* meltdown,' exclaimed Sadie, wide-eyed with sympathy.

Fran started to mumble something but Francesca cut in. 'Fran has an amazing voice,' she said quickly. 'One day you'll all hear what she can do.'

'I can hardly wait,' said Zara smoothly. And then, to Fran's intense relief, the bell for registration went.

It was just as well that Fran had plenty of recklessly selfish wish-fulfilment to distract her, because the whole day long all anyone seemed to be talking or thinking about was the auditions. General opinion was that the final contest came down to Francesca or a girl from Year Eleven, who'd come after her and given a rousing rendition of a recent R&B hit. Some people (most of whom were female) held that the R&B girl had the stronger voice, others (who were more likely to be male) argued that this was outweighed by Francesca's superior stage presence. 'Which,' said Zara, 'simply means Francesca's the one they'd prefer to get naked.' Francesca's reaction to this was the same as her reaction to any enquiry or comment concerning her performance: a roll of her eyes and a shrug.

But in the end, as Fran knew it would, it was

stage presence that won the day. She could tell it had just by the way Francesca walked across the schoolyard to meet her after the last bell had gone. Francesca held her head high and there was a kind of suppressed excitement in her movements that her composed expression couldn't disguise. 'Congratulations,' said Fran.

'Oh, Fran, do you mean it?' Suddenly Francesca looked guilty and triumphant and pleading all at once. Never mind all those shrugged shoulders and just-a-bit-of-fun remarks; Fran could tell that Francesca had wanted this to happen very much indeed. In fact, her next words confirmed it. 'I didn't much care about winning, not at first, but then everyone started going on and on about it, like one big massive wind-up . . . and, honestly, you should have heard that other girl. I mean, she was *really* good. But then I found a note from Rob Crawford in my locker and – well –'

'Congratulations,' said Fran again. Then, feeling this was slightly inadequate, she gave her a hug. 'You'll be brilliant. Lucky Firedog.'

Francesca laughed. 'We'll see. I have to have a proper rehearsal with the band before things go any further. They might think better of it.'

'No they won't. You'll knock 'em dead, I know you will. Just don't forget the rest of us once you're a rich and famous rock chick, OK?'

Francesca gave her a mock punch. 'Yeah, right.

If I'm going to be a famous rock chick, you're coming with me every step of the way. I'm going to need all the support I can get among all those hulking great boys.'

Hulking great boys . . . and the insanely adorable Quinn Adams. In Francesca's place, Fran reckoned she wouldn't need much supporting. 'Does everyone else know?'

'Not yet.'

'Don't you want to tell them? We should go to Ronnie's, spread the good news . . . I bet Zara and Sadie will be there,' said Fran, feeling heroic.

'Let 'em wait. Right now I feel like I've already listened to enough insincere congratulations to last me a year.' The two of them set off for home together, just like any normal school day. 'Look, Fran, I'm serious about needing you around for back-up. Those auditions . . . well, I know things didn't turn out how, er, you wanted, exactly, and maybe that's partly my fault, but I can make it up to you. This Firedog thing is something we can do *together*.'

'You're the girl who won a place in the band, not me,' Fran said quietly.

'Yes, but you can still come to all the rehearsals, gigs . . . everything. I'll make sure of it. It'll be so much fun. And just think,' she added slyly, 'of all the opportunities for you to get up close and personal with the lovely Quinn.'

'Be his next Looking-Glass Girl, you mean? As if.'

'Why not? The thing about you, Fran,' said Francesca, shaking out her hair, 'is that you always give up too easily. Now, for this band rehearsal on Saturday, what do you think I should wear?'

The ensuing discussion was long and detailed, but mostly one-sided. Fran's mind was elsewhere, as it had been for the majority of the day. Why not, indeed? *Seven wishes*, went the whisper inside her head, *seven chances for my heart's desire.*

By the time she got home, Fran was feeling dizzy with anticipation. There had been hundreds of moments throughout the day when she had touched the chain around her neck and felt her pulse rate quicken in expectation. Should she . . .? Could she . . .? Each time, however, something had stopped her. Excitement was still fizzing through her like champagne, but she was also beginning to give thought to the challenges ahead. If the old fairy tales were to be believed, wishes were rather slippery things and should be handled with caution. The last thing she wanted was to be rushed into asking for something she might regret, or accidentally wasting a wish on something useless.

From the smell in the hall, it seemed that Mrs Roper had burned the dinner again. Fran crunched her way to the kitchen through a light scattering of Lego bricks and peanut shells, and found her mother flapping her hands over the smoking toaster. Bread, not beans, then. Beth was sitting on the floor, playing with one of Fran's old Barbie dolls and a corkscrew, while her brother and one of his friends flicked peanuts at each other on the kitchen table.

'Fan, Fan!' cried Beth, beaming happily from under the table. She was trying to wind the corkscrew into her curls. 'Come play hair wiv Bethy!'

'Hello, darling, good day at school?' asked Mrs Roper distractedly. 'Sorry about all the smoke. I was just fixing the boys their tea and then this blasted machine went and nuked itself again – Mickey, will you please *stop* that.' A peanut had just ricocheted off her neck.

The normally dutiful Mickey snickered, and flicked the next peanut at Fran instead. He always acted up when his friend Lucian came over. The two had first met on a cereal commercial and were now working together on the Crumble Bite campaign, which they had been filming that afternoon.

Fran sat down at the far end of the table from Mickey and forestalled the next round of peanut-flicking with a glare. 'Mum,' she asked, 'if you could wish for anything you wanted, what would it be?'

'Wishes? Goodness, well I – no-no, Bethy, give the nasty corkscrew to Mummy now –' Mrs Roper had just spotted Beth attempting to drill the corkscrew into one ear. 'Fran, do you think you could get that thing off her while I answer the phone? It might be your father, you see, and . . .'

Ten minutes later, after the telephone had been answered, the peanut supply confiscated, and Beth's howls of fury had somewhat subsided, Fran tried again.

'Seriously, Mum, what would you wish for?'

Mrs Roper heaved a sigh. 'Right now, probably a full-time nanny-come-housekeeper.'

'I would wish for World Peace,' said Mickey gravely.

'I'd wish that all the poor little children in Africa would be given a lovely present,' said Lucian, not to be outdone. 'Or,' he added thoughtfully, 'for a decent cameo in the next Harry Potter film.'

Back in the privacy of her bedroom, it occurred to Fran that seven hours of the world's best house-keeper wasn't such a bad idea for a wish. Like one of those lifestyle gurus, maybe – someone to tidy up the house and give the Roper family all the tips they'd need to turn into a model of sophisticated living . . . Or would Ash think something as trivial as a home makeover was a waste of his powers? Even though she suspected that worrying about what your genie thought of you wasn't quite the done thing, Fran was anxious to prove that she wasn't just another snivelling female with a whale fixation.

Suddenly feeling very apprehensive, Fran smoothed her hair and straightened her jumper before, with a deep breath, she released the ring from the chain around her neck and slipped it on to her finger. She twisted it first left, then right, then left again. Once more, before she quite knew what was happening, there was a flickering brightness, a swirling haze and then the Slave of the Ring was standing before her. This time he swept her an extravagant bow. 'Fair Mistress,' he said. 'I am yours to command.'

'Oh, er, hello again,' said Fran, giggling nervously.

Ash straightened himself up and dusted an imaginary speck of dust off his trousers. 'So what can I do for you today?' he enquired briskly. 'Luxury refreshments? Exotic entertainment? Or is it top-class travel you're after?'

'Wow . . . it's almost like having a fairy god-father!'

'It is not in the least,' said Ash frostily. 'I am a hot-blooded Arabian prince, I'll have you know, under a cruel (not to mention tedious) enchant-ment. *Fairies* have nothing to do with it.'

Fran had forgotten how touchy Ash was, though she supposed she'd be fairly irritable too, if she was imprisoned in a ring and forced to provide other people with luxury refreshments and top-class travel for eternity.

'I didn't mean to be rude. Look, do you, er, want a seat?'

The genie took this as an invitation to stretch out on her bed. Rather disconcertingly, he then rose a couple of inches in the air and floated above the duvet, bobbing gently. 'OK,' he said, sighing, 'might as well get it over with. What's the first way in which you intend to mess up a wish-fulfilment, waste the ring's powers and bore me rigid in the process?'

Fran was now less sure than ever about what she wanted her first wish to be. She'd been quite taken by the lifestyle guru idea, but Ash's mention of exotic travel and entertainment had opened up a new wealth of possibilities. As far as wish-fulfilment went, seven hours on a desert island in the company of Heath Ledger couldn't be too bad.

'I haven't made my mind up yet,' she said cautiously, playing for time. 'I thought that maybe I should talk things over with you first.'

'Wonders will never cease! What do you want to know?'

'Um . . . I'm not sure . . . well, what do most people wish for?'

'Stupid things, but that's mostly because they're girls.'

'Girls aren't stupid!' said Fran indignantly. 'Just because people were all sexist pigs in whatever Dark Age you were born in doesn't mean the rest of the world hasn't matured in the meantime.' Then she went hot and cold at her daring.

To her surprise, Ash merely laughed. 'Oh, I've got a healthy respect for girl power, don't you worry.' He sat up, then floated back down to bed-level. 'But as I think I've mentioned before, the people who get their grubby hands on this ring always tend to be a) female and b) infatuated. It's a terrible combination. "Please, Mr Genie,"' he said, fluttering his eyelashes and putting on a whiny falsetto voice that made Fran giggle in spite of herself, '"I'm *soooo* in lurve with Maximus/ Ethelbert/ Mr Darcy. If you don't use your magic to make him kiss me I think I'm going to *die*." And then they go all weepy-eyed and snot-nosed and you can't get a sensible word out of them for hours.'

Fran resolved not to mention her own hopeless crush issues until a bit later. 'OK, so what would *you* wish for?' she began to ask, but before she could finish her question her brother came into the room.

'Haven't you ever heard of knocking?' she demanded.

'But I did knock, Fran, I promise,' Mickey said, freckled face shining with sincerity. 'You didn't hear me because you were talking to someone.'

Ash was floating above her bed again. 'Cute kid,' he remarked.

Mickey, naturally, was oblivious. 'Fran, do you have an invisible friend?'

'Of course not! Don't be silly.'

'Well, I think an invisible friend would be really cool.' Then, solicitously, 'In case Francesca doesn't want to come round any more.'

'Another Francesca, hmmm?' said Ash, a speculative look in his eyes. 'I take it she's the other girl in most of your photographs. Quite a babe, by the looks of it.'

'Mind your own business,' said Fran sharply. Mickey, naturally, thought she was talking to him and a hurt, reproachful look came into his eyes. 'Mickey, wait – I didn't mean you –' But he had run from the room. Fran frowned at Ash. 'Can't you keep your comments to yourself when I'm talking to someone?'

'My most humble apologies, Your Worshipfulness-On-High,' said Ash, voice dripping with sarcasm. 'Heaven forbid that I should ever forget my place as a lowliest of your slaves.'

'Don't be silly, of course I don't—'

'*Silly?* Somebody of my pedigree and prowess, condemned to wander the earth at the beck and call of dim-witted schoolgirls! I don't call that silly. I call it *tragic*. If only one, just one, of my clients would be a proper level-headed man . . .'

'Oh for goodness sake!' exclaimed Fran. 'I do wish you would—'

Who knows what would have happened next if Fran's parents hadn't chosen that moment to stand at the bottom of the stairs and yell for assistance. Her mum wanted help getting things ready for supper, her dad demanded to know what she had done to upset the timer on their ancient video machine. There was an unmistakable note of desperation in each voice. With a parting glare, Fran twisted the ring on her finger at the same time as Ash – eyes flashing – clasped the bracelet on his upper arm. A minute later, Fran was clattering down to join her family, not entirely regretful that her second genie-session had been cut short.

Fran felt uneasy about parting from Ash on bad terms but she didn't have much opportunity to dwell on it. By the time supper, homework and parent-soothing was over, she felt far too tired for negotiations with a short-tempered genie with a superiority complex. She was determined not to be bullied into spending any of the ring's magic before she was ready. And anyway, there would be plenty of time for wish-fulfilment over the weekend.

In this she was mistaken. Saturday was both Granny Roper's birthday and the afternoon when Mickey had a callback for a big advertising campaign, and so it had been arranged that Mickey and his dad would come straight from the audition to join the rest of the family at Granny Roper's house for tea. But then Mrs Roper announced that she and Beth were leaving after breakfast to spend the day with Beth's godmother, who was on a flying visit to London. This meant that Fran was now going to have to accompany her father and Mickey to the casting instead of going directly to her grand-mother's. Fran thought this was a terrible idea. Why couldn't she stay at home, then go by bus or train to join the rest of the family at teatime? But Granny Roper lived right out on the other side of the city and Fran's mum wouldn't hear of it.

Fran was simmering with resentment as she climbed into the back seat of the car. Hanging around in some hotel corridor while her little brother charmed the socks off various advertising hotshots was definitely not her idea of a good time. It wasn't even as if she was particularly looking for-ward to tea with Granny Roper either. Her grandmother would invariably begin the conversa-tion by asking if Fran was 'courting' yet and tended to murmur, 'My goodness, what an appetite!' when-ever Fran reached for another helping of cake. She called Mickey her Little Prince and obsessively taped every single one of his television appearances to show her cronies at her bridge club.

However, even Fran could appreciate that this latest job was a big deal. Kisco, one of the UK's lead-ing brand names, was launching a new type of cake bar – the 'Kookie' – and needed a boy and a girl to play siblings in a series of TV commercials. The final casting was taking place at a plush hotel and Kisco had hired a cutting-edge advertising agency to conduct the campaign.

As soon as Mr Roper, Mickey and Fran arrived at the hotel's reception, they were swept up by a Kisco representative. Her name badge identified her as Eva and she brandished her clipboard in a menacing sort of way. 'OK, so he's the kid from the Little Troopers Agency. Is that one supposed to be auditioning too?' she asked Mr Roper with an abrupt jerk of her head in Fran's direction. 'No? Thank Christ for that. I thought she looked a bit old for this gig.' Soon they were trailing after the clickety-clack of Eva's heels as she led them along a dimly lit beige corridor before arriving in a brightly lit beige conference room. One end of the room was set up with a group of chairs and a table of complimentary Kisco-brand refreshments. Three other boys of Mickey's age were already there, along with four girls aged about twelve and an assortment of mums and dads making desultory conversation over the Kookie cakes.

Mr Roper gave a polite nod to his fellow minders and settled down to read his newspaper. Mickey followed suit with the jumbo puzzle book he always took with him on these occasions. Some of the kids looked bored, some looked sprightly, but all of them had the air of seasoned professionals. If anything, it was the parents who were shifting around self-consciously and stealing furtive glances at the competition. As for Fran, she headed straight for the complimentary snacks. Might as well make the most of things.

She'd already got through her third Kookie cake by the time Eva reappeared, accompanied by an older man whose greying hair was set in gelled spikes and who wore oversized purple-rimmed glasses. He introduced himself as Fergus, the creative director of the Kookie launch project. 'It's gonna be funny, it's gonna be funky, it's gonna be fresh and, yeah, maybe a little bit kooky too,' he announced to the room before congratulating everyone on reaching this final stage. 'We think you're *all* winners, yeah? Total stars.'

Eva then stepped forward to explain that the children would be seen individually in alphabetical order, on a boy–girl basis, before being put into pairs for the final part of the casting process. 'Check out the sibling interaction. See who's cool with who, yeah?' put in Fergus. The whole business, they promised, would be over in just under two hours.

Fran groaned to herself – in two hours she could eat an awful lot of those cake bars. It didn't help that she'd just received a text message from Francesca: LEAVING FOR BAND SESSION AT Q'S HSE NOW. SO XITED. WISH U WERE HERE. X. Yes, today was definitely a day for comfort eating.

Hoping to take her mind off her stomach, Fran began to look around for some distraction. The three other boys waiting with Mickey had the same sort of look as her brother – i.e. they were 'character' kids rather than child-model types. The girls, on the other hand, were like a troupe of mini-Sadies. They twirled their hair and simpered in a so-adorable-you-could-slap-them kind of way.

'Mummy, what's that girl doing here?' enquired one of the mini-Sadies in a penetrating whisper.

'Shhhh, Perdita, darling,' said her mother with a pretend embarrassed glance at Fran. 'I think she's waiting for her brother.'

Perdita looked Fran up and down disparagingly. 'Oh. Well, if I get to play her brother's sister in the advert it will be a bit silly, won't it? I don't look anything like *her*.'

'That's why you're an actress, darling. You pretend things and people believe them.'

Perdita pouted. 'Everyone pretends stuff.'

'Yes, but, darling, you're a *professional*.' She shot another glance at Fran, this time a smug one. 'Lots of people wish they had your kind of talent and opportunities, poor things.'

And it was then, like a thunderbolt, that inspiration struck.

'Dad, I've, um, left a magazine in the car. Can you give me the keys so I can go and get it?'

Five minutes later, Fran was in the hotel's underground car park, breathless and trembling with suppressed excitement. It seemed deserted, but just to be sure she was safe from prying eyes, she didn't get out the ring until she reached a sheltered spot to the side of a large van. In a trice, Ash was standing on the tarmac beside her.

'Ash! I've decided on my first wish!'

'Really? How unspeakably thrilling.' His arms were folded across his chest and he looked even more haughty than usual. Whoops. Fran had momentarily forgotten that they hadn't parted on the best of terms.

'Please, Ash, don't be mad. I didn't mean to offend you earlier.'

'Very gracious of you, I'm sure.'

'I said I was sorry . . . look, I don't have much time. Can I have this wish or not?'

'That would depend.' Now he was checking his profile in one of the van's wing mirrors.

'But I thought you were bound by the Great Seal of Whatsit to—'

'To Serve and Obey, I know, I know. I'm just the hired help, here to cater for your every whim . . . Nice of you to put me in my place. Again.'

Fran sighed. There was no getting through to him in this mood. 'I'm sorry I've upset you. And I have a lot of respect for, er, what you do. But I really do need this wish.' She took a deep breath. 'So I want you to . . . I would like . . . I wonder if . . .'

'Get *on* with it.'

* * * * * ✱ 75 ✱ * * * * *

'Right. Fine. This is it then. I want to be special. I want to be the one who's chosen for a change. I want to be noticed. I wish that somehow, someone, somewhere would pick me out for something high-profile and showbizzy and exciting.' She paused and discovered she was shaking. 'Please.'

'OK.'

'OK . . . is er, that it?'

Ash was still lounging by the side of the van, looking down his nose at her with that maddeningly superior expression of his. 'What did you expect? A heavenly chorus?' Well, no. But a roll of drums, a flash of light or a puff of purple smoke might have been nice . . . 'Take it from me, babe, you've got your wish. And now – unless, of course, there's any other little matter of life and death I can help you with – I will beg your leave to depart.'

His last words floated in the air, for Ash had done his vanishing trick even more abruptly than usual. Fran couldn't help thinking that it was the genie equivalent of slamming the door in your face.

Fran made her way back across the car park with the hairs on the back of her neck tingling with anticipation. She wasn't an impulsive sort of person and was a little shocked by the speed and recklessness with which she'd plunged into this first wish, especially after all her earlier caution. But perhaps this was the right way to deal with magic after all – to go with the flow, let instinct and timing play their part. Now all she had to do was sit tight and wait for the magic to work in its own mysterious way. Anything could happen!

Her favourite daydream of a spotlit stage swam before her eyes, then melted into the vision of a red carpet thronged with fans. The roar of applause. Her face, airbrushed into perfection, beaming from posters and plasma screens. *The moment I saw her*, a disembodied voice was saying, *I knew Fran Roper would be perfect for the part* . . . Curtains parted – lights blazed – cameras flashed – a fanfare trumpeted –

She had just pressed the button for the lift up to reception when there was the sound of screeching tyres behind her. A large van had driven up and parked at a crooked angle in the middle of two bays. It was closely followed by a big shiny black car. The doors of the van opened and number of people jumped out and started unloading cameras and lighting equipment from the back. More people were clambering out of the car, waving clipboards and muttering into mobile phones.

'Hello! Stop! Wait right there!' A young woman with a shiny forehead and an extremely harassed expression came racing up to Fran. She smiled ingratiatingly. 'How would you like to be on TV?'

*

Five minutes later, Fran was sitting in the hotel lobby while her new friend asked her to 'call me Maggie' and invited her to 'tell me all about yourself'. Before Fran could open her mouth however, Maggie had moved on. 'Now then, Fran, do you believe in magic?'

'I'm not sure,' said Fran cautiously, one hand going to the chain around her neck. 'I suppose we all *want* to, don't we?'

Maggie nodded encouragingly. 'That's right, Fran. Everyone wants to have a little magic in their lives. That's why all of us here –' she waved a hand towards the rest of the people dashing about the lobby – 'are so thrilled to be involved in this particular project.'

'What project's that then?'

'Well, I work for a PR company, you see, which deals with a lot of media personalities. And right now we're working with one of our most exciting new clients. Let me tell you, this guy is going to be *huge*. He's already a superstar in Russia, he's massive in Japan and he's on the verge of hitting the big time in the States. Meanwhile, it's our job to help break him into the UK.'

This was getting better and better. 'So who is he? Would I have heard of him? Is he a pop star? An actor?'

'Not *exactly*.' Maggie ran her hands through her

hair. 'His name is Boris Gublovsky and he's a very talented sixteen-year-old magician from Russia.'

'Oh.' Fran did her best not to look too obviously disappointed but . . . Boris, the Boy Magician? Was this Ash's idea of 'high-profile and showbizzy and exciting'? To be honest, she had been hoping for something a bit more red carpet, a little more rock 'n' roll. After acquiring her very own genie, it was hard to be impressed by some kid who pulled rabbits out of a hat for a living.

Maggie seemed to know what she was thinking. 'You've heard of David Blaine, right? Before he started doing all that endurance stuff in plastic boxes? Boris's talents are kind of similar – in his own totally unique way, of course. Very streetwise, very hip.'

Streetwise and hip sounded good to Fran. 'So, er, how do I come into it?'

'Well, Fran, tonight is the night when Boris is appearing on *The Len Fisher Show*.' Maggie paused to let the significance of this sink in: Len Fisher was a hugely popular comedian who now had his own prime-time chat show. It was showbiz, certainly, but of the ultra-camp variety, thought Fran, repressing a twinge of unease. 'Boris has to fly to the States this evening and so we've already pre-recorded his interview with Len. But then Len had this great idea that they could also show a hidden camera clip of Boris in action, mixing with ordinary people and amazing them with his stunts. I'm sure you've seen Len's show?' Fran nodded. 'Great. Then you know how he likes things a little zany, a little unpredictable . . . Anyway, to cut a long story short, Paragon TV sent a crew over to Boris's hotel – that's this one, obviously – and we're going to shoot some material right here, right now, and somehow get this thing wrapped up in time for the show tonight.'

'I thought the whole point of being on a hidden camera is that I don't know it's happening?'

'In *theory*, that's true, yes, but this late in the day we don't want to leave anything to chance. The fact is, some people come across better on camera on others . . . it might sound weird,' said Maggie, a faraway look in her eyes, 'but the second I saw you I just *knew* that you would be perfect.' Fran smiled to herself. 'So, er, are you available?'

'Well, sort of—'

'Great! Terrific!' Maggie turned round and gave a thumbs up to another girl hovering with a walkie-talkie. Immediately, various people swooped down on Fran. They were all thrilled she could help. She'd love every minute. Boris was such a sweetie. Len's show was such a blast. Had she met Rick, the cameraman? Scott, the director? Had she met Angie, Becks, Steve? Would she like anything to eat first? To drink? Was there anyone she should call?

That was a point. Fran explained the situation with Mickey and the audition, but almost before she'd finished speaking someone was hastening off to clear things with Mr Roper. It seemed that since she had a genie on her side nothing could stop her; everyone was delighted for her, everyone was eager to help. Scott, the director, explained the procedure for the shoot.

'The hotel has a cafe, right, so er – Fran, is it? OK, Fran, you'll be in there chilling out and then we'll have Boris come over. As far as you're concerned, he's just a regular guy, OK? Bit of chit chat, bit of interaction, then, hey presto, he does his stuff. Amazement all round.' Obviously, the whole 'hidden camera' business was a fake, but Scott and his team were anxious to make the film look as real life as possible. 'So there won't be any rehearsal, OK? As soon as Boris walks into this cafe – bam! – the cameras will roll. Don't stress, just be nice and natural, and if you look a bit uncomfortable, that's natural too. Keep things real. Then, if you're cool with it, we'll maybe do a little interview with you afterwards, get some feedback, OK? Sound good? Yeah? Excellent.' Then he dashed off to take a call from the head of hotel security. Meanwhile, Maggie had disappeared upstairs to 'bring Boris up to speed'.

'Is there any way I could change my clothes?' Fran asked Angie with some anxiety. She was wearing a jumper her granny had sent her that was hand-knitted in a deeply unflattering green wool –

fine for a tea with an elderly relation, not so good for a TV debut. If she wasn't going to be airbrushed, surely some kind of makeover was part of the deal.

'Sure, sure!' said her new friends and people were sent bustling hither and thither. She was taken into a large bathroom where somebody dabbed various powders on her face, smeared some incredibly gloopy gloss on her lips and re-arranged her hair. Someone else found a tight pink T-shirt that Fran squeezed into in one of the cubicles. She barely had time to glance in the mirror before being whisked off to the cafe where she was set up in a corner with a large coffee and a magazine. The piped music droning in the background was replaced with a CD of current hits and the couple of hotel guests sitting at the tables were politely ushered out. For a film that was supposed to show Boris live and uncut with the Great British Public, the team from Paragon seemed very anxious to leave nothing to chance.

Once Fran and her cappuccino had been positioned to everyone's satisfaction, the lighting adjusted, the sound tested and the camera crew poised for action, events ground to an unexpected halt. The star of the show had got 'just a teeny bit delayed', announced Maggie, a glint of desperation in her eye, before dashing out to the lobby again. Cue more mutterings into various mobiles. The hotel manager, who had come to 'supervise' filming, kept rolling up his sleeve to examine his watch. Scott began to bite his nails. Steve handed round triple shots of espresso. Fran, meanwhile, took the opportunity to send a text to Francesca: OMIGOD I'M GOING 2 B ON LEN FISHER SHOW 2NITE!!! HOPE UR HAVING FUN WITH FIREDOGS. SPK SOON X.

As a matter of fact, the full impact of what was happening was only just hitting home. OK, so this wasn't *quite* what she had in mind when she'd made the – admittedly vague – wish, but she was determined to make the most of it. After all, she was going to be on a prime-time television show! With a teenage Russian superstar! Who was bound to be exotic and mysterious but – unlike the other magical being of her acquaintance – non-patronizing, non-sarcastic and one hundred per cent human . . . Russians tended to have good cheekbones, right?

The next moment a commotion at the entrance of the cafe announced that Boris had, at last, made his appearance. Not that much of Boris was immediately visible, since he was surrounded by three immense bodyguards, as wide as they were tall, who only shuffled away once their charge got in range of the cameras. 'And *action*,' said Scott softly. Someone was approaching Fran's table. She kept her eyes resolutely fixed on an article about hair-removal cream and clasped her hands in her lap to keep them from shaking. Someone was now hovering by her chair in a purposeful manner.

'Pliss, is this seat taken?'

'Ah – um – no –' said Fran, looking up at last. 'Hello.'

'Plissed to make your acquaintance,' crooned Boris the Boy Magician, and at once planted a sloppy kiss on the back of her hand. He didn't let go of her hand afterwards, but stood there, stroking it gently and gazing into her eyes.

Fran stared back in utter dismay. Boris did indeed have cheekbones you could slice cheese with, but he was also wearing tight black leather trousers with pointed shoes and had his hair gelled in an elaborate Elvis Presley-style quiff. His orange T-shirt bore the legend 'Babe Magnet' in metal studs. 'Vood you mind if I sit myself by you?'

'Um, no –'

Boris sat down and pulled his chair next to hers so close that their knees and shoulders were touching. There was a strong smell of aftershave. Eau de Chlorine with a hint of pineapple. 'I am Borees,' he announced. 'You?'

'Fran.'

'Fan. A lovely name. You are a lovely English honey, I zink.'

Fran couldn't think of anything to say so she took a sip of tepid cappuccino.

'You are hot for ze Russian boys, Fanny?'

Fran nearly choked on her coffee. Some of the froth had gone up her nose and it took her a moment to recover. 'The name's Fran. F-R-A-N. And you're the first Russian boy I've ever met.'

'Yes, but I am *special* Russian boy.' Boris leaned in with a conspiratorial smirk. 'I can show you ze many, many tricks.'

At this point Fran couldn't help glancing over to where Maggie was standing. So this was Mr Hip-and-Streetwise, Eastern Europe's answer to David Blaine! No wonder they didn't want to film the action on hidden camera. Any normal person coming face-to-face with Boris and his aftershave would probably have run screaming for mercy by now.

Boris was reaching for her hand again. 'I am zinking ve vill make vonderful magic together,' he leered. Then, quite casually, he took a couple of sugar cubes from the bowl beside her and crushed them between his fingers. As the powdered sugar fell to the table, he opened his hands to reveal a tiny red rose, which he presented to Fran with a flourish.

'Amazing.' Even after coming face to face with a genie, Fran was impressed. The Boy Magician smirked complacently. Next, he tore a page from her magazine and began to shred it into an empty teapot that had been left on a neighbouring table. When the pot was full of shredded paper, he replaced the lid and clicked his fingers over the spout, before proceeding to pour steaming turquoise liquid into her coffee cup.

Fran shook her head in admiration. 'That was, oh my gosh, incredible. I can't . . . well, I can hardly believe it.' For a moment, she had completely forgotten about the cameras. She did not, however, fail to notice when Boris slipped his arm around her waist and gave her a lingering squeeze. 'I impress you, Franny?'

'Will you please stop *doing* that,' she hissed, moving her chair to a safe distance.

'Very well, Fran – vood you like to see me do my most amazing miracle?'

'Er, OK.'

'You like to dance, Fran?'

'Not particularly.' This didn't sound good . . .

'I am zinking you are a most hot dancer, Fran. OK. Pliss stand to clap your hands and shake ze booty with me.'

'*What?* No. No way.'

'But for ziz magic it is most necessary, Fran. A very, very special trick for a very special honey, yes?'

'No,' said Fran firmly. This was getting ridiculous. She cast a pleading look in the camera crew's direction.

'And cut!' said Scott. 'OK, do we have a problem? Because we don't have time for problems. No. Time. At. All.'

Boris shrugged extravagantly. 'Ze lady, she does not want to cooperate.' He strolled over to admire his quiff in the mirror behind the counter.

Maggie hurried over. 'Fran, is something wrong?'

'He wants me to *dance*! To bop around the cafe like a lunatic! For some stupid trick!' Fran felt bad about interrupting the filming but there was no way she was shaking her booty for Boris Gublovsky's gratification.

'Boris is a complete professional, Fran – and this is performance art, remember? It works because it's spontaneous, a little "out-there" . . .'

'Yeah, but if this was real life and I didn't know about the camera and *The Len Fisher Show* and everything there's no way I'd do it. There's no way *anyone* would do it.'

Maggie closed her eyes and rubbed her forehead. 'Right. How about if you weren't on your own? What if more people came into the cafe and joined in too, would you feel better then?' She shot an enquiring glance at Scott, who shrugged and rolled his eyes.

'Fine. Whatever. Let's just get a move on. You OK to go with that, er, Fran?'

'Uh, maybe . . .' she said doubtfully. But Maggie was already summoning over Becks and the hotel manager to explain the situation. The latter could be heard to mumble something about Health and Safety Regulations but seemed, on the whole, far from reluctant to grab his fifteen seconds of televisual fame. A couple of minutes later, he had exchanged his suit jacket for a barista's apron, Becks and Maggie were poised at the entrance of the cafe and Boris and Fran were back in their original positions.

'And . . . *action.*'

'Pliss to make hot dance moves with me,' said Boris again.

'I'm not sure I understand,' said Fran, playing for time.

'Pliss to clap your hands and waggle ze hips and I vill show you sexy magic for a sexy lady. Give me your energy and we'll make funky moves together, yes?'

There was a long pause. Then Fran – very slowly, very reluctantly – got to her feet.

'*Everybody* in ze house get ready to dance!' declared Boris, spreading his arms wide. Every movement made his leather trousers squeak. 'Here you – yes, you two lovely English honeys – you will help me make my magic, yes? And ze coffee-making man! All such lovely English peoples! Move to ze music! Yeah!' Boris clicked his fingers and, whether by accident or design, the background track changed to a pulsing eighties rock anthem. The volume seemed a lot louder too. He clicked his fingers again and the lights in the cafe dimmed. Fran exchanged apprehensive glances with her fellow recruits.

'In a circle, peoples!'

They shuffled into place.

'Clap your hands, peoples! Stamp ze feet! I need

to feel your energy, yes? Make ze body sway to ze funky beat!'

By now the music had got very loud. Fran, Maggie, Becks and the hotel manager began to move their feet from side to side, supplemented by the odd shoulder wiggle and sway of the hips. The manager, who was really getting into the spirit of things, attempted an impromptu groin-thrust.

'Here ve go, peoples, here ve go!'

Boris stood in the centre of the circle, eyes closed, brow furrowed with concentration. As the others began to clap in time with the music, uncertainly at first, but then with increasing enthusiasm, Fran saw to her disbelief that Boris's feet had risen at least three inches from the floor. For about thirty seconds he hovered there, floating in the same way as Ash had done above her bed, but with the strain of the effort showing on his face. Then, as they all looked on, transfixed with astonishment, the music came to the end of the track and Boris's feet returned to earth. Everyone burst into spontaneous applause.

'That was *incredible*,' said Fran at last. 'How – what – how did that – did you—'

'But I am zinking you haf magic too, Fran. I am under ze spell you cast, yes?' He took the rose he'd conjured and dabbed her playfully on the nose with it. 'Maybe you vill become my beautilicious assistant.'

'And . . . cut,' said Scott, with a heartfelt sigh of relief. 'Phew. Well done, everybody, I think we've got a great little scene there. Fantastic work, Boris, as ever. Nicely played, er, Fran.'

Maggie was now hovering by Boris anxiously. 'Great. Terrific. Wonderful stuff. Boris, I'm very sorry, but you need to leave for the airport in ten minutes *max*. So if we—'

Boris heaved a long-suffering sigh and, after patting his quiff into place, got ready to leave. Every step was accompanied by a whole symphony of trouser-squeaks. 'Ah, such lovely honeys, ze English girls. I vish that ve vill meet again,' he announced, making one last grab for Fran's hand and kissing it with moist appreciation. Then the three giant bodyguards closed around him and he was gone.

The next fifteen minutes or so where taken up with what Scott called the debrief, in which they pretended to break the news of the 'hidden' camera to Fran and she gave her reaction to her encounter with Boris. She was too dazed to really take anything in but did her best to smile and nod in the right places. Then, all of a sudden, it was over and she was shaking hands with everybody, grinning away and assuring them that, yes, it had been a wonderful experience and, yes, she'd be sure to watch the show that night. She tottered out to join her father and Mickey in the lobby with the feeling that maybe she didn't have the stamina for a life in showbiz.

'Cool, Fran! You've met a real live *magician*!' Mickey was hopping up and down with excitement. 'Did he have a wand? A broomstick? Was he like Harry Potter?'

Fran blinked at him. She was feeling tired, thirsty and not a little confused. 'Sort of . . . no . . . not really . . . though he can do some amazing stuff.'

'Well, we'll be able to see for ourselves, won't we?' put in her dad. 'We can watch the show together at your Gran's.' He gave her a hug. 'What a wonderful experience for you, love.'

'Yeah,' said Fran. 'Magic.'

Both Mickey and Fran fell asleep in the car during the brief journey to Granny Roper's house. It had been a long afternoon for both of them. Although she only dozed off for ten minutes or so, Fran woke up feeling groggy and disorientated. She was still wearing the hot-pink T-shirt she'd worn for filming, her face felt smeary with the make-up they'd given her and one of her eyes kept sticking together. Before they left the car Fran insisted Mickey and her dad wait while she changed back into the jumper she'd originally been wearing and tried to tidy herself up a bit using the mirror over the dashboard. It was only then she discovered that a dusting of cocoa from her cappuccino was still clinging to her lipgloss.

'I can't believe nobody *told* me!' she wailed for the twentieth time as the family assembled round the table for tea and birthday cake.

'I'm sure that's only because no one even noticed,' Mrs Roper said soothingly, as she had on the nineteen previous occasions. She herself was oblivious to the fact that Beth was busy smearing jam into her hair.

'Have some more cake, pet,' her granny suggested. 'If you scrape off the buttercream I'm sure it won't be so fattening. Now, Mickey, my love, I know you had a very special audition today. Come and sit by Granny and tell me all about it.'

While Mickey recounted his latest adventures in advertising, Fran went over and over everything that had happened since she'd summoned Ash in the car park. The more she thought about events the more deeply uneasy she felt . . . Boris might be talented, but he was still the biggest nutcase she'd ever met. And she had volunteered – on camera – to 'make ze body sway to ze funky beat' with him! Never mind Boris's amazing levitation skills, how would her nearest and dearest react to the sight of Fran shaking ze booty on national television? Fran went hot and cold at the thought of all the people who might be watching the show that night.

Francesca would be sure to tune in of course, but what about Zara and Sadie? And Quinn?

At six thirty everyone was equipped with yet more cups of tea and at six fifty the whole family lined themselves up in front of Fran's grandmother's TV. At six fifty-five the video was set to record and then, at seven on the dot, the room filled with the jaunty theme tune everyone knew so well. *The Len Fisher Show* always opened with a different song-and-dance routine and this evening it was a troupe of drag queens dancing the cancan. As the dancers formed a ring of muscular legs in fishnet stockings and frilly pink knickers, Len rose from the middle of them atop a gold pedestal. He was dressed in a tweed coat and jodhpurs, he carried a tasselled riding crop and his hair was dyed a brilliant turquoise. 'WELL HELLOOOOOO, LUVVIES!' he cried, to cheers and whoops from the studio audience.

The first half of the show passed in a blur as far as Fran was concerned. There was a spoof of the latest Hollywood blockbuster, a comedy quiz with a couple of minor soap stars and a round-up of the week's tabloid headlines. Finally, Boris's – and Fran's – moment of glory arrived. Len pranced across the stage with a couple of rabbits (their fur dyed turquoise) under each arm. 'WHO BELIEVES IN MAGIC, LUVVIES?' he asked in his top-volume squeal. 'WE DO!' roared back the audience as a shower of glittering stars fell from on high. 'WE DO! WE DO!' squeaked Mickey and Beth, bouncing up and down on the settee.

Boris's interview wasn't live, but it was very much in the style of the rest of the show, full of crazy swooping camera angles, random bursts of music, and slapstick from Len. The Boy Magician was dressed just as badly as Fran remembered – this time he was wearing a zebra-striped tank top and orange flares – though next to Len's blue Mohican he didn't look quite so out of place as he had in the hotel's cafe. But although the rest of Fran's family were in raptures over Boris's trick with an exploding champagne bottle and vanishing chihuahua, Fran was finding it hard to concentrate on the wonders before her. Any moment now . . .

'And now,' said their host as the interview clip ended and the camera cut back to Len live in the studio, 'let's take a wee peek at what young Boris gets up to when he's not schmoozing us lucky show-biz types. Ladies, gents, luvvies and all, I am proud to present – BORIS GUBLOVSKY'S CANDID-CAMERA CONJURING TOUR!!!!!' Cue more music, applause and – suddenly – a shot of Fran engrossed in her magazine. A wild cheer went up from the Roper audience.

At first Fran almost didn't recognize herself. For one thing, the camera angle was crooked and the scene slightly out of focus in what was doubtless a deliberate attempt at the 'hidden camera' look. For another, her five-minute makeover was more radical than she'd realized. Had she *really* been wearing all that sparkly blue eyeshadow? With her high ponytail and clinging pink T-shirt she looked like one of the wannabe Sadie-clones, but – oh, dear God – was that a roll of *fat* hanging out over her jeans? She knew the T-shirt was a little too tight for her but this was a disaster . . . and that was even before they got to the bit when she snorted cappuccino foam up her nose. Trust Fran to spend her fifteen minutes of fame wearing a cocoa moustache. Even the dancing drag queens had more class.

Strangely enough, everyone else – studio audience and Roper family alike – seemed to think the whole thing was a work of comic genius. 'That Russian kid is *hilarious*,' said her mum, wiping tears of merriment from her eyes. 'How on earth did you manage to keep a straight face?'

'My goodness,' said her gran, 'he's a bit of a cheeky one, isn't he?'

'Fran, is Boris going to be your boyfriend?' enquired Mickey.

By the time the dance session started, Fran had buried her head under a cushion and was whimpering with shame. Surely it all had to be some hideous nightmare . . . surely this couldn't be happening, not to her . . . She had a fleeting hope that once the Boy Magician had made his exit and it was just her talking to Scott she'd manage to salvage some dignity from the occasion, but no such luck.

'So, Fran, do you believe in magic?' asked Scott's voice from off-camera.

'I didn't used to but now . . . well, who knows what's out there? So yeah, yeah I do.' The screen Fran giggled nervously and played with her pony-tail. The real Fran bushed and blushed again.

'"There are more things in heaven and earth . . ." and all that?'

'Definitely.'

'How did you feel when you realized you were being filmed?'

'Totally shocked – I'd never, ever have guessed. I'm still reeling. It was a complete surprise.' Pause. 'I really hadn't a clue.' Pause. 'Honestly.'

'And what's the likelihood of you becoming Boris's beautilicious assistant? Is he in with a chance?'

'Erm . . . he's very, um, talented but . . .'

'Not your type?'

'Yeah. I guess I don't usually go for dark men.' The screen Fran squirmed with embarrassment. So did the real one. 'And I think maybe he's a bit, like . . . immature?'

The scene split into a particularly unflattering still of Fran licking cappuccino foam off her finger next to one of Boris patting his quiff and then, finally, they were back in the studio. 'Poor old

Boris,' said Len, shaking his head, 'I guess he'll have to go polish his wand on his own then!' Once again, the audience erupted into laughter. Mr and Mrs Roper exchanged glances. Granny Roper pursed her lips. Mickey looked confused.

There and then, Fran decided that Ash was one dead genie.

'I thought you only used your powers for good! No injury or mischief allowed, you said! Serve and protect and all that rubbish!' Fran had waited all morning to get the living room to herself and now she and Ash were stood in front of the TV, where the Borisgate tape was playing for a second time. She wanted Ash to witness his crime at first hand.

'I'm sorry, but I still don't see what all the fuss is about,' said Ash, who was refusing to rise to the bait. 'I think you come across rather well. That T-shirt looks quite cute – better than the boring shapeless stuff I've seen you in before.'

'*Excuse me*, but I'm not about to take fashion tips from some guy who's spent the last millennium or so in his pyjamas.'

The genie merely arched an aristocratic brow. 'Yes, well, if I'd known I was about to be banished to a ring for eternity I would obviously have made more of an effort with my wardrobe. Besides,' he added, admiring his reflection in the window, 'this look's a classic.'

Fran realized they were straying off the subject. 'That's not the point. The point is I have made a total, utter idiot of myself in front of eight million people and it's all your fault. You deliberately sabotaged my first wish! Admit it!' Fran – good old Fran who never liked to make a fuss, Fran who hated shouting – was, for the first time in her life, spoiling for a fight.

But Ash wasn't listening. As usual. Instead he was fiddling with the remote control, a frown of concentration on his face. 'Aha – here we go!' The television was now showing a Sunday-morning game show. 'The greatest inventions of the modern age: miniskirts and breakfast television . . . By the way, I thought that Boy Conjuror of yours showed precocious talent. Are you sure he's not a minor warlock?'

'Stop trying to change the subject! Don't you feel the *slightest* bit guilty about what's happened?'

Ash turned off the TV and got to his feet. He looked at her sternly. 'Let's get one thing clear, all right? I. Am. Not. To. Blame. For. Sloppy. Wishmaking.' She started to protest. 'No, listen to me, Fran. You were overexcited and emotional and you didn't think before wishing. I've seen it happen a thousand times. A girl names some starry-eyed, daydreamy aspiration that means everything and nothing and then acts all outraged when it doesn't work in the real world . . .'

'I can't believe I'm hearing this – Mr Magic pops out of a ring and tells *me* to get a reality check!'

'Look, I'm here to grant wishes, not work miracles, OK? Next time try and be a little more specific.' He sighed and ran his hands through his hair. 'I don't *enjoy* seeing you lot screw everything up, you know. I'm sure it's just as emotionally exhausting for me as it is for you.'

'OK, but why don't you try being a bit more helpful then? A bit more patient?'

'Easy for you to say. You try being trapped in an enchanted ring for a few centuries and see where patience gets you.'

That brought her up short. 'I didn't mean – well, no, you're right. Sorry. Poor you . . . it must be awful.' Fran was feeling guilty again, but once more Ash managed to completely wrong-foot her.

'Oh well, it's not *all* bad. In fact, it can be quite fun, if you get a good client and aren't stuck in some godforsaken hole like Uzbekistan. Or Idaho, even.' He flashed her a brilliant white smile. 'One of these days I should write my memoirs.'

Fran smiled back at him. It was hard to stay annoyed with Ash for long – and anyway, she needed to keep him in a good mood if she was going to make a success of the remaining wishes. Right there and then, Fran resolved to take a new approach to genie-maintenance. From now on she would make a special effort to show Ash how much she valued his advice as well as his wish-granting skills. She would consult him and include him in all her plans. She would be the model client: calm, rational and sweet-tempered at all times. He, in turn, would grow to respect her, to put that little bit of extra effort into making every wish come true. After all, she still had six chances to win her heart's desire, and she wasn't going to let some git of a genie get in the way.

When Fran woke up on Monday morning she had that cold, queasy feeling you get before an exam or a visit to the dentist. On average, eight million people tuned in to watch *The Len Fisher Show* and it would be just her luck that seven hundred and sixty eight of them were the pupils at her school.

Francesca's view was that Fran was taking everything Far Too Seriously – 'people will be laughing *with* you, not *at* you, silly' – but then Francesca was feeling guilty for alerting Zara and Sadie and all the Firedogs as soon as she'd got Fran's OMIGOD I'M GOING 2 B ON LEN FISHER SHOW text. At the time she thought she was being wonderfully efficient in spreading the good news, but in hindsight she couldn't help thinking she should have been just a little less quick off the mark.

None the less, Fran tried hard not to let her own gloom spoil Francesca's obvious high spirits. She'd made up some excuse to stop her coming round on

Sunday, because she just couldn't face pretending to be thrilled with Francesca's success with the band while her own venture into showbiz had gone so horribly wrong. Instead, she'd listened on the phone while Francesca laughed like a drain for about ten minutes ('Did he *really* ask you to polish his wand?') and then gushed for half an hour about how exciting it was to rehearse with a proper band, how friendly all the Firedogs were once you got to know them and how complimentary Quinn had been about her voice. Francesca never gushed, as a rule, and Fran found it hard to know how to respond. So on Monday morning she was relieved to find that Francesca was back to her usual under-stated self, even if her conversation was still ninety per cent full of Firedog. This time she even remembered to say, 'Next time, of course, you'll have to come along too,' and 'One of these days, the others really must hear you sing.'

As they approached the entrance to their class-room, Fran's steps grew slower and slower. Matters weren't helped by the fact she'd just caught sight of Zara and Sadie enthroned on the fire escape with Rob Crawford in attendance. Fran's pace ground to a halt.

'Come on, Fran, don't be so wet,' said Francesca impatiently, pulling her by the arm. 'You'll have to face everybody sooner or later. Hey, guys.'

'All hail the Firedog's foxiest rock-chick,' said

Zara, clapping slowly. 'Not forgetting Magic Boy's beautilicious assistant. Congratulations to one and all.'

'I think the Firedogs are super-lucky to have you, Francesca,' said Sadie with a simper in Rob's direction.

'Right you are,' said Rob. 'We thought it was about time the band got ourselves some eye-candy.'

'That so?' Francesca smiled coolly. 'Let's hope you don't choke on it.'

Rob grinned back, a little uncertainly. Had she just made a dirty joke? Or was it some kind of insult?

'By the way, hon, *loved* the dance moves,' said Sadie to Fran. 'They were, like, majorly retro.'

'Didn't know you had so much rhythm in you, Roper. Maybe you should branch out, do some, you know, private performances?' said Rob with a wink and a leer.

'Morning, everyone.' It was Quinn. Quinn! Looking adorably just out of bed, with his mussed-up hair and sleepy eyes, slouching into the collar of his shirt as if it were part of some ironic style statement rather than a bog-standard school uniform.

'Hi, Quinn,' said Francesca casually. 'You know Zara and Sadie, right?' Quinn nodded at them. 'And this is Fran.'

'Of course, the other Francesca.' He smiled

warmly at her. 'Doesn't it get confusing, both of you having the same name?'

'Oh, Fran's always been just Fran,' said Francesca.

'Or, as she's more usually known these days,' put in Zara, 'Fanny Potter, Magician's Assistant Extraordinaire. Did you see the show, Quinn?'

'Sure. Francesca must've sent me, like, five texts to remind me.'

'Poor Boris,' sighed Zara. 'Most of Britain knows that Fran's not interested in immature, dark-haired, boy magicians . . .'

'. . . and could that be,' chimed in Sadie, 'because she's got a thing for older, blond, boy musicians?'

Quinn acted like he hadn't heard. 'I thought the whole thing was pretty cool, actually – as a satire on the cult of celebrity of course.'

'Er, of course,' said Fran, dazzled.

'It was heavily improvised, right?' he asked, giving her a knowing look.

'Uh, sort of . . .'

'As spoof characters go, that Boris Gublovsky is a work of genius,' Quinn continued, 'but I still think they could've spent a bit more effort on the stunts. Take that levitating trick, for example – you could *so* obviously spot the wires.'

'The thing is –' Fran began, then stopped. If Quinn wanted to think her idiocy at the end of a camera lens had actually been a witty spoof of celebrity culture, that was fine by her. Who knows how Boris had done his stunts, anyway? A week or so ago she too would have been looking out for the wires. Post-Ash, however, she couldn't be quite so sure.

'Right,' said Quinn, hitching his bag over his shoulder. 'I guess it's time Rob and I got a move on. See you later girls.'

Fran blushed. Sadie giggled. Zara tossed her head. Francesca, however, rolled her eyes. 'Quinn's a nice enough guy but could he *be* any more up himself?' she muttered to Fran as they made their way towards their classroom.

'What do you mean?'

'All that pretentious crap about satirizing the cult of celebrity for starters. No offence, Fran, but I don't reckon the people who make *The Len Fisher Show* would recognize irony if it slapped them round the face.'

'Well, maybe Quinn was trying to avoid embarrassing me,' said Fran defensively. 'You know, take the pressure off.'

'Ah yes,' said Francesca, laughing. 'Quinn Adams, the answer to a maiden's prayer. You have to hand it to the boy – he's got the manly-yet-sensitive thing down to a fine art.'

Fran started to argue but thought better of it. If Francesca couldn't see Quinn's inner as well as outer beauty then she wasn't going to force the point.

And anyway, right now she had other issues to deal with . . .

'Hiya, Fran – got any rabbits up your sleeve?'

'Oho, ze vonderful Ms Roper! Still moving to ze funky beat, yes?'

'There you are Fran – I thought you'd gone and done a vanishing act!'

'Does anyone know how to say "abracadabra" in Russian?'

And that was just the teachers.

'So how did it go?'

Ash, for once, managed to sound mildly sympathetic. They were in her bedroom with the radio on loud and the door locked to forestall any interruptions. Fran was still on her mission to butter Ash up while bringing him up to date with modern life in general and her own experience of it in particular, and to this end she'd provided him with a selection of relevant publications – *Time Out*, *National Geographic*, a copy of her school's annual magazine and *Glamour*. She'd even let him switch stations on the radio, away from Radio One to some weird pirate frequency that seemed to play nothing but thrash metal. At present he was floating just below the ceiling, happily engrossed in a pull-out lingerie guide from *Glamour*, and nodding his head in time to the music. Meanwhile, Fran was lying on her bed trying to compose a list of Heart's

Desires, colour-coded in order of a) importance and b) feasibility. Even with seven hours of top-notch magic at her disposal, Fran was coming to terms with the fact that a trip to the moon might be more trouble than it was worth.

Now she sighed and put the list to one side. 'How you'd expect – lots of sarky comments and stupid impressions of Russian accents. Or English dance moves.'

'Are you quite unpopular then?' enquired Ash casually.

'Of course not!' Fran said indignantly. I'm just . . . you know, average.'

'I see.' Ash turned to a double-page Wonderbra ad and helped himself to a fistful of tortilla chips – another of Fran's little enticements. Apparently genies didn't need to eat or drink as such, but Ash assured her they could, quite happily. (In fact, he'd even requested a peanut butter and jelly sandwich the next time around – 'A taste I developed on my Idaho excursion. And some single malt Scotch whisky might be nice.' Fran said she'd see what she could do, but honestly there *were* limits . . .)

'Maybe I'm not the class princess,' Fran continued, 'but I get on with loads of people.'

'Fine. Let's see 'em.'

'What?'

Ash floated down to ground level. 'Much as I adore looking at pictures of young ladies in their underwear, it is also a poignant reminder of all I have lost. So, rather than wallow in self-pity, I think it's time I had a introductory guide to your socio-educational environment.' He pointed at last year's school magazine. 'Maybe it will put your paranoid witterings into context.'

Fran was taken aback. Her plan had been to drop Ash little hints about her life, loves and pursuit of happiness, but so subtly that he barely noticed how she was drawing him in. This sudden interest in her life was rather unsettling. What was he expecting her to provide, exactly? A blow-by-blow account of every friend or foe she'd had since first-year juniors? A breakdown of her homework timetable? A performance-related assessment of the Year Ten netball team?

As it turned out, this was pretty much what Ash was after. 'Show me something about this Francesca of yours,' he commanded. And, 'Do English schools have cheerleaders?' And, 'Which of your teachers has the lowest opinion of you?'

Fran decided to work backwards. 'Well . . . Mrs Barnstaple – she's head of PE – says she's never met anyone so uncoordinated. And Mr Mayhew, my English teacher, thinks I'm pretty dismal.'

'Your English sounds perfectly adequate to me,' said Ash, 'though your syntax tends to deteriorate when you're emotional.'

'Not that kind of English. I mean studying books

and plays and stuff. Anyway, Mr Mayhew wrote in my last report that "Fran has the poetic sensibility of a tub of margarine."'

'Hmm. So what about the cheerleaders?'

'They're only in America, I think. But we do have our equivalents; you know, the ultra-popular girls—'

'Show me.'

Fran rolled her eyes but found herself turning the pages until she found a photo of Zara and Sadie and a few others at last year's Christmas concert, where they'd gone round collecting money for charity dressed up as angels in glittery dresses and tinsel wings. 'Delightful,' said Ash. 'And these, I suppose, are their male counterparts.' He was pointing to an action shot of the school rugby team.

'No way!' Fran couldn't help giggling. 'They're all such meatheads. Well, I guess some girls like them, but . . .'

'I see. So most girls at your school are attracted by the studious, intellectual type.' Ash had found a photo of the Science Club, wonky specs and nervous grins galore.

'Er, not *exactly* . . . I suppose I – we – girls I know –' She stopped and tried again. 'I suppose the really popular guys are the ones who do cool stuff outside school. There was this one boy, right, who was an amazing graffiti artist. He used to get into loads of trouble, but then he got a scholarship to Art

College and all the girls had such a crush on him. And now there's this group of lads who have their own band . . .'

'Show me,' said Ash again.

'I don't think – oh, hang on.' She found a picture of a Year Eleven geography field trip with Quinn and Rob standing together at the back of the group. Quinn's face was blurred, otherwise she would have saved the photo for the soapbox under her bed. 'That's Rob, the guitarist, and, er, that's Quinn. Everyone reckons he's the most talented one in the band. He writes all their music and sings, too. He's got the most amazing voice – really intense. He's very poetic.'

'Oho, is he indeed?' said Ash who, Fran now realized, wasn't looking at the photo at all but was examining her instead. His face had a little smirk on it. 'How *very* interesting.'

Damn it. Fran was trying very hard to keep her cool but it was difficult when Ash was looking at her in such a smug, knowing sort of way.

'And how does the lovely Francesca fit in to all of this?'

Fran frowned. 'You've already seen my photos of Francesca.'

'I meant how does she fit into the cheerleader-and-boyband set-up.'

'She's . . . she's just my friend. My *best* friend. She gets on with everybody. As a matter of fact,' Fran added defiantly, 'she's joined this band I was telling you about and she's going to make sure I get to come along to all the rehearsals and everything.'

Ash didn't say anything, but looked thoughtful. Fran was suddenly fed up with his questions.

'What about you, then?' she challenged.

'What about me?'

'I want to hear something about *your* life. I want to know what it's like to live in a magic ring, for instance.'

'Well, once you get inside, it turns into a marble palace filled with chocolate fountains and half-naked dancing girls.'

'Really?'

'No. When I'm not busy bringing magic and sparkle to people's lives, I go into hibernation. Boring, but true.'

'Oh. Tell me something about your pre-genie life then.'

'Like what?'

'Like . . . how did you first get into the ring?'

Ash gave her a long, brooding look. 'Girl trouble,' he said darkly.

'Boy trouble,' said Mr Mayhew. 'Or a cash-flow crisis. Dysfunctional parent. Peculiar rash.' Pause. 'Frankly, I don't know and I don't care. Because mesmerizing as your thoughts must be, it's time you sat up, switched on and PAID SOME FRIGGING

ATTENTION.' His hand slammed down on the front of Fran's desk.

Fran jumped. She had been miles away, speculating about the mystery of Ash's past and plotting the questions she'd put to him as soon as she got back from school. What with Wish Number Two up for grabs, and Francesca's recent invitation to hang out with the band on Friday night, Fran's head was full to bursting with daydream material.

'As I was saying,' Mr Mayhew continued, 'the next few weeks will be spent studying Emily Brontë's Victorian bodice-ripper, *Wuthering Heights*. Moronic twaddle, needless to say, but as far as the National Curriculum goes, Ours is Not to Reason Why.' Mr Mayhew was in a particularly poisonous mood after seeing one of his fellow graduates from the Milton Keynes College of Performing Arts appear in last night's *EastEnders*. 'Everyone should've finished the book by now, so I expect you're longing to get stuck into the emotional core of the text. And what better way to do so than with a little improvisational exercise on the central love story?' Everyone groaned. 'Oh yes, my friends. A dramatic dialogue between hero and heroine, distilling the key themes of destructive passion and the clash of Nature versus Culture . . . Ms Roper, how kind of you to volunteer! I am sure you will make a wonderfully impassioned Cathy. And for the dashing and dangerous Heathcliffe . . . hmm . . . let's see . . .' He surveyed the class morosely. Little bastards, the lot of 'em. 'Wayne Roberts. Perfect.'

Wayne lumbered to his feet, sighing. He knew that resistance was futile.

'Right, Fran, come and stand opposite Wayne. Remember, Heathcliffe is the love of your life. Both of you are reckless, romantic and D-O-O-M-E-D. Try and visualize yourselves on a windswept Yorkshire moor, if it'll help.'

Fran and Wayne stared at each other in dismay. Fran had actually quite enjoyed the book, but in the horror of the moment she found she could remember very little of either hero or heroine, let alone basic plot. They ate lots of porridge, she recalled, and did a great deal of running around and shouting in the rain.

'I love the moors,' she said at last.

'Yes,' said Wayne, 'they're so . . . windswept.'

Pause.

'It's nice to be in Yorkshire,' observed Fran. 'In the rain. With you.'

The class tittered and Mr Mayhew gave an impatient flick of his thinning blond locks. 'Let's inject some emotion, people. A bit of fire. Wayne, you're supposed to be a force of nature. I want to see some snarling animal passion, OK?'

'Grrrrrrrr,' said Wayne faintly.

Fran put a hand to her brow.

'NO, NO, NO!' Mr Mayhew strode up to them.

God, how he despised amateurs! 'Look, it's not like I'm asking you to perform frigging *Beckett* . . .' They stared back at him blankly. 'Never mind . . . Right, one more attempt. Heathcliffe, tell Cathy that you'd rather die than be without her. Cathy, at least *try* to look broken-hearted.'

'I would rather die than be without you,' repeated Wayne obediently, to howls of laughter from the class.

'Oh dear,' said Fran. 'I'm really sorry – d'you want to come and have some porridge instead?'

Morning break found Fran on a comfort-eating mission to the chocolate machine. 'Are you sure you don't want any oats with that?' asked Zara, taking a swig of Red Bull. 'I've heard that porridge is the new Prozac.'

'Don't be silly.' Sadie sipped daintily from her can of cherry Coke. 'Fran's not heartbroken, just, like, totally humiliated. Poor bunny.'

'Give her a break,' said Francesca at last. 'It's not as if any of us lot could have done any better.'

'Pity,' said Zara with a contemptuous glance at Wayne, who was busy stuffing himself with caramel bars in the corner. 'I could have done with some raw animal passion this morning.' She sauntered towards the door. 'Right, I'm going outside to have a fag. Coming, girlies?'

Sadie and Francesca began to follow after her,

though Fran was still hovering undecided by the chocolate machine. As Zara passed Wayne she turned towards him and bared her teeth in a snarl. 'GRRRRRRRR! Ooh, you bad sexy beast you!' Her and Sadie's shrieks of laughter could still be heard long after the door shut behind them.

'Er, sorry about that,' Fran muttered to Wayne. He was now shredding his chocolate-bar wrappers into tiny pieces, eyes fixed on the floor. 'Look, Zara's just—'

'What, you think I let that stupid cow get to me?' asked Wayne. To her embarrassment, she saw that there were angry tears in his eyes. 'No, it's that bastard Mayhew I'd like to kill. Every sodding week he has me prancing around his stupid classroom. Like I'm a performing animal or something. And you know what? It wouldn't happen if I was thinner or cooler or looked like Quinn Adams.'

Fran grimaced sympathetically. She knew he was right – Mr Mayhew never bothered the popular crowd. As she hurried off to catch up with the others, Fran couldn't help feeling a little bit guilty about Wayne, even though it wasn't really anything to do with her.

'You're not still obsessing about that English lesson, are you?' demanded Francesca as soon as she saw Fran's glum expression.

'Sort of—'

'You know what's really annoying about you, Fran?' said Zara, 'you're so *feeble.*'

'Yeah, it's like Mr Mayhew majorly senses weakness. I mean, he's never picked on me or Zara, has he?' put in Sadie cheerily. 'He's got, like, some kind of a *doormat* radar.'

'They've got a point, you know,' said Francesca. 'Maybe next time you should tell Mr Mayhew where to get off.'

Fran stared back at her in incomprehension. Sure, Mr Mayhew shouldn't be allowed to get away with always picking on people like her and Wayne, but there was no way in hell there was anything she or anyone else could do about it.

Or was there?

Two minutes later Fran was standing in the 'Out of Order' girls' toilets by the sports hall, while Ash wrinkled his nose and complained that she never took him anywhere nice. Fran, however, had more important things on her mind than blocked drains.

'Ash, do you think I'm . . . feeble?'

He gave a snort of derision. 'I wish. You've been chewing my ear off about something or other practically ever since we met. On our second encounter you called me a sexist pig, as I recall.'

He was right, Fran realized to her surprise. Somehow she was quite capable of holding her own with an overbearing genie, but when it came to normal, non-magical folk, maybe she *was* a pushover. Well, now was her chance to fight back. She might not be able to bring peace to the Middle East, but here was a wrong to be righted, and humiliation to be avenged. Mr Mayhew had made far too many people's lives a misery for far too long.

'OK then, here's the deal. I'm going to make my second wish and maybe it's a little bit sudden, but I really think it's a good one. You remember I told you about my creep of an English teacher, Mr Mayhew? Well, I've decided it's time somebody taught *him* a lesson.'

'What, so you want me to turn him into a tub of margarine for seven hours?'

'Tempting . . . but no.' In a few brief sentences Fran filled Ash in on Mr Mayhew's teaching methods. 'Everyone knows Mr Mayhew hates kids and that what he really wants to be is a famous actor. All right then – this is his chance. For the next seven hours, I wish that Mr Mayhew would believe he's a mega-successful actor, and that he's come here to star in a one-man show. I want him on stage, in front of everyone and giving *us* the performance of a lifetime.' She looked at Ash somewhat anxiously. 'What do you think?'

'Very nice,' he said approvingly. 'A very neat little wish.'

'And . . .?'

'And you may consider it done, O my Mistress.'

Ash was busy admiring himself in the mirror above the sink. Even under the harsh strip lighting his bronzed skin and glossy black hair shone with health. 'You know what? Now that we've finished business you should give me a guided tour of the place. It'd be fun. You could show me this Quinn of yours and I could see where all the British-style cheerleaders hang out. Hey,' he said, eyes gleaming, 'next time around, how about making a wish in the girls' changing room?'

Fran gave him a look. She wasn't about to make any more concessions to Ash before she made sure Wish Number Two was an all-singing, all-dancing technicolour success.

Julian Mayhew's day was looking up. That *Wuthering Heights* exercise had been a stroke of genius, even if he said so himself – Wayne Robert was always good for a laugh and he'd found the ideal foil in that rather dumpy, nervous-looking girl. The one who blushed all the time. Plus, he had just hit upon the perfect project for his least favourite group of Year Nines: an ensemble dramatization, in mime, of Dylan Thomas's *Do Not Go Gentle Into That Good Night*. Yes, with a little bit of creative thinking, even a crappy job like his had its compensations . . .

Afterwards, the general consensus in the staffroom was that Julian Mayhew had been behaving perfectly normally until the end of break on that fateful Tuesday. There had certainly been no outward signs of the crisis to come, although dark rumours circulated of his last lesson before The Incident, of some trauma at the hands of the Year Ten English class that had finally tipped him over the edge. But whatever the cause, it was an indisputable fact that at eight minutes past eleven on Tuesday morning, Julian Mayhew had stalked into the staffroom in the grip of a manic delusion.

'Needless to say, it is somewhat cramped,' he announced, glancing imperiously around the room, 'but one can't expect these provincial theatres to have the facilities of the West End.'

At this time of day the room was mostly deserted, though a couple of people looked up briefly before returning to their stewed tea and lesson plans. Julian's colleagues were used to him making eccentric pronouncements by now, and tended to tune him out when he started going on about the fascist conspiracy at the heart of Equity or how the RSC's Loss was Academia's Gain.

Julian took possession of the battered sofa with a lordly smile. As far as he was concerned, he was in the green room, the room backstage in a theatre where performers rest and receive visitors. And not just any performer either. From being a thirty-something English teacher, Julian Mayhew was now – in his mind at least – an icon of stage and screen, with over three decades of acting glory behind him. On the table next to the sofa was an ancient potted fern, which he now buried his face in and sniffed appreciatively. 'How very kind. Orchids have always been a favourite of mine – a truly magnificent bouquet. I don't suppose there was a note?' he enquired of Miss Duncan, who he assumed to be some underling from the theatre's management.

'Note?' she asked, looking up from her folder in a fluster. 'I didn't see anything in your pigeonhole but you could check with the office.'

'No matter. Another of my anonymous female admirers, no doubt,' he replied. 'My agent tells me that two new fan clubs have been formed in the last month alone, you know.'

'Really?' This was a blow. Miss Duncan had always had a bit of a soft spot for Mr Mayhew and it was rather disconcerting to discover he had an official fan base. His single television appearance – in *The Bill*, 1993 – must have made more of an impression than she'd realized.

'Oh yes indeed. The latest poll for *Empire Film* magazine put me ahead of both Lawrence Olivier and Jude Law in the "British Acting Legends" league.'

'My goodness,' said Miss Duncan faintly.

'Pay no attention, pet.' This was Mr Bentley, the only other teacher in the room. 'It's just one of our

Julian's little jokes.' He rolled his eyes, then returned to his marking.

However, this remark was lost on Mr Mayhew, who had got up from the sofa and was now prowling around the room. 'Tell me, my dear, how long until the performance?'

He must mean the Year Eleven parent–student careers talk, Miss Duncan decided. Mr Mayhew was supposed to be giving a speech on the advantages of studying English at A level. 'Oh, we've got a good fifteen minutes yet.'

'Then . . . perhaps . . . some refreshment . . .?' He looked at her meaningfully. One just couldn't get the staff these days.

'Good idea. I'll go and make some tea.' Miss Duncan was thinking that dear Julian was looking rather flushed. Perhaps he was coming down with something. She decided to bring him a glass of water while the kettle boiled.

'Hmm, not bad, not bad at all,' Mr Mayhew pronounced, rolling the water around his mouth appreciatively. 'Of course, it is more traditional to save the champagne for *after* the performance, but I always feel there's nothing like a little glass of bubbly to get the blood flowing.'

Mr Bentley and Miss Duncan exchanged looks. So Julian had been drinking at break-time! This was getting serious.

'I think, Julian—' began Mr Bentley.

'*Sir* Julian, if you don't mind, my good fellow,' said Mr Mayhew.

Mr Bentley frowned. He had no patience for what he called 'Julian's acting nonsense' and he now assumed his colleague was deliberately winding him up. 'Leave him be,' he said to Miss Duncan. 'If the idiot wants to go getting tipsy during working hours, then it's his look out. Let him try explaining himself when he rolls up to this induction reeking of booze.'

'And now,' announced the Greatest Actor of his Generation, 'I will require some time alone in my dressing room to focus my thoughts and gather my creative energies ready for the performance.'

A moment later, Sir Julian had shut himself among the coats and bags in the little annexe that opened out of the main staffroom. All he needed to do was to retouch his stage make-up and run through his breathing exercises and he would be ready to go.

'Er, Julian, I think we should be making our way to the hall now . . .' Miss Duncan was hovering outside the annexe. A moment later the door swung open and Mr Mayhew emerged, head held high. Miss Duncan's jaw dropped.

Stage make-up is, naturally, designed to be seen from a distance and to hold up for an hour or two in the spotlight, so considering Julian's limited resources, he hadn't done such a bad job. In the cloakroom he'd found a cosmetic case belonging to Ms La Motte, the school's Head of Languages and an enthusiastic user of bronzer and blue eyeshadow. Mr Mayhew hadn't gone for the eyeshadow, but he'd used nearly everything else. And so his eyes were heavily outlined in black kohl, his eyebrows elongated and thickened with the same, his face caked in bronze foundation and his cheekbones highlighted with stripes of purplish blusher. From a good distance away, on a carefully lit stage, he wouldn't look too bad. Face to face in a school corridor, he was terrifying. Miss Duncan let out a moan.

Mr Mayhew smiled at her indulgently. 'Lead on, dear lady, lead on. My Public Awaits.'

Miss Duncan turned tail and fled. Julian Mayhew was clearly a very disturbed man and it was her duty, as his friend and colleague, to find somebody else to deal with him. Oblivious, Julian strolled after her, humming the refrain of 'La donna è mobile' under his breath. In a few moments – following the buzz of conversation drifting down the corridor – he had arrived at the school hall and marched on to the stage.

The audience of Year Eleven students and their parents looked up expectantly. The parents had been invited to a special lunch with the Head of Year, and were now assembled with their children for a presentation on the school's career advisory service. As Mr Mayhew took to the stage, the handful of other teachers attending exchanged startled glances – had somebody changed the running order? Wasn't Julian meant to be speaking *after* the opening address? And what on earth had he done to his face?

'Ladies and gentlemen,' began Mr Mayhew, 'it is a great honour to stand before you today. I've always said that I have been very blessed in my career, which has been – I'm sure you'll agree – an exceptionally long and successful one.'

Several students snickered. Trust Mr Mayhew to turn some boring speech into a complete joke.

'So you may be surprised to learn,' the great man continued, 'that when I was first approached with the idea for *An Audience with Sir Julian Mayhew*, I felt unequal to the task. How could I possibly condense a lifetime of critical acclaim and commercial triumph into a mere hour or two? But as my good friend Dame Judi Dench said to me, "Julian, you owe it to your Art and – more importantly – *you owe it to your fans.*"'

The mums and dads in the audience stirred uneasily, while an ironic cheer went up from a group of lads in the back. They didn't have a clue what Mr Mayhew was up to, but they were determined to make the most of it. The students in the front row, who had got a good look at the drag-queen-style make-up by now, were nearly passing out with hilarity. Meanwhile, the realization was dawning on Julian's colleagues that somehow, somewhere, something had gone Very Wrong. Ms La Motte hurried off to fetch the deputy head, while the remaining teachers argued in whispers over what should be done.

Of all this, Mr Mayhew was blissfully unaware. As far as he was concerned, he was playing to a packed house on the opening night of his one-man revue. 'I will begin,' he announced, 'with my Hamlet.'

After a whirlwind rendition of 'To be, or not to be', Mr Mayhew launched into a song and dance routine from *Fame* followed, in swift succession, by extracts from Chekhov, Tennessee Williams, Jacobean Revenge Tragedy, and *Wuthering Heights: The Musical*. He was equally happy to play men, women and children, sometimes all at once. By the time he'd started on the madness scene from *King Lear*, his audience was either transfixed with astonishment or helpless with hysteria. A small crowd had gathered by the entrance to the hall and its numbers were growing, as word spread through the corridors and teachers from the neighbouring classrooms came out to see what all the noise was about.

Hovering at the back was Fran, who was struggling to come to terms with a wish fulfilment that had exceeded her wildest expectations. She supposed she should feel proud as well as pleased, to see Mr Mayhew get his comeuppance in such a spectacular fashion, but instead she felt slightly queasy. Mr Mayhew was a sadist, all right, but surely nobody deserved to be seen running around a stage howling like a dog with a pair of gym knickers on their head?

The answer came from behind her shoulder. 'There is a God,' Wayne Roberts said raptly, his pudgy face suffused with joy. He looked an entirely different person. Then he caught Fran's eye and grinned. 'Y'know, for the first time in my life, I'm actually *glad* I came to school today.' And suddenly Fran felt a whole lot better.

At long last, somebody had the presence of mind to find the pulley that closed the curtains. These drew shut on the never-to-be-forgotten sight of Mr Mayhew wringing his hands and ranting 'Out, damned spot!', in between singing snatches of 'A Spoonful of Sugar' from *Mary Poppins*. It was, everyone agreed, a truly legendary performance.

Six hours later, Fran and Ash were sitting on the wall by St Augustine's Church, debating whether spending a wish on vengeance made someone a bad person.

Although news of the sensational events in the hall had spread through the school like wildfire, what went on after the curtains closed and the hall had been cleared of spectators was not quite so clear.

It was rumoured that Mr Mayhew had been led off and locked in the deputy head's office, where he spent the rest of the afternoon covering hundreds of sheets of paper with his autograph while various senior staff members debated what to do next. At some point – so the story went – a doctor had been called to the scene, only to be mistaken for a paparazzo by the patient. In the ensuing scuffle, Mr Mayhew had made a break for freedom, and was last seen hailing a taxi to take him to the Ivy. He claimed to be meeting Kevin Spacey there for dinner.

'At least the seven hours are up,' said Fran, 'and Mr Mayhew can go back to normal. Whatever that is. I just hope I haven't caused any, you know, per-manent damage . . .'

'Who cares?' said Ash, who was bored with the whole conversation. 'It's too late to be wringing your hands over it. And anyhow, I thought you'd had enough of being feeble.'

'Yes, but I don't want to be *evil* either.'

'Evil my purple-smoking arse. Fran, you have led a truly sheltered life.'

'So tell me about your life then. Evil powers, girl trouble and everything. C'mon Ash, I really want to know . . .'

A passer-by glanced at her briefly, then moved on. Fran had hit upon an ingenious technique for talking to Ash in public, by attaching herself to the hands-free kit on her mobile. All the same, their conversations must make for interesting eaves-dropping.

'*Please?*'

Ash seemed to be thinking about it. Finally, he sighed deeply, began to speak, stopped, then sighed once more. When he spoke again his voice was deep and dark and throbbing. 'Very well, O my Mistress. The most secret pains of my heart shall be stripped bare for you. The darkest sorrows of my soul shall be laid before your feet. Hear then, O Fair Commander of a Most Accursed Ring, the story of my enslavement.' Then he switched back to his normal voice. 'OK, so what you have to realize is that in ancient Baghdad I was considered *seriously* hot.'

'Because you were a prince?'

'Er, yes . . . yes, that too. But mainly because of my natural charm and good looks. Anyway, there was this one babe – princess – who was particularly infatuated. And don't get me wrong, she was a gorgeous girl: plenty of cash, family tree going right back to the prophets, perfect teeth. The thing was . . . one, she had a hell of a temper on her, and two, I just wasn't ready to settle down. So in the end, I sent a letter saying that I didn't really feel the same way, plenty of fish in the sea, fleas on the camel—'

'Wait a minute. You dumped her by *letter*?'

'Of course,' he said irritably, 'I could hardly send her a text message, could I? Moreover, just sending a letter was a considerable risk, since the whole affair was strictly hush-hush. Even in Baghdad's more liberal circles, certain protocols had to be respected . . . did I mention the family tree?'

'Sure you did. Right after you said how rich she was.' Fran's sympathy for Ash and his enslavement was beginning to wear thin.

'Now, I knew that she was well connected but what I *didn't* realize was that she happened to be the Grand Vizier of Baghdad's third wife's second cousin's niece.' Ash paused impressively.

'And that was bad because . . .?'

'Because the Grand Vizier of Baghdad at that time happened to be a fairly powerful enchanter. And it turned out that his third wife had picked up some Dark Art tips along the way, which she'd kindly shared with her second cousin, who couldn't resist passing them on to her favourite niece. Next thing I know, I'm reeling home through the bazaar after a night out celebrating the joys of bachelor life, when there's this blinding flash and – ping! – I wake up a genie.'

'Wow . . . and there's no way of releasing you from the spell?'

'Eternal banishment *means* eternal banishment, Fran. In fact, it does exactly what it says on the ring.' This time his sorrowful expression didn't look as if it was done for dramatic effect.

'But what if someone made a wish to make you

human again – oh, I see. It would only last seven hours.'

'If I were human . . .' began Ash, then fell silent. It was getting cold and dark and Fran's breath turned misty in the air, but Ash's didn't. Ash wasn't affected by hot or cold, rain or shine, hunger or thirst. He could turn into smoke or float in the air, but he couldn't move more than seven paces away from the ring. He was invisible – nonexistent – to every person in the world save one. It must, thought Fran, be a bit like being a ghost.

Finally Ash spoke again. 'You can't cheat magic, Fran. Or fate.' He was smiling at her – a wry, rueful smile that she hadn't seen before. 'But some wishes are more powerful than others. More powerful than enchantment even . . .'

Fran wasn't quite sure she understood, but before she could ask him to explain her mobile began its insistent beeping. It was her dad, and he didn't sound happy. Where had she been for the last hour? Who was she with? When was she coming home? Still making her excuses, she climbed down from the wall and set off on the five minutes walk to home. Fran would have liked to ask Ash more about the wishes that are more powerful than enchantment, but while she was speaking to her father he had disappeared back into the ring of his own accord. Perhaps he wanted to be left alone.

*

The questions started again as soon as Fran got through the door. It appeared that her mum and dad had been having a conference on her behaviour over the last week or so and had come to the conclusion that a) Fran wasn't herself because b) she was hiding something from them and therefore c) something must be wrong. It just wasn't like their daughter to shut herself in her room for hours on end or stay out late without telling them. Not to mention all those long, late-night telephone conversations.

While Mickey and Beth played tickle-monsters under the kitchen table, the pans boiled over on the stove and the ringing of various phones competed with Beth's *Sing Along with Noddy* tape, Mr and Mrs Roper attempted to get Fran to open up. It wasn't that they didn't respect her privacy, her mum assured her, but they just wanted to make sure nothing was wrong. Why was she so distracted all the time? So secretive? 'If it's a boy you're seeing,' said her mum, 'I'd hope you would feel able to tell us about it, love. We don't want to pry, but we know that your teenage years can be a very difficult time . . .'

Fran slunk up to her room feeling a rat. She'd assured her parents that everything was fine and she'd just been a bit preoccupied with 'school stuff' lately, but she wasn't sure they'd believed her. In fact, she felt so guilty about all the secrets she was keeping from them she'd even told them about going along with Francesca to the Firedog band rehearsal on Friday night. They had made various encouraging noises but she suspected that the threat of sex, drugs and rock 'n' roll would probably be a lot harder to deal with than the news that their daughter had acquired a magic ring.

The end of Fran's last conversation with Ash had left her feeling unsettled and oddly shy about seeing him again. She knew it wasn't her fault he'd been enchanted, and also that life as a genie had several perks, but she still couldn't help feeling a bit guilty about . . . well, using him. On Wednesday after school she caught the number 289 bus to visit 'Oronames – Local Convenience' again, in the hope of finding out something more about the ring. But the bus was no longer on diversion and the driver denied all knowledge of the previous route or any mysterious corner shops along the way.

Fran decided that, as Commander of the Ring, it was her responsibility to take an interest in Ash's psychological well-being. The trauma of being shut up in a ring must have left him with some terrible emotional scars, and probably quite a lot of repressed anger . . . Unfortunately, the next time she spoke to Ash she found him in a particularly insufferable mood. At times like this it became all too clear why his ex-girlfriend had turned to the Dark Arts.

'I'm thinking of reworking my intro,' he announced. 'All that "Jewel of Arabia" and "Lion of Baghdad" stuff is starting to sound a bit old school.'

'I thought it was part of the package. Like the luxury pyjama bottoms and purple smoke.'

'There's no need to be flippant. Presentation is very important in my line of work. Anyway, punters like a bit of razzmatazz. What do you think about "Ash the Adorable, Delighter of Damsels"?'

'More like "Ashazrahim the Up-Himself, Irritant of the Unwary",' she muttered.

For a moment Fran thought Ash was going to go and do the rampaging dust-cloud thing as he drew himself up into his full height, his lip curled and his eyes flashing. A couple of weeks earlier and she might have been cowering under the bed. But Fran had got the genie's measure by now and instead of cowering she started to laugh. It wasn't long before Ash's mouth began to twitch too, in spite of himself.

'Women! Honestly!' He tried to sound stern. 'It's always the same – you start off all gushing and grateful and weepy-eyed, I give you what you want and then you start taking liberties. What's a genie got to do to get some respect round here?'

Fran decided to take her chance. Ash had clearly never suffered from low self-esteem in his life, but there was a wider issue at stake here. 'I do respect you, Ash,' she said, 'and back in the days when you were a prince I'm sure people thought very highly of you. But don't you want to be *more* than respected? What about being liked?'

'Liked? But genies are *eternally* popular – as long as they're granting wishes, not dispensing death, that is . . . And thanks to the Sacred Seal the latter is not an option for yours truly. Worse luck.'

'Well,' she said, pressing on, 'don't you want to be liked for yourself, rather than for your wish-granting skills? In your line of work you must get to know a lot about people, on account of all that heart's desire stuff, but do your, er, clients ever get to know *you*? The real Ash, I mean, not the Resplendent Lion of Adorable Thingamabob.'

'Are you saying you don't like me?' Ash was looking distinctly nonplussed.

'No, of course not!' This wasn't going quite how she planned. 'I'd like you even if you weren't granting my wishes.'

'But you think I'm rude and conceited and patronizing.'

'How did you—'

He shrugged. 'That's what everyone thinks.'

'Oh. Anyhow, I just meant . . . well, being a genie must be a bit, um, lonely. So I thought . . . I wanted . . . I'm glad you felt able to tell me about your ex-girlfriend, that's all. And if you ever want to, er, talk about anything . . .'

She steeled herself for some devastatingly sarcastic put-down, but in fact Ash was looking nearly as awkward as she was.

'That's very kind of you,' he said at last. 'Most clients don't bother with the social niceties. And, to be honest, they usually seem a bit of a wasted effort for all concerned. But it's nice that . . .' His expression was still rather puzzled. 'Thank you, anyway.'

Fran soon had other things on her mind than Ash's emotional welfare, for Friday was the day when she was going to Quinn's house to join the Firedogs after their rehearsal. Ideally she would have liked to watch the practice too, and not just because of all the opportunities for Quinn-ogling – she was genuinely interested in the music-making process. But Francesca explained that the band was quite strict about having no distractions when they were rehearsing. 'And you'd probably get bored anyway,' she said, 'listening to Rob fluff his chords and Quinn swearing at him and then the amplifier lead coming loose all the time.' She already sounded like a veteran Firedog.

As for Fran, she knew that in the normal scheme of things there was no way someone like her would even have dared to make eye contact with these gods of the Upper School, and so something that only two weeks ago had been beyond her wildest dreams had abruptly become a potential nightmare. 'What's that kid doing here?' she imagined Jez or Rob saying as they looked her up and down in a disgusted sort of way. Two things held her nerve. The first was the thought that if the evening went truly badly she could always summon Ash and wish for instant charisma or charm. The second was that Francesca hadn't invited Zara and Sadie. 'It'll be just the two of us,' she promised, 'so we'll have to present a united female front. Those boys'd get away with murder, given half a chance.' And then she laughed her new, grown-up laugh.

Quinn's address turned out to be in an expensive new housing development. It was half past seven when Fran arrived, but even under the sickly street lighting the bricks looked ultra-red, the door and window frames extra-white and the brass door-knocker super-new. Although the lights were on, she couldn't hear any noise from inside and as she rang the bell Fran found she was clutching Ash's ring, as if for reassurance. A thin blonde woman opened the door. 'Can I help you?' she asked suspiciously.

'Um . . . hello . . . I'm here to see . . . my friend's in . . . Quinn's band?'

'I suppose you'd better come in then,' Mrs Adams smiled tightly, then waved a manicured hand towards a door opening off the entrance hall.

'You'll find the others in the basement,' she said, before disappearing into the back of the house. For a few moments Fran stayed where she was, her feet sinking into the mushroom carpet as she listened to the Victorian-style wall clock briskly tick the seconds away. She knew it was stupid, but she'd kind of been expecting Quinn's family set-up to be . . . well, a little more bohemian.

At last, she gave herself a shake and tried the door that Mrs Adams had indicated, which opened on to a flight of steps leading down to a second door. She decided that the basement must be soundproofed, for even now she could only hear a faint murmuring coming from the room behind. Then she pushed opened the door and suddenly everything burst into life again. This was clearly Quinn's domain, for one could hardly see the walls behind their layers of film posters and concert flyers. A battered sofa and clutter of dirty plates gave the room a scruffy, cosy sort of feel that was somewhat at odds with the state-of-the art TV and stereo, not to mention all the music-making gear on display.

'There you are!' Francesca came up and kissed her briefly on both cheeks. It was the kind of thing her mother sometimes did, but Fran hadn't seen someone of her own age do it before. Francesca, of course, looked glowing. Her hair was pinned up in a twist that was escaping in soft, sexy curls about her face, and though she was only wearing an old black shirt dress, she'd got herself some new pendant earrings. The gold droplets swung and sparkled in the light as she moved. Now she looked Fran up and down approvingly. 'You look nice,' she said.

'Thanks.' Mindful of Ash's remark about 'the boring shapeless stuff' she usually wore, Fran had screwed up her courage and chosen a fitted red shirt to go with her jeans. She'd even put her hair in a high ponytail like they had for the Len Fisher show.

'Come and say hi to everyone.' Francesca took her by the hand and was leading her across the room to where the others were standing around various bits of kit. It was clear that they'd only just taken a break from rehearsing and Rob, the lead guitarist, was having a heated debate with Liam, the bass player, as to why they kept getting out of sync at the end of the chorus. Meanwhile, Quinn and Jez were sharing a joke with Jez's girlfriend, Cath. 'The poor thing's *very* insecure,' explained Francesca as Cath shot her a dirty look.

Much to Fran's relief, nobody asked who she was or what she was doing there. The other boys nodded at her amiably enough, then went straight back to their conversations. Cath stared. But Quinn gave her a soft, secret smile and touched her on the arm. 'Glad you could make it,' he said. Then he went over to the fridge in the corner and started handing out beers while someone else put pounding guitar rock on the stereo. People began to settle down on the sofa or else lounge on the floor. Fran momentarily regretted asking for a Coke when she saw Francesca swigging nonchalantly from her bottle of lager.

Conversation soon turned to the dramatic events of Tuesday afternoon. The official line was that Mr Mayhew was on indefinite sick leave, but everyone had heard the rumours that he'd been picked up outside the Ivy restaurant on Tuesday evening, after getting into a brawl with the manager. 'They say he was found wandering up and down the street grabbing passers-by and demanding "Do You Know Who I Am?"' reported Jez in awestruck tones. 'Sick leave or not, I don't reckon we'll be seeing that poor bugger again.' Fran shifted uncomfortably, but his next remark made her feel even worse. 'Shouldn't your other two friends be here by now?' he asked Francesca. 'Sara and Katie or whatever they're called.'

'Kiddies' Corner here tonight,' sneered Cath.

'Oh leave it,' said Rob. 'I invited them. They're a good laugh even if, strictly speaking, they're still minors.' He smacked his lips appreciatively.

Fran looked over at Francesca, who merely shrugged. A moment later there was a knock on the door and the Gruesome Twosome themselves arrived. In their different ways, both of them had made a particular effort with their appearance: Sadie was in heels and a strappy lilac dress, Zara in ripped denim, black boots and several inches of eyeliner. They looked great, but when she saw Cath smirking into her beer Fran was glad she hadn't got too obviously dolled up for the occasion.

The addition of two more people gave the gathering a party atmosphere. Zara passed round her cigarettes, the music was turned up again, more drinks were handed out and the talk and laughter grew louder. Fran could hardly believe it: only a couple of weeks ago she'd spent her Friday night doing the washing-up and helping Mickey learn his lines, and now here she was hanging out with the in-crowd at Quinn Adams's house! And now – oh help, oh hell – the boy himself was coming over . . .

'You having a good time?' he asked, settling down on the floor beside her.

'Yeah, definitely.' She tried desperately to think of something interesting to say. 'Um, did the rehearsal go well?'

Quinn took a drag at his cigarette. He was looking as delectably rumpled as usual, and sitting so close that his bare arm was just brushing against hers. 'Oh, it was all right. Your friend's a bit of a star though – keeps the rest of us in line.'

He glanced over at Francesca, who was laughing at something with Liam, her head tilted so that her earrings flashed in the light. 'Francesca's great,' said Fran loyally, 'and I know she's loving being in the band.'

'That's good . . .' Quinn still hadn't taken his eyes off Francesca. 'You guys have known each other forever, right?' Fran nodded. 'Lucky you.' Then, just when she'd given up hoping he would, he turned his attention back to her. 'Maybe you should come and see the practice next time. It'd be good to get an outside opinion.' He offered her a swig from his beer bottle. Fran didn't like beer but hey, it wasn't every day she got the chance to share saliva with the most beautiful boy in the school.

'Are – are you working on a new song at the moment?' she ventured.

A faraway look came into his eyes. 'The creative impulse is always there . . . but . . . it's more of an instinct than a process, you know? Truth is, I find it hard to talk about.'

'I can imagine,' said Fran respectfully. 'It's a very personal thing.'

'I knew you'd understand.' There was a flirtatious shriek from Sadie and Rob's corner and Quinn smiled wryly. 'I can tell that *you* take music seriously.'

'Yes,' she said a little bitterly, 'but caring about music will only get you so far. Making people stop and listen is more difficult.'

'Ah, but if you show them your passion, they'll give you their confidence.' He moved a little closer so his voice was warm and melting in her ear. 'As long as you've got passion, Fran, the rest will come.

I promise.' Then he moved away again. 'You know, I'm not as self-possessed as everyone thinks . . . I still get nervous when I'm performing.'

'You? Nervous? Really?'

'Don't let on to the others though. It's our secret.'

Their eyes met and Fran felt a tingle beginning at the base of her spine. But the next moment, Sadie came over and practically sat in Quinn's lap, demanding he gave her a neck rub. Fran hoped that Quinn would turn back to talk to her again, but after he'd disentangled himself from Sadie he wandered over to where Francesca was sitting and was soon deep in discussion about a possible gig they were hoping to fix up. For the next half-hour, she didn't even manage to catch his eye and was left to hover at the edge of other people's conversations. As is often the case in these situations, the more she tried to think of amusing and interesting things to say, the harder it was say *anything*. Slowly but surely, Fran felt herself grow invisible.

Partly to give herself something to do, she went over to the sound system and began to look through Quinn's CD collection. 'Sorry, Fran, but I don't think you'll find any Britney,' said Zara, who was passing with an armful of drinks to go with the pizzas that had just arrived. 'Congratulations, by the way – all your tagging along after Francesca has finally paid off. How does it feel to be a part-time grown-up?' Better than being a full-time bitch, said Fran under her breath, watching Zara drape herself over Liam. As for Francesca, she'd turned her back on Quinn and was chatting to Jez instead. Neither Cath nor Quinn seemed too happy about this, Fran noticed with a stab of envy.

Maybe it was time to leave. But it was only a little after nine and that would be . . . well, feeble, wouldn't it? She imagined Ash's snort of exasperation and then found herself wishing that he could be here tonight; at least that way she'd have someone to talk to. Even if he was more likely to insult than support her. She decided she'd sneak off with the ring for a few minutes, just to have a quick word . . .

'We really must stop meeting like this,' drawled the genie the moment he had flickered into solid form. 'Though I must say, it's an improvement on the last glorified sewer you took me to.' They were indeed in another bathroom, although this one was a vision of gleaming blue tiles, matching towels that looked like they'd never been used and a battery of gilded taps.

'That's cos we're in Quinn's house.' Although she'd seen no sign of Mrs Adams or anyone else on her way upstairs, she kept her voice to a whisper. 'His band have had a session and now it's a sort of party. Mind you, I don't know the others that well

– expect for Francesca, that is. And Quinn. He's been really friendly.'

'And am I to understand that Quinn is the object of your every desire?'

'I guess. Some desires anyway.' Fran thought there wasn't much point trying to hide it from Ash any longer. *As long as you've got passion, Fran, the rest will come. I promise . . .*

'Hah.'

'What's that supposed to mean?'

'Nothing. Just "hah".' He folded his arms across his chest and looked at her narrowly. 'So, to recap, you're at a "sort of" party with the man of your wildest dreams who's being "really friendly". Am I right?' Fran nodded. 'Great. Then why are you hiding out in his bathroom?'

'It's hard to explain—'

'If it's so hard to explain, I think I'd better see for myself.' He stretched himself and moved towards the door, the faintest wisp of smoke curling at his feet. 'Come on, Fran, you must have got me out of the ring for a *reason*. So if you want to make another wish and you're still dithering over the right one, then it makes sense for me to see what you're up against. I'm here to help, remember?' He smiled at her winningly. 'Besides, I've had centuries of experience at this sort of thing.'

Fran thought about it. He had a point – it *would* be useful to get an outside opinion, and for all his rude remarks about infatuated females Ash must be a bit of an expert on the lonely-hearts scene.

'OK. But only on the condition that you don't take the mick out of me later. And that you stick to silent observation, not sarky comments.'

'You'll hardly know I'm here,' he promised as she unlocked the door. Then, with a whoop of exultation, he turned a mid-air cartwheel in the hall.

It didn't seem that anyone had noticed her absence; at any rate, when she walked back into the basement room – invisible genie by her side – everyone was too busy watching Sadie demonstrate her dance routine from the audition to pay her any attention. Sadie was more than a little wobbly on her feet, and she was giggling hysterically, but if anything this only enhanced the performance. Fran went back to pretending to sort through the CDs.

Ash was looking around him with lively interest. 'This is *much* better than your room,' he said. 'A proper bachelor pad. Which one's lover-boy?'

'Blue shirt,' she said, disguising her words with a cough and jerking her head in Quinn's direction.

Ash marched over for an inspection. He peered right into Quinn's face – only an inch or two from his nose – but Quinn continued to laugh and clap at Sadie's dance moves, oblivious. 'Hmm,' said Ash. 'Looks a bit vacant to me – and I'd be *very* surprised if those blond highlights are natural. Still, takes all sorts . . . hello, hello, who have we here?' Zara had just sauntered by, en route to the last slice of pizza. 'There's something about this one that reminds me of my ex-girlfriend.' He gave a shudder. 'Do you happen to know if she dabbles in the Dark Arts?'

Fran was grinning to herself at this when she realized Francesca had come over and was standing next to her.

'Are you all right, Fran-flakes? I've hardly had a chance to speak to you all evening.'

'I'm fine. I'm, er, enjoying myself . . .' Fran was uncomfortably aware that Ash was circling around Francesca, looking her up and down with a critical eye.

'Classy, for a ginger bird,' he remarked, 'though a bit skinny for my liking.'

Fran shot him a warning glance. She was already beginning to regret letting him loose like this, but now that she knew more about what being a genie really entailed, the whole Slave of the Ring/Commander of the Ring dynamic had become a lot more complicated. Would Ash stick to his promise to behave? And how easily would she be able to make him disappear if he didn't? She was reluctant to fetch the ring out from under her top in full view of the room. But while Fran was debating her next move, Sadie came over to join them – walking straight through Ash in the process.

Fran gasped in horror. She couldn't help it; everything about Ash seemed so fundamentally *solid* that even though she knew he was invisible to everyone else she found it incredible that Sadie hadn't realized she'd just stepped through a mass of flesh-and-blood genie. But no, all that happened was that Ash, or Fran's image of Ash, flickered slightly, and the next second Sadie was standing in front of, not behind him.

'Is something wrong, Fran-flakes?'

'Cos you're looking *totally* freaked out,' said Sadie. 'Like maybe you're gonna puke or something.'

'Lovesick, one might say,' put in Ash.

'Well, don't,' Fran muttered out of the side of her mouth.

'What was that?' asked Francesca.

'Nothing. I was just, er, clearing my throat,' said Fran. 'Maybe I'm coming down with something.' She coughed some more, for dramatic effect.

'Poor honeybun,' cooed Sadie. 'Let's hope it's not something nasty.'

'Too late for that,' said Ash, shaking his head regretfully, 'I mean, come on, the guy wears *blond highlights*.'

'Ring!' exclaimed Fran. The others stared. 'I mean,' she said weakly, 'it's time I checked no one's tried to, er, ring my mobile. Someone might be trying to Ring Right Now.' She moved her hand towards the chain around her neck in what she hoped was a threatening manner.

Ash pulled a rude face. 'Party pooper,' he said, seconds before vanishing.

Fran heaved a sigh of relief, then realized that Francesca and Sadie were both looking at her very oddly.

'Come on, Fran, it's time we got going.'

'But it's not even ten!'

Francesca looked amused. 'Maybe so, but I think you've had enough partying for one night.'

'Hang on, you don't think I'm drunk do you? Because I've been drinking Coke all evening—'

'If you say so,' said Francesca, who clearly didn't believe a word of it. She was already shepherding Fran towards the door as if she was a wayward child 'Never mind, Fran-flakes. We'll get you a glass of water on the way out and you'll be feeling better soon.' Fran tried to protest, to convince her that she didn't need looking after, and that she was perfectly happy to stay. But what was the point? Come to think of it, she probably *had* had enough in-crowd socializing for one night. And she'd promised her parents to be back home before eleven.

'Ladies! You're not abandoning us already, are you?' It was Quinn, with Zara and Sadie on either arm.

''Fraid so,' said Francesca, 'Fran's feeling a little bit the worse for—'

'I'm fine,' cut in Fran, giving Francesca a swift

nudge in the ribs. 'Just tired, that's all. Thank you for a lovely evening.'

Sadie giggled adorably. 'Fran, hon, you can sound such a quaint old thing sometimes.'

'Ah, but that's because Fran's a true lady,' said Quinn, looking at her gravely with soft dark eyes. She tried smiling back at him – in a private, meaningful sort of way – but Zara had started feeding him bits of choc ice and the moment was gone. And it was Francesca's arm that he caught as they were going out of the door. 'Francesca, don't forget to give me a call about tomorrow, OK?' She nodded. 'Great. It won't be the same without you, you know.'

'What won't be the same without you?' asked Fran as soon as they were alone at the bus stop.

'Oh, Quinn is trying to fix up a gig and I promised to come along for the negotiations.' She explained that Quinn was friendly with the manager of his local pub, which hosted live music nights once a month. 'They're quite strict about standards though, so I expect this guy'll take one look at us and see us for the bunch of hopeless amateurs we really are. I reckon Quinn only wants me there so's they have someone to smile and look pretty.'

After the two girls reached Francesca's house and said their goodbyes, Fran lingered on the pavement for a few minutes, looking up into the Goldsworthys' living room. They hadn't drawn the curtains, although it was getting on for eleven, and the scene within was lit with a soft, rich glow. She decided Mr and Mrs Goldsworthy had just come back from a dinner party or trip to the theatre, because Mrs Goldsworthy was looking even more elegant than usual, in a backless evening dress. Mr Goldsworthy had a well-groomed head of silvery hair and black-rimmed designer spectacles. He had just poured his wife a glass of wine and she was laughing, tilting her head back in just the same way her daughter did. It was like watching a glossy TV advert, something for posh chocolates or perfume perhaps. Then Francesca herself came into the room and the curtains were drawn. Fran turned to trudge the last few minutes home.

There were no lights showing when she arrived, but she found her parents slumped fast asleep in front of the television. It was still switched on, and there was a clutter of wine glasses and Chinese take-away cartons on the floor. After tonight, Fran was finally realizing what she was up against – it was a terrible thing to be jealous of your best friend, but it was even more terrible to realize that you couldn't even class yourself as competition. Slowly but surely, Francesca Goldsworthy had moved out of her league.

Mickey had got the part in the Kisco commercial. When Fran came downstairs at eleven, it was to find the table laid for brunch – posh china and the milk in a jug! – and her mum was making celebratory pancakes. 'Though it will be nothing but Kookie cakes from now on mind,' Mr Roper joked. 'We'll have them with milk for breakfast, between two slices of bread for lunch and smothered in gravy for dinner. Celebrity endorsement is a serious business you know.'

Mickey was alarmed. 'Will I *really* have to eat them with gravy?' Then he squared his small shoulders. 'I suppose I'd get used to it,' he said bravely.

Fran put an extra dollop of chocolate spread on her pancake. She was sure that if Mickey told the Great British Public that a marshmallow cake dunked in gravy made a tasty treat they'd rush out to try it in droves. It was all about charisma. That, and being adorably small and earnest and saucer-eyed. She didn't reckon that Mickey could still sell stack loads of Crumble Bites or Kookies or whatever if he had buck teeth and pimples. And what if Fran were a size-ten hottie with legs up to her armpits? Would it be her, not Francesca, who Zara and Sadie and Quinn and the rest were falling over themselves to be friendly with?

'Charisma is something you're born with,' was Ash's verdict. 'It's nothing to do with looks; you either have it or you don't.' This time they were sitting in the shed at the end of the Ropers' tiny garden, watching the rain ooze through the slats and eating chocolate spread out of the jar. Somewhat to her surprise, Ash wasn't bearing a grudge about the night before. In fact he hadn't referred to the events at Quinn's house at all. It seemed that even a genie thought her life was too tedious for words.

'Maybe if you're male, but it's different for girls,' argued Fran, 'because people are still more likely to judge us on our appearance.'

'Rubbish – it's all about confidence. Take Scheherazade, for example.' Fran looked confused. 'I can see you don't know your *Alf Layla wa-Layla*,' he said condescendingly, 'or, as it's also known, the *Tales from the Thousand and One Nights*, which Scheherazade told King Schahriar—'

'Oh, but I do know this,' interrupted Fran. 'There was a sultan who took a new wife every night and then killed her in the morning until the beautiful Scheherazade spun him tales to delay the execution and he fell in love with her instead.'

'Aha!' said Ash triumphantly. 'My point exactly. The *beautiful* Scheherazade, you say?'

'Well, er, wasn't she?'

'Let's just say there was a *reason* she was practically the last virgin in town. It's all very well to say she was as lovely as moonlight on roses or whatever rubbish they're spouting in the bazaar these days, but it entirely misses the point. Which is that Scheherazade survived when all the other poor bimbos copped it because she had charisma. And intelligence. And a talent for making up cliff-hangers.'

Fran digested this for a while. Maybe if she started whispering action-packed thrillers into Quinn's ear she'd be able to keep his attention for more than five minutes, but somehow she didn't think so. 'I think it's time we put your theory to the test,' she said.

'And how are we going to do that, my Sultana of Sagacity?'

Fran was prepared for this and reached down for a magazine she'd brought along to the shed with her. Several of its pages were marked with coloured stickers. The first one marked a photograph of a model sitting beside a fountain. 'See this girl? I want you to make me look like her for the next seven hours. Only,' she said, turning the pages hastily, 'I want to have long chestnut hair, pale skin and violet eyes like the girl in *this* advert, and I want to be wearing what the girl on page forty-two is dressed in. In the clothing size to fit the first girl, obviously.'

It was an irresistible wish, even if Fran said so herself. Naturally, people would think it extremely odd if she suddenly shrunk down to a size ten and acquired movie-star teeth but then went back to her normal self all in the space of seven hours. This way, however, she would be able to truly feel like a

Beautiful Person, even if it was only for a little while. And, thought Fran, a gorgeous girl could get a lot done in seven hours, if she played her cards right . . .

The genie, however, was unimpressed. 'I preferred it when you were being vengeful. Shallowness is such a boring vice.'

'And hypocrisy is such an irritating one,' said Fran defensively. 'I saw you looking all the girls up and down yesterday. Judging them. Judging Quinn cos you don't like his hairstyle or whatever. I bet you wouldn't have listened to Scheherazade for more than five seconds before deciding she wasn't your type.'

'Then that would have been my loss,' Ash said quietly. He sighed. 'This is about last night, isn't it? Trying to make an impression on the boy band and their groupies? Honestly, Fran, they're not worth the effort. Trust me.'

Fran raised her brows. 'Sorry, but my mother warned me never to trust men with smoke coming out of their trousers.'

Ash raised his brows back at her. 'Dearie me. Little Miss Butter-Wouldn't-Melt: that's what I thought when I first saw you. And yet underneath that sweetly blushing exterior you're about as bashful as a marauding roc.'

'Roc?'

'Scary man-eating bird.'

'I tend to leave the man-eating to Zara.'

Ash laughed. 'Fran . . . one of these days you're going to realize just what you're capable of.' He gave a funny little half-smile. 'And you know what? I'm kind of sorry I won't be there to see it.'

Fran's attention had already moved back to the task in hand. 'Think of it as a scientific experiment if it will make you feel better. This is my chance to see if you and my mum and all those chat-show hosts are right and it truly is personality, not looks, that make a difference in life.' Ash rolled his eyes but didn't say anything. 'Look, the rest of my family are going out for the afternoon at two, so I don't want to officially make the wish until then. But when the time comes, are you going to be OK with it?'

'Your wish, your waste,' he said shortly, and that was that.

Mr and Mrs Roper were not happy when Fran informed them she was opting out of the family trip to the cinema that afternoon, though her excuse that she had lots of homework to catch up on wasn't something they could object to. They did, however, protest at the news that she was spending the evening with 'friends from school' again. 'But we have to go out tonight! To the Goldsworthys' wretched cocktail party, remember? I was counting on you to babysit!' wailed her mother as she struggled to strap Beth into her pushchair. Mr Roper was dashing about trying to decide whether it was more urgent to find his shoes, glasses or car keys. Mickey, meanwhile, was reciting his Kisco lines for the five-hundredth time since brunch.

'So why didn't you ask me about it properly?' demanded Fran. 'You shouldn't just assume I'm going to be available.'

'But – you always – I always – flippin' hell –' Mrs Roper had just been poked in the eye by Beth's flailing foot. Fran, however, was not in the mood to sympathize. Everything was such a *mess*, as usual, and not just the babysitting arrangements. God knows how, but globules of raw pancake batter had somehow transferred from the kitchen and were now festooning the hall carpet.

'There, there,' said Mr Roper distractedly. 'I'll ask Jenny from next door to pop round . . . aha! Gotcha!' He had just found his shoes, with the keys tucked in one toe and his glasses in another. 'Are we ready to go now? Everyone got everything, yes? That's right, wave bye-bye to Fran, Bethy . . . wait, love, let me give you a hand with that pushchair –'

More bustle. More squeals. More soothing. Finally, the door slammed shut. And five minutes later Fran was twirling before the mirror in her bedroom. 'So,' she said coyly, 'how do I look?'

'Predictable,' said Ash. The expression in his eyes was hard to read: ironic, amused, deliberately indifferent. 'And I don't reckon that chest of yours is real,' he added before disappearing into the ring.

Oh well. If Ash was determined to be in a grump it was no skin off her (finely sculpted) nose. Fran practised blowing a kiss with her juicy new lips, then shook out her mane of chestnut hair and smiled sweetly at her reflection. A beautiful stranger with huge violet eyes and peachy-perfect skin smiled back at her. Her legs were long and slim, encased in tight black trousers and sexy black boots. Her waist was narrow, her breasts a voluminous swell beneath a scoop-necked silk top in aquamarine. Real diamond studs sparkled in her ears. This girl wasn't just gorgeous, she was stylish and glamorous too.

The thing was, she wasn't strictly a girl: twenty-something young woman was nearer the mark. Which wasn't *quite* what Fran had in mind when she'd first dreamed up her new face 'n' body shopping spree. It would mean some readjustment to her plans, certainly, but it was nothing she couldn't handle. And on the subject of handling . . . cautious prods revealed her magnificent bosom to be curiously unyielding. She tried a few star jumps, but her chest stayed firmly in place even though her new bra was little more than a wisp of chiffon. Oh my gosh, Fran thought dizzily, Ash was right – I've just had a boob job! What would my granny say?

Although she told herself there wasn't much

point in being an über-babe if there was no one else around to appreciate it, it took several false starts before she was able to tear herself away from the mirror in her bedroom. Another fifteen minutes was spent in front of the mirror in the hall while she practised introducing herself in her breathy new voice. She decided to call herself Sabrina. 'Sabrina von Schwarzkopf,' she crooned huskily to the coat stand, 'and the pleasure's all mine.' It took a further ten minutes to find a baseball cap, dark glasses and baggy sweater she could use as temporary camouflage while she snuck out of the house. So what with one thing and another, it took nearly an hour of dawdling before she was ready to set off on the Firedog trail.

Thanks to her conversation with Francesca the night before, followed up by a few crafty text messages, Fran knew the band were meeting the manager of the Three Lions pub at three that afternoon. She was sure a busy pub would provide plenty of opportunities to 'accidentally' bump into Quinn and Co., and as for her cover story . . . well, it was still a work in progress, but when the time came she was confident that Sabrina's charms would carry her through.

The expedition got off to a bad start when Fran reached the bus stop only to see the one she wanted pulling away. However, after one gawp at Ms von

Schwarzkopf, the driver screeched to a halt and even waited for her to totter along the pavement in her teeny-tiny heels (the boots were proving to be better suited to posing in than walking in). His patience was rewarded with a mega-watt smile from Sabrina and resentful grumbling from the rest of his passengers. The female ones, that is.

As Fran approached the Three Lions she reluctantly pulled on the hat and baggy sweatshirt again. It would have been fun to make the kind of dramatic entrance that would have the punters spluttering into their pints, but she wanted to keep a low profile for now. Fran didn't have much experience of pubs, other than going out for an occasional Sunday lunch with her family, but she decided this one must be quite trendy in spite of the dingy dark wood and maroon-painted walls. The clientele were mostly what her dad called 'yuppie types' and there were lots of flyers for music festivals and trendy art shows, plus a poster advertising 'live music, first Saturday of every month', pinned to the wall by the bar. And sure enough there, sitting round a table in the corner, were Quinn and Francesca and the rest. They were deep in conversation with an older guy she didn't recognize, but who was presumably the man in charge of booking the bands.

Fran went over to the bar and pretended to study the food menu. Every step she took seemed to have a wiggle in it, either because of the boots or because Sabrina's body was naturally programmed to shimmy. Even with the hat pulled down over her face, and the Page-Three-Girl bosom under wraps, the barman was eyeing her with open admiration. 'What can I get you, gorgeous?'

'Oh . . .' Fran realized she didn't have clue what a girl like Sabrina would choose to drink. Francesca had all *Sex and the City* on DVD and Fran seemed to remember something called a Cosmopolitan featured quite heavily. But this didn't look the sort of place to serve cocktails. 'Um . . . I'll have an orange juice, thanks.'

'Here you go. Freshly squeezed, just the way you like it.' The way he looked at her chest as he said it made 'freshly squeezed' sound rather disgusting. Fran took her drink and slunk off to the table next to Quinn's, trying to be as unobtrusive as possible. Soon she had her head buried in a newspaper someone had left behind, pretending to be engrossed in the property ads while she listened to the conversation on her right.

It seemed that Quinn's friend was willing to give Firedog a chance to perform in the music night two weekends from now, though they'd have to do an informal audition before the offer was official. 'And if I see any of your kiddie school chums lurking around my bar, the deal's off. The same goes for all you budding rock stars. No boozing today and *definitely* no boozing on the night. I've got my licence to think of, understand?'

The Firedogs scowled into their glasses of Coke but assured him this wouldn't be an issue. Then everyone shook hands before the manager was called away to sort something out at the till.

'I'd better be on my way too,' announced Francesca. 'I'm supposed to be meeting Sadie and Zara in ten minutes.'

'Is it a private party or can anyone join?' asked Rob. 'Cos after last night, I reckon me and Sadie have some unfinished business, if y'know what I mean.' There was chorus of sniggers.

'I suppose you can come if you want,' said Francesca without much enthusiasm. From the scraping of chairs it seemed as if the other lads had decided to take this as a general invitation. Fran began to panic – she'd only just arrived and her quarry was leaving! And if they were all going to someone's house an introduction would be nearly impossible to pull off . . .

But today, it seemed, was her lucky day. 'I still need to sort out with Steve when we're going to do this audition,' said Quinn. 'So I'll catch you guys up in a bit, OK?' As the others were shuffling noisily out of the pub, he went over to the bar to have another word with the manager. An opportunity like this was almost too good to be true.

Fran counted up to ten, crossed her fingers for

luck, and took a very deep breath. She removed the hat and sweater and fluffed up her hair. Then she sauntered over to the bar. 'Excuse me,' she said in Sabrina's husky purr, 'but I couldn't help overhearing you earlier. Am I right in thinking that you're a musician?'

Quinn turned around and literally did a double take. His eyes widened and he gulped. Several times. 'Er, yeah, yeah that's right. A musician. Yeah. That's, uh, me.'

'But how *fascinating!*' cooed Fran. It was hugely gratifying to see Mr Sex God himself reduced to red-faced incoherence in the exact same way she was whenever Quinn was around. 'And so you have your own band . . . er . . .?'

'Firedog. But that's just the band's name . . . I'm not called Firedog. Obviously. I'm, um, Quinn. Pleased to meet you.'

'I'm Sabrina von Schwarzkopf,' said Fran, running a hand through her chestnut locks, and opening her violet eyes very wide. 'And the pleasure, Quinn, is all mine.'

She waited expectantly but Quinn was beyond the power of speech. 'Let me try to explain myself.' Improvisation wasn't Fran's strong point and yet she found herself launching into her story with reckless ease. 'I'm a writer, you see, and at the moment I'm researching a novel about life in an up-and-coming guitar band.' Dramatic pause. 'So you can *imagine* how excited I was to find myself sitting next to the exact sort of group I want to feature in my story. Talk about coincidence . . .' Fran leaned in even closer and spoke in a confiding undertone. 'I don't suppose you'd be willing to have a little chat about your experiences, would you? You would? How *wonderful* . . . that'll be two more orange juices, please,' she told the gawping barman as she took Quinn by the arm. 'And now, Mr Firedog, why don't we sit down here and you can tell me *all* about yourself.'

Quinn, it appeared, was more than happy to talk about himself and his life as the lead singer, songwriter, founder and 'artistic director' of Firedog. In fact, once he'd recovered from the whole shock 'n' awe treatment, it wasn't long before the famous Quinn Adams charisma began to assert itself. He retousled his hair, smiled his dreamiest smile, gazed into her face with his most soulful expression and made a heroic effort not to let his eyes drop to her heaving bosom more than once every ten seconds or so. Fran, meanwhile, made a heroic effort to stick to her cover story and not throw herself, gibbering, into his arms.

So it was just as well Quinn didn't need much prompting. Fran made the occasional scribble in the notebook she'd brought along but otherwise concentrated on smiling and nodding in the right places and trying out Sabrina's silvery laugh. After twenty minutes on Quinn's musical influences, Quinn's musical awakening and Quinn's sense of musical destiny she decided it was time to bring the conversation round to more personal matters.

'I suppose you must already have quite a lot of fans? Female fans in particular?'

Quinn's bashful shrug was charm itself. 'Some . . . maybe . . . well, you know how it is . . .'

'And is there anyone special in your life at the moment?'

'Er, no. Not right now, anyway. It can be difficult – being so wrapped up in the band and everything—'

'Lonely too, sometimes?'

'I guess . . .'

'Ah, but I'm sure it's this sensitivity which makes your performance so full of feeling . . . so rich in heartache,' breathed Fran, forgetting that she wasn't supposed to have heard Firedog play. 'Tell me, Quinn, would you say that you have been damaged by your past? By someone who didn't treat you as you deserve, perhaps?'

'Well, now you mention it, my ex-girlfriend *was* a total witch.'

Aha! She knew it! There really was a secret love trauma in Quinn's life! But before she could pursue this further she found his gaze fixed on her with new intensity. 'And what about you?' he was asking 'Do you ever feel, er, lonely?' Quinn was ever so slightly blushing but he had a glint in his eye.

There was a breathless pause.

Fran leaned across the table towards him. Their eyes met. Their pulse rates quickened. Their hands touched . . . Quinn's fingers were brushing the tip of Sabrina's perfectly manicured nails . . .

And then, all of a sudden, reality came crashing down.

Quinn's fingers were stroking *Sabrina's* perfectly manicured nails – not Fran's slightly chewed-looking set, with the traces of glitter varnish she hadn't got around to removing. Quinn wasn't holding hands with Fran the schoolgirl but Sabrina the twenty-something maneater. Boy-eater. She snatched back her/Sabrina's hands as if they had been burned.

'I'm afraid you'll have to excuse me,' she said with Sabrina's brightest smile, 'but I have to use the loo.' She was already backing out of the nearest door.

While Quinn was left to sweat it out in the bar, Fran locked herself in the pub's toilet, taking a long, hard look at the stranger in the mirror. The con-artist-turned-cradle-snatcher in the mirror. OK, so Fran wanted to experience being beautiful for a few hours. Fine. Then this had provided the opportunity to get some inside info on the boy of her dreams. Also fine. But that, she told herself sternly, was as far as things were going to go. Maybe if she'd been magicked into a fifteen-year-old sexpot the situation wouldn't have begun to feel so, well, sleazy, but it would still be deeply unfair on *both* of them.

Sabrina's reflection was sulking now. C'mon, surely just one teeny-weeny kiss couldn't hurt? 'There's no need to look like that,' Fran said aloud, 'because I'm not going to back down.' Never mind all that theoretical debate about whether personality or looks made the real difference in life: holding hands with Quinn, kissing Quinn, would only mean anything if it was done as her real self. Otherwise the achievement would feel as false as Sabrina's breasts . . . wouldn't it?

'Sorry about that,' she said briskly when she got back to where Quinn was sitting. 'Let's see, where were we . . . Oh yes. Firedog's musical influences.'

Quinn looked confused, trying to work out if he'd imagined the sexual tension that had seemed to be crackling in the air only a few minutes ago. He liked to think that if he had a sixth sense, it was dedicated to picking up on flirtation, but then he'd never met a girl – woman – like Sabrina before. Why had she snatched her hand away like that? Was it because she could tell his palms were sweating?

'. . . and now,' this violet-eyed vision of loveliness was saying, 'that we've got to know each other a little better, do you think there's any chance of being introduced to the rest of the band?'

'The Firedogs?'

'Exactly.' The Human Venus had already gathered her things and was heading purposefully towards the main door. 'I've *so* enjoyed our chat but I think the time has come to put the other members of the band in the picture.'

'I'll, uh, give the guys a call,' said Quinn, dazed.

It turned out that the others had congregated in a cafe a few minutes down the road from the Three Lions. Their reaction to Quinn arriving in the company of someone who looked liked they'd sprung straight from *The OC* casting couch was mixed, to say the least. Whereas you could almost hear the collective thud as the boys' jaws hit the floor, Zara and Sadie's expression was openly hostile. Francesca blinked – several times.

'Hi everyone, I'd like you to meet Sabrina von – er, Sabrina. We met in the pub.'

Fran permitted herself a flirtatious smile, then moistened her lips in a suggestive manner. Envious disbelief flitted across the faces of the entire party. Even Francesca looked taken aback.

'Sabrina's a novelist,' said Quinn reverently. 'She's writing a book about a group of friends in a band. We've been having a chat about the whole, you know, songwriting thing and now she wants to talk to you guys.'

'If that's all right with you,' added Fran, fluttering her eyelashes as if her life depended on it. The boys did everything in their power to convey that this would be very all right indeed, before simultaneously leaping up to offer her their seats. Zara and Sadie replaced their scowls with smiles of dazzling insincerity.

'Have you had anything published before?' enquired Francesca when everyone was finally settled.

'No, this is my first novel.'

'So you don't have any previous writing experience?'

Fran resented the implication of this. 'Actually, I've done a lot of work on magazines. Lifestyle magazines mostly.'

Everyone looked suitably admiring. Francesca raised her brows. 'Great. What kind of work would that be?'

'Um . . .' Fran thought back to a career talk her class had recently had from a local journalist. 'Proofreading, copy-editing, that sort of thing . . . I started off doing a work placement at *Uncut*. It's a design magazine; you might not have heard of it.'

'Funnily enough, my dad's a contributor,' said Francesca coolly. Fran suppressed a smile – this was exactly why she'd chosen the title. 'So who do you know there?'

There was an ever-so-slightly challenging note in her voice.

'Maisie O'Donnol, of course. And I did a bit of

work for Declan, before he moved to *Time Out*.'
That'd show her. Maisie was the editor and Declan
the former art director at *Uncut*; Fran had heard Mr
Goldsworthy complaining about both. 'But I got
bored with doing the behind-the-scenes stuff, that's
why I've turned to novel writing. Creative freedom
and all that.'

'Sounds fantastic,' Rob leaped in eagerly.

'Amazing,' chorused Jez and Liam.

'Just tell us what you want to know,' said Quinn,
surreptitiously moving his chair so that his thigh
was resting against hers.

The Firedogs were surprised to learn that Sabrina
was more interested in seeing them 'interact as
friends and musicians' rather than do a formal
interview, but they were happy to oblige. Even Zara
and Sadie managed to suppress their natural resentment in favour of ingratiating themselves with this
glamorous newcomer. Sadie preened when Sabrina
asked about her accent, but was less pleased by the
observation, 'Californian? *Really?* Sounds more
Aussie to me – but maybe that's your south London
twang coming through.' Fran took even more satisfaction in asking Zara, 'So are you in the band or are
you just another groupie?'

Midway through Rob's monologue about the
time somebody in Tesco 'nearly' mistook him for
Chris Martin, Fran thought she heard her name
mentioned. The girls had given up on ingratiating

themselves with Sabrina and were busy gossiping at the end of the table.

'. . . so Fran texted you, like, *five* times to find where you were going, what you were doing, right?' Sadie was saying to Francesca. 'I'm surprised she hasn't tracked us down by now.'

'It's like she's your poodle,' said Zara. 'I don't see how you can stand it – it would drive me insane.'

'Fran's been my friend ever since I can remember.'

'Oh, I know,' said Sadie hastily, 'Fran's a real honey, don't get me wrong. It just seems, well, a bit *freaky.*'

'She's not a freak,' said Francesca, rolling her eyes in an amused sort of way. 'She's, you know . . . sweet.'

Gee, thought Fran, thanks for the ringing endorsement. Sabrina's face was turning pink with Fran's discomfiture and she noticed Quinn was looking at her anxiously. 'Are you all right, Sabrina? Can I get you a drink or something?'

'That's ever so kind of you, but I think it's probably time I got going.'

This announcement was met by a chorus of disappointment. When Fran finally managed to convince them that her mind was made up, it seemed that her departure was the cue for everyone else to get going too. At any rate, all the boys stood up and attempted to escort her, en masse, out of the cafe. The other girls were left to trail behind. Everyone congregated on the pavement outside, Quinn and Rob taking position either side of Sabrina; Jez, Liam, Zara and Sadie hovering the rear. Only Francesca stood apart, looking bored.

Fran was just trying to decide how to make an appropriate exit – how formal should she make her goodbyes? If she went to the bus stop would they all start following her? – when a sleek silver car drew up alongside the pavement in front of her. The window rolled down and an impeccably groomed male head leaned out.

'Francesca?' he asked. 'Is that you?'

It was Mr Goldsworthy, on his way home after a meeting with a client. Catching sight of his daughter together with her new friends from the band he had naturally pulled over to say hello. Now he got out of the car and introduced himself. When he reached Sabrina, Fran was relieved to see that Mr Goldsworthy was too much of a proper grown-up to do the whole jaw-dropping, lip-smacking routine she was beginning to brace herself for. It had been fun at first, but the novelty had started to wear off.

'A pleasure to meet you,' said Mr Goldsworthy smoothly.

'Sabrina's researching a novel,' interjected Francesca. 'She says she's worked at *Uncut*.' Again there was a slightly suspicious note in her voice.

'Really?' Mr Goldsworthy turned to Fran with new interest. 'Who do you know there?'

Fran went into her name-dropping routine a little nervously. She needn't have worried, however – Mr Goldsworthy immediately launched into a one-sided discussion about the internal politics at *Uncut*. Now and again Fran chipped in with some comment she'd heard Mr Goldsworthy make in the past: 'Maisie's ambitious, but she's got no people skills,' or, 'I think commissioning the Llewelyn-Bowen column was a mistake.' Mr Goldsworthy was so obviously impressed that Fran soon found herself confiding in him about the trauma of writer's block. Meanwhile, the rest of the party shuffled awkwardly on the pavement.

'Dad, it's time we headed off,' said Francesca at last. 'We need to get some practice in before our audition at the Three Lions tomorrow. So's we can get that gig I told you about.'

'Did you? How exciting,' Mr Goldsworthy said vaguely. 'Well, don't let me keep you . . . I take it you're not going to be around for the party this evening then. What a shame.' A thought occurred to him and he turned to Sabrina. 'My wife and I are holding a small drinks party this evening. I don't suppose you would like to come? It's going to be very informal, just friends and neighbours, but I could introduce you to my friend Fabian Harlow. He's a publisher, rather high-powered I believe, and

I'm sure he'd be happy to talk to you about your book.'

'How very kind,' Fran heard herself saying. And before she knew it, she was putting Mr Goldsworthy's card into her pocket. Francesca's expression was far from friendly. It was definitely time to go. 'Right. Bye, guys, thanks so much for helping with my research and everything . . . I'm sure you're all, er, headed for great things.'

'You'll let us know how the book's going?' said Quinn, trying to catch Sabrina's eye for a last lingering look. Unfortunately the expression in his own was desperate rather than meaningful. 'In fact, you could always, er, give me a call if you think of anything else you'd like to know . . .' He passed her an old bus ticket with his number scribbled on the back. Fran tucked it away with Mr Goldsworthy's card and treated everyone to a final radiant smile.

'It was *fabulous* meeting you all,' she said. 'Truly inspiring.' Then she turned on her heel and made off down the street at Sabrina's speediest wiggle. Things had gone better than she'd hoped, but she didn't want to push her luck.

The afternoon's charm offensive had given Fran an appetite and so she took Sabrina off to a fast-food bar where she had great pleasure in ordering super-extra-ultra size everything. After all, Sabrina and her twenty-four-inch waist could take it. As she sat on a bench outside, tucking into her second burger, she saw the woman sipping diet lemonade next to her looking at her with hatred in her eyes. Fran didn't blame her. She'd probably hate Sabrina too.

Once energy levels were restored, it was time for a little retail therapy. Fran usually hated shopping for clothes – the bewildering array of garments that never seemed to be in the right size or cut, the cramped changing rooms with unflattering mirrors, the trauma of squeezing into something that had looked effortlessly chic in a magazine but proved to be hideously impractical in real life . . . As Ms von Schwarzkopf, naturally, it was a whole new experience. Even though she didn't buy anything, all the shop assistants were falling over each other to be of service. Luckily, Sabrina had a special expression for freezing out unwelcome attention: a stare 'n' sneer combo that even managed to silence a group of lads who'd followed her around the lingerie department, making rude comments.

Fran felt her next stop should be a posh West End bar, where Sabrina could schmooze with other glamorous types, but being beautiful was strangely exhausting and by the end of the day all she wanted to do was to go home and kick off those crippling heels. So, much as she hated large social events full of people she didn't know, she decided that the Goldsworthy's drinks party would be an honourable compromise. Before she went, however, she decided to summon Ash to give him an update on the situation.

'Oh. It's *you*,' frowned Ash when he appeared in the living room.

'Of course it's me! Who else would it be?'

'You're still the scary purple-eyed lady. I don't like talking to you when you look all different. It's very disorientating.'

'And there I was thinking you were a fan of man-eating birds . . . Don't you find my new look attractive then?' She couldn't resist giving a wiggle of Sabrina's hips.

Ash shrugged. 'I'm not saying you – *she* – isn't harem-stocking material. It just so happens that Sabrina isn't my type. Anyway, I thought you'd be sucking face with the bottle blondie by now. Or did I misjudge the guy and it turns out he's more interested in kindred spirits than heaving bosoms?'

She knew he was only taking this line because he wanted to prove his point about Scheherazade and natural-born charisma. But there was no need to for him to be so superior and judgemental about it, she flounced her hair in Sabrina's most contemptuous manner. Then she tried out Sabrina's über-appealing pout in combination with a tremulous widening of her violet eyes. 'I know you don't approve of this wish, but there's no need to be such a *meanie* about it. Or Quinn, for that matter.'

'Dear gods! If you could just stop obsess –' It

seemed as if Ash was about to let rip, but at the last moment he seemed to think better of it. 'All right . . . all right . . . I suppose if this transformation thingy is weird for me it must be even weirder for you. And you've obviously done pretty well so far. But you know I'm always available if you get into one of your messes, OK?'

Fran resented the reference to 'her' messes, but decided to let it go for now. 'That's ever so sweet of you, Ash,' she said in Sabrina's most treacly manner, 'but as you can see, I'm doing fine. In fact, I'm off to a very glamorous cocktail party now. With grown-ups. *Real* grown-ups.' Not immature boys, she added to herself, who think a few hundred years stuck in a ring gives one some kind of moral authority.

The party was already in full swing when Fran arrived a little after seven. Mrs Goldsworthy met her at the door, looking elegant in a black cocktail dress. If she was disconcerted to find Ms Schwarzkopf oozing sex appeal on her doorstep, her gracious smile didn't show it.

'I'm Marina, you must be one of Richard's friends.'

'Well, sort of. We met this afternoon outside a pub.'

'Is that so?'

Mrs Goldsworthy's smile was looking a little

fixed, but before Fran could explain things further Mr Goldsworthy himself arrived in the hall.

'Sabrina! So glad you could make it.' He kissed her lightly on both cheeks. *Mwah, mwah.* 'Sabrina's a novelist,' he explained to his wife, 'who's been talking to Francesca as part of her research for her book about rock bands. She used to work at *Uncut*, you know.'

'Really?' said Mrs Goldsworthy. She was looking at Sabrina through narrowed eyes – in exactly the same way her daughter had, in fact. 'And who do you know at *Uncut*?'

Fran sighed and once again prepared to launch into her spiel. Thankfully Mr Goldsworthy got in first. 'Oh, she knows the whole gang. We've already had a good natter about it all. Agrees with me completely about the Llewelyn-Bowen debacle.'

'How gratifying,' said his wife drily. She took Sabrina's arm and began to shepherd her up the stairs towards the drawing room. 'Do come and meet the others.'

Before she had time to feel nervous, Fran walked into the thick of the party, introduced herself to several scary-looking grown-ups and plunged into a stream of chit-chat. As long as she smiled nicely, asked polite questions and then responded to the answers in an interested sort of way, conversation flowed quite easily. A few people tried speaking to her in bimbo-friendly words of one syllable, but even though her real self was younger than everyone else there by nearly two decades, Fran just about managed to hold her own.

She also discovered that, 'And what do you do?' was a multi-purpose conversation filler and almost as boring as all those questions adults liked to ask you about Favourite Lessons and Forthcoming Exams.

'I'm a writer,' she said brightly for the tenth time in an hour. 'And what do you do?'

'I'm a publisher,' said Fabian Harlow, with a well-oiled smile. 'What a propitious coincidence.' He sized up Sabrina again, but more carefully. There was nothing more tedious than desperate wannabes demanding one publish their masterpiece, but Fabian prided himself on his business instinct. Sabrina's cleavage had 'bestselling author' written all over it. 'I'd love to hear about your work.'

'Um, well, there's this girl who's in love with a guy who sings in a rock band. Then her best friend joins the band and so the first girl, the heroine, gets the chance to hang out with them all and starts to, like, *really connect* with Qui – the rock star, I mean. But she can't tell him how she feels because whenever the best friend (who's very glamorous) is around, it's like the first girl doesn't exist.'

'And is there a happy ending?'

'I hope so,' said Fran fervently. Then, remembering

she was supposed to be making a pitch, added, 'it's very light-hearted.'

'Sounds delightful – Bridget Jones meets *Spinal Tap*,' purred Fabian. They could hold the launch party at the Ivy . . . a nice bright jacket for the book . . . a nice short skirt for the author. 'Chick-lit isn't my personal area of expertise alas, but perhaps you could pop round to the office next week and we could discuss it further? Let me give you my card.'

And off it went to join Mr Goldsworthy's card and Quinn's bus ticket. I'm getting quite a collection thought Fran as she turned to see what the commotion was at the other end of the room. It was her parents: arriving late as usual, full of apologies as usual, and in such a flap that Mrs Roper had already managed to knock a wine glass off the mantelpiece. She had dressed up for the occasion, in quite a smart blue trouser suit, but her hair was already coming loose from its clips and Fran could see a Bolognese-coloured spot on the lapel of her jacket. It looked as if Mr Roper had let Mickey practise knotting his tie again.

'Asylum seekers from the domestic front no doubt,' murmured Fabian. Fran gave him Sabrina's iciest stare and went off to join the Ropers. She suddenly felt quite protective of her parents, adrift in the Goldsworthys' designer drawing room. It struck her that most of the guests had been selected according to the same criteria as the flowers, canapés and Mr Goldsworthy's shirt: as a complement to the decor.

By the time she reached the other side of the room, her parents were talking to Marina. Fran had a feeling Mrs Goldsworthy and Sabrina hadn't quite hit it off and so she hovered at the edge of group, pretending to be lost in admiration of a flower 'installation' of a single white orchid and a gold-dusted twig.

'Francesca has really come into her own this year,' Mrs Goldsworthy was saying. 'That awkward adolescent stage can be *such* a bore . . . thank God the girl has finally acquired a bit of poise.'

'Yes, your teenage years can be hell, can't they?' said Mr Roper. 'Fran seems to be doing all right, but it's hard to tell sometimes.'

'She's a dear girl,' said Mrs Goldsworthy vaguely.

'I'm a little worried about this band business though,' put in Mrs Roper. 'I know Fran's not directly involved but—'

'We don't want it to become a *distraction*, I agree, but these days extra-curricular activities are almost as important as grades – it's never too early to start thinking about university applications you know.'

'I was thinking more about . . . well, the boys in it are a couple of years older than our two, aren't they?'

'Francesca's so mature in her tastes it's only natural that she should seek out older friends. And to tell you the truth, I'm not sure the school is stretching a girl of her abilities sufficiently . . . Richard and I were thinking about sending her to Ashton Court, but she's reluctant to leave her friends behind of course.'

'Of course,' echoed the Ropers faintly. Ashton Court was a madly posh boarding school on the other side of London.

'Do excuse me,' said Marina with a charming smile, 'but I simply *must* have a word with the Fothering-Gills.'

Fran's parents exchanged glances and sighed. Socializing with the Goldsworthys was always a bit of an ordeal, and now that alarmingly glamorous girl – some model or actress friend of Marina's no doubt – was bearing down on them.

'Hello there,' she said. 'I met some friends of your daughter's this afternoon. Am I right in thinking she's the Other Francesca?'

And somehow, before they quite knew how it happened, Mr and Mrs Roper found themselves telling Sabrina all about Fran and her talent for singing, how good she was with her younger siblings, how much they all relied on her and how they sometimes worried she didn't feel appreciated enough. 'We're just so busy all the time,' said Mr Roper.

'I think she needs a bit more confidence, you see,' said Mrs Roper. 'But now she's got these older friends and has started to stay out late we can't help worrying.'

'Please don't,' said Fran earnestly. 'It's only because I – she – er, well, I remember what I was like at that age. It meant so much to know my parents trusted me. And your daughter sounds like a responsible sort of girl.'

'Oh yes, she is. She's wonderful, really. Keeps me in line.' Mrs Roper laughed, a little embarrassed. 'Sorry to ramble on like this, we must be boring you stiff.'

'Not at all.'

'You're very kind.' Mrs Roper looked searchingly into Sabrina's eyes. 'It's the strangest thing . . . but I can't help feeling I know you from somewhere. Have we met before?'

'I don't think so,' said Fran, backing away. Her mother couldn't possibly see through the genie magic, but the sudden scrutiny was making her nervous. Plus, she'd just caught sight of the time – it was ten to nine and at nine o'clock Sabrina the Sex Goddess would be replaced by Fran the Schoolgirl: untidy plait, chubby legs, chewed nails and all. 'Nice meeting you but I've just remembered I'm running late for . . . um . . . something.' She reached the door, passing Mr Goldsworthy on the way – 'Lovelypartythankyouverymuchforhavingme,' and began to hurry down the stairs. A large man was standing at the bottom, smoking a cigar, and when she tried to get past he deliberately moved to block her way.

'Now, now,' he said, wagging a meaty pink finger at her, 'I can't be letting all the pretty girls run away, can I?'

'But I'm late—' Fran was horribly aware of the minutes ticking away.

'I'm sure your boyfriend can wait a bit longer. Treat 'em mean keep 'em keen and all that.' He chuckled at his own joke before slipping one arm around her waist.

Fran stared back at his piggy face with disgust. How would he react if he knew who Sabrina really was? But this had given her an idea.

'Oh, I haven't got a boyfriend,' she said, wide-eyed. 'I only turned fifteen last month and my parents wouldn't like it. They're still upstairs at the party you know.'

'Fifteen! Ha! Ha! That's a fine joke!'

'It's true,' said Fran sadly, 'I'm very . . . over-developed for my age.' She bit her lip shyly. 'It's a terrible burden. The local Child Protection Officer says he's never known anything like it.'

The man attempted a chuckle, but he was looking uncertain and Fran took the opportunity to slip past to the door. She just managed to totter to the end of the road before her vision filled with purple haze, her body prickled from head to foot, and Sabrina and her violet eyes vanished into the night.

*

'So I was right,' said Ash when Fran had reached the end of her report, 'charm *is* simply a matter of self-assurance. You couldn't have held your own among those posh party types just by being doe-eyed and pouty.'

'It's easy to be sociable when you know you're a sex bomb. As far as Quinn and the other boys were concerned, Sabrina could have been deaf and dumb and they'd still say she was the most fascinating personality they'd ever met.'

'Yes, well, if Quinn even has *one* track for his mind to run on then I'd be very surprised,' Ash sniffed. 'And in this day and age, if a man can't appreciate a fine mind above a fine cleavage then, frankly, he's not worth the effort.'

'You are such a fraud.' But Fran couldn't help laughing at Ash's sanctimonious expression.

'Seriously, though, if you had the chance to permanently turn into Miss Sultry von Birdbrain would you take it?' Ash asked.

Fran thought it over. No matter what Ash or her mother said, looks *did* make a difference to your experience of life: being irresistible was a power as well as a pleasure, exhausting and addictive. As Sabrina, she had taken risks and made choices that she wouldn't – or couldn't – have done as Fran. She remembered the all-conquering radiance of Sabrina's smile, the ruthlessness of her sneer. 'I don't know,' she said at last. 'It's complicated.'

They were walking past the department store where Sabrina had gone shopping the afternoon before and Fran stopped to look at the window display. She'd been talking to the genie under cover of her hands-free phone kit again, but it had been a slightly disjointed conversation as Ash got distracted by other pedestrians, billboards and passing cars. Now he was gazing longingly after a silver Jaguar. 'Flying carpets may be fuel efficient,' he said, 'but where's the sex appeal?'

'There's no need to rub it in,' said Fran crossly. She hadn't heard the flying carpet reference, being lost in admiration of an itsy-bitsy sequinned dress in the window. On Sabrina, she knew, it would look a million dollars, but on her . . . She sighed heavily, and Ash turned to look at her again. 'You know what you need?' he said. 'Positive reinforcement.'

'So you're a psychoanalyst now, as well as a genie.' The hands-free cord had come detached from her phone and she was getting odd looks from the occasional passer-by, but she was past caring. London streets were full of nutters mumbling to themselves.

'No, but I'm a first-class flatterer.'

She was about to tell him not to be daft when he raised a hand to forestall her. 'Wait.' Ash cleared his throat, smiled dazzlingly, and swept her his most extravagant bow – only for an old lady laden with carrier bags to walk right through him. Fran couldn't help giggling; he looked so outlandish in the middle of that grey street with its dingy shoppers. Like a peacock in a car park.

'Celestial Maiden!' he declaimed in a ringing voice. 'Siren among Schoolgirls and Princess among Patrons! Will you permit the most devoted of your slaves to exalt your splendour to the skies?'

'Er, go on then.'

His hands were clasped to his chest, his eyes half-closed and his whole body atremble with feeling. 'O Priceless Pearl of Albion,' he cried, 'O Gilded Lily of London Town! Your eyes are the silver of a midwinter sky, your skin is soft as ripe apricots, your mouth is sweeter than a honeycomb and your silken hair . . . aah,' he sighed, a look of rapture on his face, 'it is a net to trap kisses in!' Dramatic pause. 'Fair Mistress, you have but to say the word and I will stride the earth for you, endure fire and ice for you and shake the pillars of heaven to their foundations – all to lay your heart's desire at your feet.' He paused for breath and gave her a wink. 'There. Feel any better?'

And although she knew he was only messing around, something about that wink *did* make her feel better. Lots.

O Priceless Pearl of Albion Fran was saying to herself dreamily during Monday break. *O Gilded Lily of*

London Town . . . I wonder if Quinn has noticed I have skin like ripe apricots? On the seat next to her, Francesca was wittering about something, but she'd stopped listening ages ago. All morning Francesca hadn't stopped going on and on about Sabrina and what a stuck-up bimbo she was. Francesca certainly didn't buy all that novel-writing crap. It was just a bid for attention. Francesca wouldn't be surprised if Sabrina had some sort of personality disorder – predatory people were always insecure. And really, she wasn't *that* attractive. Not when you got close.

'. . . disgusting, don't you think?'

Fran was idly winding a strand of hair round one finger. She'd worn her hair loose this morning and Quinn had given it a friendly tug as he'd swung past on the way to class. *A net to trap kisses in* . . .

'Don't you think? Fran? FRAN!'

'Oh. Sorry. Um, what don't I think about what?'

'Honestly! You could at least *try* to keep up. I was saying that it was totally disgusting the way all the boys were leching over that plastic-pumped stick insect. You should have seen Quinn – like a slobbering puppy.'

'But boys are like that, aren't they? They can't help themselves.' This, at least, was how Fran had excused Quinn's loss of dignity on Saturday. Although she felt a pang whenever she remembered the worshipful way Quinn had gazed at Sabrina, it was obscurely comforting too. Even Quinn could feel intimidated. Even Quinn got tonguetied. Fran had a feeling that from now on whenever she came face to face with the Object of her Every Desire, she'd be able to hold her nerve.

'Well it's about time they learned some self-control. Not to mention good taste. Quinn was completely gaga.'

Fran frowned. 'Why should you care who Quinn slobbers over? You think he's immature and conceited, remember.'

'Well, I guess I'm disappointed to be proved right. Up till now, I was beginning to wonder if I'd misjudged him . . . and then it turns out he's just as shallow as the rest of his mates. Huh. Anyway, my mum said Sabrina gatecrashed their party half-drunk and flirted outrageously with every man in the room.'

'She didn't –' began Fran indignantly, then realized her error. 'She didn't!' she said again, in tones of pained disbelief.

'I know, can you believe it? Mum and Dad were still rowing about it when I got home. Zara says it's because Sab—'

'Zara and Sadie met this girl too?' asked Fran, all innocence.

'Oh . . . yeah . . . I said I'd hang out with them

for a bit after I'd gone to the Three Lions. Sadie's really keen on Rob and wanted me to give her some advice about him and all that. I meant to give you a call, but what with Sabrina and everything I forgot.'

Just like you 'forgot' to mention you were auditioning for Firedog, Fran added silently. To change the subject, she asked how the meeting with the Three Lions manager had gone. Francesca pulled a face.

'It was OK. I mean, we got the gig . . . but the truth is, we're not as hot as everyone seems to think. This is strictly between the two of us, of course.' At the sound of Francesca's old confiding tone, Fran's spurt of resentment died away. 'We've about one and a half decent songs which we play to death and then the rest of the time we do this really crap cover stuff. And somehow I don't reckon all the practice in the world is going to turn Jez into a halfway decent drummer or stop Rob doing his ridiculous guitar riffs. Quinn definitely has a talent for song-writing, but he hasn't come up with anything new for a while.'

'I'm sure he's working on something at the moment,' said Fran vaguely. 'Everyone knows that inspiration can't be hurried.' And she returned to remembering the soft tug of Quinn's hand on her hair, how he'd called back over his shoulder to her in greeting. *Fran,* he'd said, *we need to talk. There's something I've been meaning to ask you.*

After school, Fran decided to go on another shopping expedition, this time to the local record store. It was about time she updated her CD collection and she'd seen a couple of albums at Quinn's house that looked really good. Of course, there was always the hope that relations with Quinn would get to the point where she could borrow some of his stuff and then have deeply felt discussions about it afterwards. Maybe he would want to listen to some of her own CDs too. At any rate, it was important that when she saw him again she had plenty to say for herself. She might not be Sabrina von Schwarzkopf any more, but she could still dazzle him with her insightful remarks on the contemporary music scene.

Nevertheless, it was with slightly mixed feelings that she realized Quinn himself was standing on the other side of a large DVD dumpbin display. What's more, he was deep in conversation with Rob Crawford. Fran decided that, just for the moment, discretion was the better part of valour, and retreated round the corner to debate her next move. Then she heard her, or rather Sabrina's, name.

'Honest to God,' Rob was saying, 'that Sabrina babe was sex on a stick – I can't believe that she came on to you in the pub. No wonder the other girls are still spitting about it.'

'Even Francesca?'

'Don't get your Y-fronts in a twist. We all know Francesca's a girl who likes to play it cool.'

'While being seriously hot.'

'Exactly.'

Behind the corner, Fran felt a stab of misery.

'C'mon Adams, tell it to me straight,' Rob continued. 'On the off-chance Ms Babe-O-Rama doesn't get back to you any time soon, Francesca's next on your hit list, right?'

'Let's say I'm still refining my strategy.'

So Quinn had plans, did he? Fran shrank further back into her corner – whatever happened, they mustn't see her now. But Rob's next words sent her heart plummeting.

'Maybe you should have a word with her little buddy.'

Oh God . . . please . . . I don't want to hear this . . .

'Fran?' said Quinn. 'I'm working on it. She's a nice kid.'

'And hopelessly devoted,' said Rob, sniggering.

'But of course.' They both started to move off. 'It's a wonderful thing,' added Quinn, 'puppy love.'

For a long while Fran didn't – couldn't – move. She was frozen to the spot with shame. You idiot, she told herself. You stupid, self-deluded child. No wonder Rob had laughed. Everything about her felt bruised and aching, as if she'd been in a fight. She covered her face with her hands, indifferent to the other customers milling about, and longed for a puff of smoke she could vanish in.

She didn't know how long she stood there, but after someone had barged past her for the fifth time – treading on her toes in the process – she managed to pull herself together enough to creep out of the shop. The movement of her feet seemed to function quite independently from her mind, which was stuck in a loop of every Quinn Adams Moment since she'd first crashed into him in the music suite . . . well, it felt like years ago. But that's what comes of living in a fantasy world, she told herself bitterly: you lose all sense of perspective.

In the glass wall of the bus shelter, Fran caught her own eyes staring back at her, like those of a ghost.

> *It's a looking-glass world*
> *For the looking-glass girl,*
> *Lost in a whirl*
> *Of smiles and champagne . . .*

'What did you just sing?'

It took a moment or two for Fran to realize the question was addressed to her, by another girl loitering outside the shelter. She hadn't even realized she'd been singing aloud. Perhaps I really *am* going mad, she thought. 'Sorry,' she mumbled. 'It's nothing.'

'It's not nothing,' said the girl in a belligerent sort of way. She put her hands on her hips. 'Sing it again,' she commanded.

'No thanks,' said Fran defensively. 'I don't want to.' Who did this girl think she was, the music police?

'I know that song,' said the girl, glaring now, 'and I want to know where you got it from, OK?' Although she was all of five feet tall, there was something rather menacing about the way she was squaring up to her. From feeling weepy and melancholic, Fran was starting to get hacked off. For all she knew, this girl could be mentally unbalanced. Or a mugger, hoping to distract her before making a grab for her bag.

'You can't know the song, because it was written by a friend of mine,' Fran snapped. 'Though for your information, it's called "Looking-Glass Girl".'

'No it's not. It's called "Looking-Glass Boy".'

'What?' Fran stared at her. 'How would you know?'

'Because,' said the girl grimly, 'I wrote it.'

For a while the two of them just stood there, staring at each other. Fran's thoughts were whirling so fast she was literally lost for words – but the weird thing was, it didn't occur to her to accuse this girl of lying. She wasn't even as shocked as she thought she'd be. Tonight was clearly a night for revelations, a night where a lot of things began to fall into place. 'I think we need to talk,' she said.

'Suits me.' The two of them walked a little way down from the bus stop and found a wall to perch on. 'Though I reckon I can guess what the little toerag has been up to.'

'Er, by toerag do you . . . um . . . do you mean Quinn, Quinn Adams?'

'The one and only. I'm Amira, by the way.'

'Fran.'

Close to, Amira was less scary than Fran had at first feared. She was both extremely small and extremely pretty, and even while sitting on the wall, her whole body was bristling with energy. 'So you know my skunk of an ex, do you?' she asked. 'Still posing as the musical genius, I'll bet, with those no-brain mates of his.'

'*Quinn* is your ex-boyfriend?'

Amira snorted. 'Summer fling, it was – the heat-wave must've addled my brain. Actually fell for his "poor sensitive soul" crap. Can you believe it? Hah!'

Fran looked at her with new respect. She was ready to bet this was the 'total witch' of an ex that Quinn had mentioned to Sabrina. And she thought he was suffering from the trauma of a broken heart! 'So what happened?' she asked.

'Ugh, he fed me these lines about how he was really turned on by the "art of inspiration" and how much he longed to share my "creative processes". So, lots of nagging later, I showed him some of the stuff I was working on at the time. I thought he was hoping to find weepy pages of "Quinn Adams is My Love God" sop, now it looks as if I underestimated the scumbag. The copyright-pirating plagiarist scumbag, that is. And where does he get off,' she demanded, working herself up into a rage again, 'messing around with my lyrics? Looking-glass *girl* indeed! What the hell is that s'posed to mean?'

'Can you tell me how it's really meant to go?' asked Fran timidly.

Amira's expression softened. 'Sorry. I'm raving, I know. I'll try and put a lid on it – deep breaths and all that. And since you asked so nicely . . .'

> *It's a looking-glass world*
> *And he's a looking-glass boy,*
> *My heart's just a toy*
> *And he's playing his game.*
> *It's a looking-glass world*
> *And he wants a looking-glass girl*
> *To lose in a whirl*
> *Of smiles and champagne.*
>
> *It's a looking-glass world*
> *And they're having a ball,*

But I'll never fall
For his words again.

No, I'll never fall
For his words again.

Her delivery was matter of fact and a little off-key: a demonstration, not a performance. Fran shut her eyes and saw Quinn crooning into the microphone as he had the day of the audition, remembered his languid, caressing voice, the wistfulness in his eyes that had seemed to hint at a secret heartache . . . *No, I'll never fall for his words again* her own voice echoed softly, after Amira had reached the end.

Amira looked at her shrewdly. 'Fooled you too, did he?'

'Yes, but I never – we weren't – well, it doesn't matter. It's a great song, no wonder Quinn wanted to pinch it.'

'Bet it wasn't the only one. Bastard.'

'So you've written a lot of stuff?' Fran asked in awestruck tones.

'Oh yeah. Some of it's a bit crap though . . . I'm still experimenting.' She looked at Fran again, in an assessing sort of way. 'You've got a well-nice voice, you know. I usually have to leave the vocal stuff to the others.'

'Others?'

But Amira was distracted by the ringing of her

mobile. Although she didn't answer the call, she jumped down from the wall and began to dust off her jeans. 'Look, I should have got going twenty minutes ago but . . . do you live round here?'

'Not far. Milson Road.'

'Tell you what then. Do you want to meet up again tomorrow after school? Now that I'm not going to kick your butt for music piracy, I reckon you and me have a lot to talk about. Like what we're going to do about that swine Quinn.' And Amira's face set in a very fierce expression.

By the time she and Amira had exchanged telephone numbers and said their goodbyes, Fran hardly knew what to think or how to feel. She knew that she was going to have to take action of some kind – let Francesca know, let everyone know, what a cheat Quinn was – yet whenever she tried to think clearly about the situation the same mocking words squirmed through her head. *Puppy love* and *hopelessly devoted*. But although Quinn's remarks in the shop still bitterly stung, the humiliation was balanced by a growing sense of indignation. And if he'd managed to fool someone as tough and smart as Amira, then maybe Fran wasn't as dumb as she thought. Maybe.

What would Ash think, she wondered. Would he laugh and say 'I told you so'? Tell her off for being a snivelling female? Oh God, it was just so *humiliating*! But although she couldn't face telling him the news, at least not just yet, she didn't want him to think she was avoiding him either. Fran was in need of distraction and company, and though Ash could be A-grade irritating on occasions, right now he was all she had.

'Tell me something about the other owners of the ring,' she said, as they sat in the garden shed with a plate of peanut butter and strawberry jam sandwiches between them. The sandwiches were OK, but Fran felt very close to splurging a wish on a tub of triple-choc-fudge ice cream.

'So many girls, so little time . . .' mused Ash, licking peanut butter off his fingers. 'What about them?'

'You must have lots of stories about girls who had their hearts broken. Or who wasted their wishes on rubbish men.'

'Huh. The latter would apply to practically every client I've ever had. I can't go into specifics though – it's prohibited by the Commander-Slave Confidentiality Clause.'

'What's that supposed to do? Keep you from selling your story to the tabloids?'

'From spilling your grubby little secrets to my next owner, actually. Just like the Sacred Seal prevents me from blasting you with a thunderbolt. All part of the service. But why the sudden interest in broken hearts, O Mistress Fair?'

'Nothing,' she said quickly, looking down to

avoid his eyes. Every so often a wave of misery would flood through her and she would have to clench her fists until it passed. 'Tell me something . . . cheerful instead. A funny story or whatever. From when you were in Baghdad.'

'To Hear is to Obey.' The genie thought for a while. 'Hmm. Well, there was this one time me and my mate Sindbad—'

'*The* Sindbad? As in Sindbad the Sailor, who went on all those famous voyages and discovered the Valley of Diamonds and fought the—'

'No, that was his grandpa. And let me tell you, once he got out his travel journals the old man could bore for Baghdad . . . Sindbad Junior, on the other hand, was famous for mixing the meanest iced-sherbet cocktail in town. We used to visit the camel races together, go serenading outside the Grand Vizier's harem block . . . the usual boys'-night-out stuff.' Ash's face lit up at the memory. 'Oh, and we came up with this great scam to flog old oil lamps in the bazaar. We told customers that all they had to do was tie a lamp to their loin cloths, then if they got undressed and stood outside in the next full moon, rubbed the lamp and sang a little song about sausages, a genie would appear.' He laughed heartily. 'Incredible how many fell for it.'

'Don't you feel guilty for ripping people off like that?'

'Not when there are so many gullible morons in

the world. Fact is, if somebody one hundred per cent *wants* to believe in something, then they usually will.'

'You're right there.' She bit her lip.

'Fran . . . are you, er, feeling all right?'

'A little queasy. Too much peanut butter perhaps.'

He was looking at her rather anxiously. 'Are you sure that's it? Nothing's wrong? I wouldn't want you to think . . . I mean, I do feel *slightly* bad about those oil lamps but it was hundreds of years ago—'

'It doesn't matter, Ash.' Fran sighed. 'And you're right: people believe what they want to believe. However idiotic it looks in hindsight.'

Since Fran felt that if she had to see Quinn again she would be sick, he was naturally the first person she saw when she and Francesca arrived at the school gates. He was talking to Miss Duncan in a special, confiding sort of way, and even from several metres away she could see how pleased and flattered Miss Duncan was. Francesca gave a contemptuous snort.

'Look at the sad old bag. All of a flutter because Quinn is turning on the charm.'

Fran felt a twinge of fellow-feeling for Miss Duncan, but she was relieved by Francesca's words. Right from the start, she remembered, Francesca hadn't been taken in by Quinn's knight-in-shining-armour act. The sad fact was that if the events of yesterday hadn't happened, Fran would have said Quinn was letting Miss Duncan go all gooey on him out of the goodness of his heart. 'I know,' she said, 'he's just showing off how irresistible he is. It's pathetic.'

Francesca stared. 'Dreary Duncan's the pathetic one. She's always had the hots for the poor guy.'

'It's not as if he tries to discourage her though. It's not as if he tries to discourage *anyone*.' Maybe this was the right moment to tell Francesca some of the things she'd learned yesterday. How had Quinn put it? *I'm still refining my strategy . . .*

'You've changed your tune.'

'Ah yes, the tune,' said Fran darkly. 'I think you'll find the *tune* is the crux of the matter.'

Francesca gave her an odd look. 'Look, Fran, is something wrong? You've been acting strangely all the way to school.'

'Have I? Well, I've got a lot on my mind at the moment. In fact, there's something I need to tell you . . .' Fran stopped to collect her thoughts, trying to find the best way to begin.

'And it's not just this morning either,' Francesca swept on. 'Sarah Potock told Zara that she'd seen you out on Sunday afternoon being *really strange*. Talking to yourself and laughing and waving your hands about.'

Fran gritted her teeth. 'I hope you told her that was ridiculous.'

'I'm only repeating what Sarah told Zara,' said Francesca with a toss of her head. 'I can't be expected to defend you for something I don't know anything about.'

'Can't you? Funny – that's what I thought friends do.' And Fran set off to the Middle School entrance alone. Her warning about Quinn and the Firedog's bogus musical credentials would just have to wait.

Fran spent the rest of the school day avoiding people. Although Francesca had cornered her after registration to apologize – 'You mustn't take these things so seriously, Fran-flakes' – she wasn't in a particularly forgiving mood. Especially as every time she put her foot outside a classroom she seemed to see a Firedog. Typical. After all those weeks of lurking around the music suite hoping in vain for a glimpse of Quinn, the one time she wanted to avoid him, he and his mates were suddenly everywhere. Then, as she was buying a Coke from the drinks machine at the end of the day, she turned round to find the man himself standing beside her.

'Hey,' he said, smiling down at her, 'how's it going?'

'Fine, thanks,' she said curtly. Slowly but surely she could feel her face going red, this time with annoyance rather than adoration. Unfortunately, this crucial difference was lost on a group of Year

Sevens loitering near by, who were grinning broadly.

She moved away, but Quinn fell into step beside her. 'I hope you don't mind, Fran, but I've got a massive favour to ask.' She dug her nails into her palm. 'I thought me and the lads should buy something to give to Francesca after our gig on Saturday, as a sort of welcome-to-the-band present. But seeing as you know her best . . . well, do you think you could come shopping with me after school tomorrow? I'm in serious need of inspiration here.'

'So I've heard.' Somehow she managed to look him in the face and smile. 'But I'm afraid I'm busy tomorrow . . . I guess you'll have to steal ideas off somebody else.'

'That's a shame.'

'Oh, I'm sure you'll manage. From what I hear, you've had a lot of practice.'

She sketched a wave and hastened off down the corridor. Quinn was left slightly puzzled by the conversation, though he was gratified to see that Fran looked really quite pretty when she was flustered. He always tried to make a special effort with the shy ones – they became almost reverent with gratitude. And that way, he told himself complacently, everyone was happy.

By the time she had located number thirty-three Augustine Crescent, Fran was regretting she'd agreed to meet Amira after school. She was tetchy and tired and, post-Quinn, in a particularly unsociable frame of mind. What's more, she could tell from the music and laughter blaring out of the front room that Amira had company. Fran pressed the doorbell with serious misgivings.

The door crashed open as Amira came whirling to meet her. 'Fran!' she said, giving her a bone-crushing hug. Before Fran could react, she took her by the hand and dragged her through the door and into the front room. 'I hope it's OK but I've already told the others about you. We were meant to be having a session today anyway and – she's here, everyone! Hey, you lot! It's *her*!'

The three other girls in the room all stopped mid-conversation, turned and stared. One of them went over to switch off the stereo and in the sudden silence Fran felt her heart thump uncomfortably. 'Uh, hello,' she said nervously.

'Jamelia, Zoë and Naz,' rattled off Amira, 'collectively known as the Stamping Butterflies. A bunch of undisciplined, incompetent bimbos—'

'Otherwise known as the hottest girl band in Greater London,' finished the girl called Jamelia, giving Amira an affectionate shove. 'Don't listen to her, Fran, she's a slave driver.'

'Simon Cowell's scarier sister,' said Naz.

'But without his charm,' put in Zoë, passing Fran a bowl of pretzels. 'You know, I'm actually beginning to pity poor Quinn once Amira gets her talons into him.'

'You're at Conville Secondary, aren't you?' asked Jamelia. 'Do you know a girl call—'

'This is a Council of War, not a mother's meeting,' said Amira, rapping on the coffee table to call them to order. 'We all know the crime, so let's talk punishment.'

But in spite of Amira's most ferocious efforts, the Council of War did not run with much military discipline. As time wore on, the stereo was switched on again, more provisions were fetched from the kitchen, and among all the shrieking and giggling Fran soon forgot to feel awkward. Everyone was full of questions about Firedog and what kind of music they were into and how seriously people took them. It was good to think of Quinn in almost impersonal terms, and Fran found she was even able to talk about his godlike status at school in a jokey, offhand sort of way. Amira listened to this with a slight frown on her face.

'The thing about Quinn,' she said, 'is that he can turn on the charm, but he doesn't have a clue about girls, not *really*. The only reason he gets away with it is that he's so good at playing Mr Bleeding Heart that he almost believes it himself. Huh, he's probably even convinced himself that he wrote all my songs by now.'

Fran found it hard listening to Amira talk about

Quinn with such an authoritative air, and so she took the opportunity to ask some more about the Stamping Butterflies. To her surprise she found that Amira was the manager, rather than a member.

'Can't sing,' she said brusquely. 'And anyway, everyone knows the people with the *real* power in the music industry are the ones behind the scenes.'

'Is that where you want to be?' Fran found it hard to believe that someone who could write something as special as 'Looking-Glass Boy' wasn't interested in performing it.

'Course,' said Amira. 'I'm going to be a Pop Svengali. The Pete Waterman of my generation. Got it all planned out.'

'Meanwhile, we're the guinea pigs,' said Naz cheerfully. 'One day she'll have us doing the teeny-bopper cheerleader thing, the next it'll be all grungy hair and tormented soul stuff.'

'And what are you doing now?'

Naz, Jamelia and Zoë all looked at each other, then, on cue, burst into song: *Don't make me cry, sweetie-pie/ Let's have some fun, honeybun.*

It was the girl-band hit that Sadie and chums had performed at the Firedog audition, but nearly unrecognizable thanks to the blues/gospel treatment the Stamping Butterflies had given it. Each word throbbed with wildly exaggerated yearning, each note was drawn out within an inch of its life. *Doh'nnnnn make me cryyyyyyyy* . . . When they got to the end, Amira climbed on to the table to conduct a repeat of the chorus, motioning to Fran to join in. It was impossible to take the performance seriously as they all swayed in a line, every gesture awash with melodrama, until the last harmony died away and everyone collapsed on to the floor in a fit of giggles.

When they had somewhat recovered, Amira turned to Fran. 'Now you do it on your own,' she commanded. 'Go on – let's hear it.'

Fran was overcome with confusion. 'Oh, no,' she stammered. 'I couldn't.'

Confronted with a group of expectant faces, Fran's old self-consciousness returned. These girls were so at ease both with themselves and each other, so careless with confidence, that she couldn't bear it if she dried up in front of them. She shook her head again, and determinedly changed the subject. 'Don't you think it's time we got back to the Evil Scumbag issue?'

Fran had a point: they'd had nearly two hours of discussion and still nobody could decide whether legal action or GBH was the most appropriate penalty. She was slightly surprised that Amira, for all her rantings and ravings, was the one most in favour of doing things by the book. Presumably she was already looking ahead to her world-conquering career in the record industry. 'You have to issue a writ first,' she said knowledgeably, 'then you get an injunction and *then* –' eyes gleaming – 'you sue for damages.'

However, getting definitive proof was still an issue. It was eventually decided that Zoë would go undercover with a Dictaphone to the Three Lions gig, then once the evidence was on tape Jamelia's brother, who was studying law, would be called in to advise the best thing to do with it. It all seemed a bit vague to Fran – making a record of Quinn's crime was all very well but what then? What if Quinn persuaded everyone that Amira was trying to rip off *his* music, not the other way round? All the same, she was relieved that some sort of plan was in place. And she was even more pleased by the way the Stamping Butterflies took her own involvement for granted.

Although Fran dreaded sharing her recent discoveries with Francesca, she was still almost as reluctant to confess all to Ash, especially after his snide remarks about deluded females and gullible morons. When she finally came clean that night, her account of the fiasco was as short and sharp as she could make it.

'Well?'

'Well what?'

'Well, aren't you going to say "I told you so"?'

He looked back at her levelly. 'I'm still debating. There is a range of traditional responses to this sort of news, after all. "I told you so" is one. "Men are bastards" is another.'

'Takes one to know one,' muttered Fran. She still thought dumping someone by letter came fairly high on the Rogue Male measurement scale.

'Ouch.' Ash, however, didn't look unduly insulted. 'One thing I *have* learned through my centuries of servitude, is that the fairer sex are screwed over with depressing regularity.'

'Yeah, and as I remember, you think we're all snivelling wimps who bring it on ourselves.'

'Indeed. Men are bastards and women are idiots – doesn't take a genius to work that one out. Or a genie, for that matter . . . But do you know what *really* annoys me? Nine times out of ten, the girls who get conned are the girls who should know better. The attractive ones, the smart ones. You weren't the first girl to turn moronic over a moron, Fran, and you certainly won't be the last.'

'Er . . . thanks.' Fran supposed this counted as moral support, genie-style.

'The question is, now that you know what the Son of a Dung Beetle's been up to, what are you going to do about him?'

'The Stamping Butterflies suggested castration.'

'The Stamping Butterflies are clearly a force to be reckoned with.' Ash got up from his chair and began to pad about the room restlessly. 'But maybe you should be more imaginative. Seven hours in a vat of boiling oil should do the trick. Or snakes. How about a pit of vipers? Go on – it'd be great.'

'He's a conceited jerk, not a child killer. I want to teach him a lesson, sure, but in a . . . constructive sort of way. So Quinn understands what he's done.'

'You think if conceited jerks realized the misery they cause it would reform them?'

'Has it reformed you?'

Ash didn't answer at once, but stood with his back to her, looking out of the window. 'Alas, we will never have the opportunity to find out,' he said lightly.

Fran was remembering Amira's comment that Quinn didn't have a clue about girls. At the time, she had thought this was just Amira being contrary, but now she wondered if she had a point. Perhaps it was true that despite – or maybe because of – his all-conquering charm, Quinn had never bothered to really think about what went on in girls' heads.

Ripping off his ex-girlfriend's music was a terrible thing to do, of course, and now that the Stamping Butterflies were on the case she hoped his crime would be exposed for the rest of the world to see. But what about the hurt Quinn had caused by exploiting her friendship with Francesca? Did he even realize how cruel this was? Did he ever think about all those other girls he led on with his tender smiles and puppy-dog eyes? For some reason, Fran thought of Sabrina, of how powerful she'd felt in the pub and later in the cafe, when she knew everyone in the room was looking at her with unrequited admiration. Quinn, she suddenly realized, must get that feeling too.

'I know what I want,' said Fran abruptly. 'I want Quinn Adams to spend seven hours looking at the world from a girl's point of view.'

Ash gave a whoop of delight. 'Oh *yes*. Let's turn him into irredeemably ugly girl for a few hours. I'll give her pimples and a squint and breath like stewed garlic. We can call her Quinnella.'

Fran shook her head. An acne-encrusted version of Quinn in skirts had plenty of vengeance potential, but the long-term repercussions of this could get very messy indeed. 'Physical transformations are too complicated. He's still going to be a boy, but one who thinks like a girl.' The genie's face lit up with an evil grin and she looked at him sternly. 'A *straight* boy, Ash. I mean it. Though you can make the female part as madly OTT as you like.' After all, there wouldn't be much point to the exercise if Quinn saw the world through the eyes of someone as self-possessed as, say, Sabrina. Or Francesca for that matter.

'You're being far too soft on him,' said Ash sulkily. 'All right, all right . . . one touchy-feely neurotic heterosexual coming up. Say the magic words and let's get on with it.'

After a bit of wrangling, Ash was persuaded to

postpone the fulfilment of the wish until noon the next day (Fran had decided that the magic would have maximum impact if Quinn's seven hours encompassed time both in and out of school). The genie made one last plea for boiling oil but his heart wasn't in it. Although he might not always approve of Fran's choices, he had to admit that, creatively speaking, her wish-making skills had come a long way.

At twenty past eleven on Wednesday morning, Quinn Adams finally summoned up enough energy to crawl out of bed. He'd been practising with the band the evening before, and after the others had gone he and Rob had stayed up until the early hours of the morning drinking beer, smoking and having long, rambling conversations on such important subjects as the Ten Greatest Guitar Solos of All Time and whether Anna Wilton or Sadie Smith had the perkiest arse. Staring blearily at his alarm clock, Quinn found he couldn't remember the conclusion of either debate, let alone what time Rob had eventually left or how on earth he'd made it up from the basement and into bed. He appeared to have gone to sleep with his socks still on.

The rest of the house was eerily silent, his parents having left for work hours ago. Since he had a free period on Wednesday mornings it wouldn't have occurred to either of them to check he was up.

Never mind. Once he got to class he could always say he'd gone to the dentist or been sick or something. Judging by the evidence in the bathroom mirror, the sick excuse was probably the most convincing. Yeah, he looked a bit rough, but there was no point stressing about it. Chicks liked the pale and interesting look. If anyone commented he'd say he'd been up all night writing love songs or whatever.

By eleven fifty-five, Quinn was feeling a new man. He'd drunk about a pint of orange juice, turned the radio on loud, had a long hot shower and was now leisurely getting his stuff together for school. He figured he was already so late there was no point rushing, especially as he was in the middle of a daydream involving, among other things, a backstage party at the MTV awards and a whole load of groupies in hot pants. As the clock chimed twelve, he had his hand on the latch ready to open the front door. It was at that moment that he felt a sudden urge to check his hair.

Oh. My. God.

Quinn stared at the hall mirror in dismay. There was this, like, major *kink* thing going on at the back of his head – a whole tuft of hair practically at right angles to everything else. Quinn had always been secretly proud of his hair, whose dark blond dishevelment could be pretty much left to its own devices after an initial tweak or two. But this . . . this was *horrific*. He couldn't go out like this. What if he, you know, ran into someone hot?

Oh. My. God.

What if Francesca saw him looking like this?

His bag fell from a lifeless hand, then he pounded up the stairs and into the bathroom, using an old compact mirror of his mother's to minutely examine the back of his head. Gel, he thought feverishly, gel was the answer. But three applications of gel later, the wretched tuft still refused to stay down. And what was even worse, he could see a spot forming just over his left eyebrow. It was going to be one of the big squishy kind, he could just *sense* it. He was falling to pieces. He was the most hideously ugly guy in the history of the world. Nobody would ever fancy him again.

OK, OK, time to calm down . . . and time for a little positive reinforcement. His chakras must be all over the place. Quinn closed his eyes and chanted softly to himself *I am a strong, sexy man. I am a strong, sexy,* confident *man.* After five minutes of repeating this mantra, he took a deep breath and picked up his bag again. He was ready to face the world.

Things improved during the bus ride to school, when this really cute girl sat down on the seat across from his and started checking him out. Unless she was just staring at his spot . . . He risked another glance and was rewarded with a tiny smile. Yessss!

Quinn smiled back and ran his hands with slow-motion extravagance through his hair, just like that guy in the anti-dandruff shampoo advert – only for his fingers to hit the gel slick at the back of his head. Eeuuw. Now the girl was smirking. He tossed his head and pretended to look out of the window, though his face was red. Whatever. She was probably a total perve anyway, eyeing up random blokes on a bus.

'Look what the cat dragged in,' said Rob, when Quinn caught up with him in the school canteen. 'Tell you what, mate, you look nearly as rough as I feel. So what's your excuse this time? Dog ate your travelcard?'

'Bad Hair Day.'

'That figures.' Rob laughed and punched him on the arm. 'And then you ran out of time to cleanse, tone and moisturize, right?'

So much for moral support. Quinn retreated into an injured silence – not that Rob seemed to notice. 'Oi-oi,' he said as they were collecting cutlery, 'Francesca's sitting over there on her lonesome. Time for a little brotherly chat, I reckon.'

'No, wait, we can't just—'

'Don't be daft.' Rob began to saunter across to Francesca's table.

'Rob, stop,' said Quinn in a frantic whisper. 'I'm just not ready for this. It will be so totally obvious.'

'What will be obvious?'

'That I, you know, *like her*,' Quinn squirmed.

Rob was momentarily lost for words. What the hell was all this about? Quinn must still be drunk or high or something. Or, more likely, taking the mick. That must be it. 'You are so full of crap, Adams.' And before Quinn could stop him he was sliding into the seat opposite Francesca's. With a sheepish grin, Quinn and his bowl of lettuce took up position next to her.

'Going on a detox?' enquired Francesca, eyebrow raised.

'A healthy diet is key to nourishing positive emotional energy. It's not something I take lightly.'

'So I can see.'

After that he couldn't think of anything to say and sat there in silent agony as Rob and Francesca chatted away without a care in the world. He was even more unsettled when Francesca's friend Fran sat down opposite and started, well, *watching* him. She must have noticed the spot. 'I like what you've done with your hair,' he mumbled, partly to distract her and partly because he genuinely thought it was looking good. 'A side parting totally suits you – makes a much better frame for your face.'

'Quinn's having a bad-hair day,' announced the treacherous Rob.

'I know the feeling,' said Francesca. God, she was beautiful when she smiled . . . it was an almost spiritual experience, thought Quinn, staring at her raptly. After a minute or so under his adoring gaze, however, her smile became a little fixed and she turned away to talk to Fran.

'I need a toilet trip,' he muttered to Rob. 'Coming?'

Rob nearly choked on his pizza crust. 'You want me to *come to the toilet with you*?' he hissed, glancing swiftly around to check that no one else had heard. 'Please tell me you're kidding.'

But Quinn had already got to his feet, one finger prodding Rob in the back. 'We'll be back in a moment, girls,' he said brightly.

Rob followed Quinn to the toilets – it wasn't as if he had much choice – but he was beginning to be alarmed. He had his reputation to think of. They both did. 'Look, mate,' he said, watching in a kind of sick fascination as Quinn got out a compact mirror from his bag and began to check the back of his hair, 'I don't know what's going on here, but you have *got* to sort it out.'

'Tell me about it. It's as if it's got a life of it's own.'

'I'm not talking about the hair, for Christ's sake. It's you. I've never seen you, well, lose it like this—'

'I know,' said Quinn in agonized tones, 'that's what I wanted to talk to you about. Every time I see Francesca I turn into this hideous, quivering wreck.'

'But – but – but you had it all worked out. Play

it cool. Be charming but sensitive. It never fails, remember. What's changed, man?'

'This one is different, Rob. I can feel it. It's like we have this . . . psychic connection.' Quinn was now leaning towards the mirror, eyes half-closed. '*I am a strong, sexy man. I am a strong, sexy,* confident *man. I am—*'

'Quinn, stop it.'

'Say it with me, Rob, it'll make you feel so much better: *I am a strong, sexy—*'

'Stop it – please –' Rob was truly frightened now. A boy from the year below had just come through the door and was staring at the both of them, frozen in incredulity. 'You have to get a grip on yourself, OK?' He grabbed Quinn by the sleeve and hustled him outside. 'Never,' he said, voice shaking slightly, '*never* do that to me again.'

Quinn, however, had just seen Fran and Francesca coming down the corridor. He clutched Rob's arm. 'Omigod! Start laughing, right, like I've said something hilarious – you know, ha ha ha, you're so funny, Quinn. Go on.'

But Rob didn't know whether to laugh or cry.

'Hello again,' said Francesca. 'Whatever happened to you two back there?'

'Boy talk . . . you know how it is.' Quinn attempted a coy smile.

'What, so you had to speed off for a heart-to-heart

in the gents?' asked Francesca. Fran's snort of laughter turned into a hasty cough.

'Actually, we were discussing strategy for the gig on Saturday,' said Rob firmly. 'And beer,' he added as an afterthought. 'Beer and football.'

'Okaaay.' Francesca wondered why everyone was looking so shifty. Even Fran seemed to be smirking about something. 'So what was the upshot of this grand strategy meeting?' Two blank faces stared back at her. 'Funny, last time I checked, I was a member of the band too. Seems I was wrong.' She turned on her heel.

'Wait, uh, Francesca,' said Quinn desperately. He took a deep breath. 'I was thinking . . . me and Rob are going to Ronnie's after school, so I wondered if you'd like to – to maybe join us?'

'We are?' asked Rob. 'Oh. Right. Yeah, we're going to, erm, strategize the gig some more.'

'All right then. Fine. You can bring me up to speed at the caff.'

'Great,' gushed Quinn, accompanied by a slow-motion hair flick. 'That'll be *great*.'

'What the hell was all that about?' asked Francesca as soon as she and Fran were safely away.

'Haven't a clue.'

'Quinn was being a total head case.'

'I know.'

'And Rob wasn't much better. But I thought Quinn was *really* weird.'

'Mm.'

'Though it was nice of him to compliment you on your hair back there in the canteen – blokes don't normally notice things like that.' They made their way into the classroom. 'I don't know what's got into him. He's usually so smooth it's scary.'

Fran raised her brows. 'Maybe it's time he stopped believing his own hype.'

Rob's afternoon wasn't getting any better. Away from Francesca, Quinn seemed to calm down a bit, but he wasn't anywhere near normal. He spent most of the afternoon staring dreamily into space or else writing little notes to pass to his friends around the class, complete with smiley faces and heart decorations. What's more, he sensed that Rob was upset about something and kept pestering him to 'talk it through'. By the time Quinn had finished explaining, misty-eyed, that Rob was his Best Friend In The World and Nobody Would Ever Come Between Them, Rob was contemplating multiple homicide.

Things didn't improve when they got to Ronnie's. The plan had been that Rob would keep Quinn company until Francesca arrived, whereupon Rob would make up some excuse to leave them to it. But as soon as the bell went Quinn lost his nerve and practically begged Jez and Liam to come along too – 'It feels like ages since I've had a good chat with my boys!' Right now, the only thing that seemed take his mind off Francesca was the dessert menu. 'Ooh look – chocolate fudge cake. I know I *shouldn't* of course, but does anyone fancy going halves on a slice?'

Jez and Liam exchanged confused glances with Rob. 'He's been like this all day,' he said wearily. 'There's nothing I can do.'

Quinn, oblivious, began passing round the milk and sugar. 'Right, time to catch up with the goss – starting with the whole Rob 'n' Sadie situation. You have to understand, Rob, I'm only saying this because I care, but I can't help feeling that the girl is only after One Thing.'

'Sure hope so.'

'You don't mean that,' said Quinn reproachfully. 'I know it's flattering on one level, but a boy can end up feeling so . . . used . . .'

'Now I really have heard it all,' said Francesca, who had arrived unnoticed and was surveying their tea party with some amusement.

Quinn sat up straight and casually pulled a strand of hair over the offending spot. *Remember: I am a strong, sexy, confident man* he told himself. 'Yeah, well, guys can feel under the same social pressures as girls, you know. We're just not so ready to admit it.'

'I get it. You want to be seen as more than just a

pretty set of pecs.' Had Francesca noticed he'd been working out then? Quinn blushed. 'Very commendable,' she said, pulling up a chair. 'It's about time you lot came to appreciate why some girls are as neurotic as they are.'

'It's tough being a woman,' he agreed.

'Do you mean it?' This was Fran, trailing behind her friend as per usual. She didn't sit down, however, but hovered by Quinn's chair, looking at him intently. It was rather unnerving.

'Of course he doesn't,' said Francesca, laughing. 'He's just trying out the lyrics for his next seduction song.'

Quinn felt as if the bottom had dropped out of his world. 'That's not true,' he said, 'in fact, that's a very *hurtful* thing to say. I can't believe you think I'm so cynical.' They stared back at him in amazement – it almost looked as if there were tears in his eyes. 'Maybe I come across as a bit of a charmer, but everyone puts up a front, you know? *Everybody* has days when they need something to hide behind.'

There was a shocked silence. Rob looked nauseous, Francesca a little guilty. As for Fran, she was smiling to herself in a satisfied kind of way.

Fran would have liked to have hung around for the duration of the wish – after all, Quinn still had nearly three hours of girldom to go – but she had promised her parents she would be on babysitting duty that evening. It didn't even look as if she would get a chance to see Ash in between attempting her chemistry assignment and getting her brother and sister fed, watered and ready for bed. Then at half past seven Francesca rang. Would Fran mind if she popped round for a quick chat? Fran, up to her elbows in Beth's bubble bath, her head spinning with molecular theory, found that yes, she did mind, but there wasn't much she could do about it.

As soon as she opened the door, Francesca pushed past her and went straight to the living room, where she began pacing back and forth and biting her lip in a nervous yet coy manner that was most un-Francesca-like. With a sinking feeling, Fran remembered the affair of the Firedog audition. She began to chew her own lip in anticipation. Mickey, who was sprawled on the floor trying to construct a Kisco bar out of Lego, soon got the hint. 'I'll be in my room, Fran, but just let me know if you need anything,' he said in a solicitous undertone.

Once Mickey had left, Francesca paced around for few more minutes, started to say something, stopped, then came up to Fran and gave her a big hug. 'Oh, Fran-flakes,' she said, 'thanks for letting me barge in like this. You're my best friend, I don't know what I'd do without you.'

'I hope nothing's wrong.' Fran had returned the hug, but it was hard to keep the suspicion out of her voice.

'Wrong? Oh no, everything's right. At least I hope so – I'm still feeling a little overwhelmed . . .'

'By what?' said Fran, although she began to think she knew the answer. She wasn't going to make this any easier for Francesca.

'Quinn.' Francesca gave an odd, nervous laugh. 'The thing is, Fran,' she said quickly, 'today's the first time I've ever got to see the *real* Quinn. After you left the cafe, right, we got talking, just the two of us, about *everything*. I mean it – thoughts, fears, ambitions, dreams. He completely opened up to me. He was so . . . perceptive . . . so *tender*.'

Perceptive. Tender. Fran supposed that there would come a time when she could appreciate the irony of the situation.

'I used to think he was a bit of a poser,' continued Francesca, 'but now I think you were right about him all along. I mean, *you* always thought he was sincere.'

'Yes,' said Fran quietly, 'yes I did. Real knight-in-shining-armour stuff.'

'But lately,' said Francesca, looking at her narrowly, 'I kind of thought you'd gone off him?'

'I suppose I have,' said Fran at last.

Francesca gave a sigh of relief, followed by a radiant smile. 'Thank God. I *knew* you'd be fine about it.'

'About what?' asked Fran again.

'Me and Quinn, of course. Turns out he's fancied

me for, like, ever! Can you believe it? Anyway, after the cafe we went for a walk in the park . . .' And Francesca proceeded to describe, in loving detail, the exact moment when Quinn took her into his arms. How gentle he was. How his kisses were so soft, so sweetly hesitant. How he walked her home afterwards and held hands the whole way.

Fran listened to this and felt a hot ball of anger beat against her chest. It was true that she was over Quinn – now that she knew his real nature she couldn't *not* be. But Francesca didn't know any this, Francesca was determined to believe that Fran was OK with the Quinn situation just like she had been OK with the Firedog audition, for the simple reason that it suited her. Francesca, she realized, hadn't bothered to find out what she really felt or thought about anything for a long time. She abruptly cut into Francesca's monologue.

'Actually, I think you were the one who got Quinn right. I think he really is an insincere poser.'

There was a spluttering sound. 'But—'

'And now he has you where he wants you, he'll go back to being his old self. Come tomorrow, I can guarantee there won't be any more heart-to-hearts over skinny lattes or holding hands by the light of the moon.'

Francesca looked hurt. 'Look, I know you had a crush on the guy, but you've got to realize that it was never going to go anywhere. Can't you just be happy for me?'

This made Fran even angrier, but she told herself she had to bear some of the responsibility for the situation. After all, it was her stupid wish that had made Francesca fall for Quinn's touchy-feely charm. 'I can't be happy for you because I know you won't be happy with Quinn. You don't know what he's really like.'

'Oh, and you do, I suppose?'

'Yes, I do as a matter of fact.' It was on the tip of her tongue to blurt out everything she'd found out from Amira – every last sneaky, sordid detail. That'd show her. But on second thoughts, why should she make life any easier for Francesca? Let her find out about Quinn's true colours in her own time. 'But you're obviously not going to listen so there's no point.'

'You're right there.' Francesca tightened her mouth, then picked up her bag and went to the door. 'I'm sorry, Fran, but it's about time you did some growing up.'

Time to grow up. Time to move on. Time to get a life. Alternatively, she could always shut herself in the garden shed and have a chat with her invisible friend.

Ash, however, was in one of his moods and listened to her description of Quinn's gush-giggle-hair-flick routine with no more than polite interest. Only, being Ash, it wasn't particularly polite, especially when she got to the Quinn–Francesca angle. He seemed unreasonably annoyed that she was so upset by it. 'If you're not infatuated by Quinn any more why should you care if Francesca's shacked up with him? Sounds to me like they're made for each other.' Then he tried to get her to use one of her last three wishes on a vat of snakes – 'I'll make it double size to fit the two of them.'

But even the thought of wishes-in-waiting didn't lift her spirits. It had all seemed so gloriously simple at the start: seven magical opportunities to become the sort of girl who Francesca would want as her best friend and Quinn Adams would want as a girlfriend. Now she was already four wishes down and with very little to show for it. Quinn was out of her life and it looked as if Francesca was too. Maybe Ash was right – good riddance to both of them. But what did that leave her with? Nothing and nobody, that's what, Fran thought sourly. Looking back over the last few weeks, all she could see were opportunities that had been missed, schemes that had backfired, and effort that had been wasted.

She tried to explain this to Ash but he only got offended. After telling her that he was sick of being taken for granted and that she was ungrateful, unreasonable and self-obsessed, he wound up by saying the sooner she spent her three wishes the better; maybe then he could finally find a client worth working for. He disappeared back into the ring with a flounce.

Knowing Ash as she did by now, Fran wasn't unduly worried by this. They'd make it up next time round. But still, his parting words got her thinking: soon all her wishes would be gone and she wouldn't even have a genie to talk to any more. It was strange to think of the ring belonging to someone else, of some other girl plotting with Ash to win her heart's desire. For a moment, the thought crossed her mind that she could postpone spending her final wish indefinitely and . . . then what? Keep Ash hanging round as a kind of pet? An invisible friend? Even if there wasn't some sort of clause attached to the ring to prevent that kind of thing happening, she knew in her heart it could never work out. Fran would just have to get used to being on her own.

Fran was determined to avoid Francesca for as long and as much as was humanely possible, and for most of Thursday morning it looked as if Francesca had made a similar resolution. She spent all her time with Zara and Sadie who, even if they didn't know what had caused the falling-out, were happy to make the most of it. Every time Zara set eyes on Fran, her lip became so curled with contempt that Miss Duncan enquired whether her tongue piercing was giving her trouble. Sadie made a point of being extra nice and super pitying. However, most of their class either hadn't picked up on the rift or didn't think it worth mentioning. Fran supposed this was as good a measure as any of how much her and Francesca's friendship had changed. From insepara-ble to expendable in a few easy steps.

So it came as a complete surprise to find that it was Francesca who was the first to crack. She didn't even wait until the end of lunch before tracking Fran down in the library in order that they could 'resolve their issues'. She revealed that she felt bad about the previous evening, that in hindsight, she'd been 'insensitive' and that she'd 'got carried away' and said things that she 'regretted'. Finally, with the air of someone announcing a huge favour, she explained that, for the moment, she and Quinn had decided to keep their newfound relationship 'strictly hush-hush'.

Francesca implied they'd come to this decision out of respect Fran's feelings, or perhaps to avoid a frenzy of media interest. A more plausible explana-tion was that Quinn was attempting to keep his options open right to the last. Fran wondered how Francesca would cope with the discovery that ninety-nine per cent of Quinn's 'perception' and 'tenderness' had disappeared along with his sudden predilection for lettuce at lunchtime. On the other hand, she was beginning to think that the trans-forming powers of her wish hadn't been responsible after all, and that Francesca's gush about Quinn's finer feelings had been just that: gush. That she'd had him in her sights more or less right from the start, and was only looking for an excuse to fall into his arms.

Lost in thought, Fran realized with a start that Francesca had come to the end of her little speech and was looking at her expectantly. 'So shall we agree to put last night behind us and start over?' she prompted.

Fran shrugged. 'OK.'

'Great.' Pause. 'I'd hate to lose our friendship, Fran-Flakes.'

'Would you?'

'Of course! I completely rely on you, you know that.'

Fran smiled a little sadly. 'Yes, I suppose you do.' She collected her things and went to the door.

'We're fine then, right?' Francesca called after her, frowning. 'Right? Wait, Fran –'

But Fran had already gone.

The rest of the school day passed without incident as Fran trudged listlessly through her usual routines. Everything seemed dull and pointless. She hadn't heard anything more from Amira, and part of her was beginning to wonder if the Stamping Butterflies were too busy refining their plans for vengeance to remember to include her. Whenever she thought about this a grey emptiness seemed to grow inside.

Then at half past four she got a message on her

mobile: CUM 2 KNGMEAD URGENT A. It appeared Amira's text-messaging style was as short and sharp as the rest of her. Even so, just looking at those three-and-a-bit words made Fran feel better than she had for days.

She was a little surprised by the venue for their meeting however, for Kingsmeade was a big indoor shopping centre, and Amira didn't seem the kind of girl who spent her free time browsing for nail varnish in glossy malls. And where exactly was she going to find her? However, as soon as Fran descended the escalator into the main atrium she realized she needn't have worried. For there, standing in front of the central fountain, their voices raised in triumphant harmony, were the Stamping Butterflies. The song was unfamiliar to Fran, a hip-hop track that she guessed must be one of Amira's compositions. Then she heard the lyrics and everything became clear:

> *Don't you melt before his eyes*
> *No, don't you fall for his lies*
> *Cos he's off-key and outta time*
> *When he starts his sweet-talking*
> *That's when you start walking*
> *Cos he's got no rhythm nor rhyme*
>
> *Heartbreaker, smile-faker,*
> *Tear-jerker, sleaze-smirker,*

Dirt-dealer, song-stealer,
Quintessential scum
Who-o-a yeah
Quintessential scum

Jamelia, Zoë and Naz were standing shoulder to shoulder, belting it out with bright eyes and even brighter smiles, while Amira presided over a small electronic keyboard. They were all wearing cute little matching T-shirts with – wait a minute – oh my God – with *Quinn's* face on them. Quinn's! A photograph, blown-up large, with CRAP IDOL printed below. Fran was almost helpless with laughter as she reached for the ring. Ash had *got* to see this.

Soon Amira was waving her over, a huge grin on her face. Jamelia and Naz gave her the thumbs up and Zoë winked broadly, all without breaking their stride. Meanwhile, a slightly confused genie hovered in her wake. 'Is it another party?' he asked hopefully.

'Shh and listen,' Fran hissed, earning a dirty look from the woman standing next to her. A small crowd of shoppers had already gathered and their numbers were growing. Fran didn't have much of a chance to join in the appreciative smiles and nudges however, for the next moment Naz and Zoë both shot out an arm and caught her own in an iron grip. And somehow, before Fran had time to react or realize what was happening, she was in the middle of the Butterflies, joining in the words of the chorus:

> *Heartbreaker, smile-FAKER,*
> *Tear-jerker, sleaze-SMIRKER,*
> *Dirt-dealer, song-STEALER*

It was easy to remember, even better to sing. Fran tossed back her hair, straightened her shoulders and smiled a fearless and unfamiliar smile. The anonymous bustle of the shopping centre was about as public a place as you could get, but somehow it didn't matter. In fact, it was liberating. With each note she felt the frustration and anxiety of the last few days surge up and out of her.

> *QUINtessential SCUM!*

'. . . We're the Stamping Butterflies,' announced Amira as the last note died away, 'and that, ladies and gents, was the world premiere of "Quintessential".' The girls had barely got their breath back when she plunged straight into the introductory chords of 'Looking-Glass Boy'. How very different it was to the performance of Fran's daydreams – those soft-focus visions of her and Quinn, crooning sweet nothings on a spotlit stage! And yet, as she heard her voice swell to join the others – low and sweet and self-assured – she wouldn't have changed a thing. Not the plasticky chill of the atrium nor the muzak filtering from a novelty candle shop nor the smell of stale syrup from the waffle stand. Everything was exactly right. Seven paces away was Ash, his eyes intently fixed on hers, his expression inscrutable.

When they reached the end of the final chorus, even the people hastening up the escalator paused to clap. They got a few wolf whistles too. Amira lost no time in doing the rounds with the collection box. Meanwhile, Fran found herself swept up in a group Butterfly hug. 'Wasn't that fab?' said Jamelia breathlessly. 'You were awesome, Fran!'

'Sorry I messed up some of the words though—'

'Don't you dare apologize,' said Zoë. 'You did great. Just like we knew you would.'

'Not bad,' said Amira, coming to join them and jingling the collection box in a triumphant sort of way. 'Not bad at all.' Then she grinned. 'Apologies for the ambush, but we reckoned if we asked you nicely in advance you'd have bottled out of it.'

'Thanks for ambushing me then. Standing there . . . all those strangers . . . I thought it would be terrifying. Not like this. It felt *amazing*.'

'Amazing,' echoed a voice from behind her shoulder. It was Ash. 'I've never seen you like that before,' he said slowly. 'All . . . shining. You were shining, Fran.'

She smiled happily back at him. The boy standing behind the invisible genie thought she was beaming at him instead and became very bashful indeed. 'But how on earth did you come up with "Quintessential"?' she asked Amira. 'Don't tell me you composed it in the last two days!'

Amira tried, and failed, not to look smug. 'Oh, it's been knocking around for a while but I was having trouble with the lyrics. Then after Monday night everything just fell into place. Cool, huh?'

'We got the T-shirts printed yesterday,' put in Naz excitedly, 'and there's gonna be matching flyers too!'

'Yeah, we're going to hand them round at our next gig,' said Zoë. 'Jamelia's brother, he's studying law, right, and he's going to tell us scary things to put in about copyright infringement and stuff. So's everyone knows the Firedog members are rip-off merchants.'

Amira explained that after much soul-searching, she had reluctantly decided that a full-on legal battle might be more trouble than it was worth. 'Mind you, we're still going to get the buggers on tape. For back-up evidence. But in the end, we figured doing things this way was more fun – guerrilla tactics and all that.'

'Our next gig is on Sunday afternoon, outside the cinema on Evan Street. You up for it?' said

Jamelia. 'We've got a T-shirt for you and every-thing.'

'Just try and stop me,' said Fran, glowing. She could hardly believe her luck. This was the most fabulous thing that had ever happened to her – apart from acquiring a genie and seven wishes of course.

She looked round for Ash, but at some point during the exclamations and explanations he had vanished back into the ring. It was probably for the best, she decided. After all, it wasn't as if he could *really* participate in the occasion. Sometimes it was hard to remember he wasn't quite . . . human.

By Friday, rumour of the Firedog gig at the weekend had spread through the school like wildfire. Since Quinn was anxious not to have their Three Lions debut sabotaged by 'a bunch of screaming kids', as he put it, the details of the gig were released on a strictly need-to-know basis, in keeping with the band's aura of oh-so-hip exclusivity. There was no chance the Firedog members would ever demean *their* artistic integrity by busking in shopping cen-tres. What was known for certain, however, was that the after-show party was going to be the stuff of leg-ends and that it was taking place at Francesca Goldsworthy's house.

Fran received, on separate occasions, a personal invitation from both Quinn and Francesca. Although she was one of only a handful of people in their year with the right connections and/or street cred to make the grade, she took a perverse satisfaction from being as non-committal as possible. Francesca was determined to act as if nothing had changed between them, but her attempts at mateyness were becoming increasingly strained.

She telephoned Fran on Friday evening, during a break from yet another rehearsal with the band. 'Just checking you're still on for the gig tomorrow,' she said in a too-bright voice. 'It'll mean so much to me to know you're there.'

'Yeah, but I'm afraid I promised Mum I'd babysit on Saturday night.' This wasn't true; in fact, the rest of the family were going to be staying with Mrs Roper's sister that weekend. Fran had got out of the visit by pleading pressures of homework.

'Oh. I see. But – but will you at least be able to make the party? Please?'

'I'm not sure.'

'*Please,* Fran, do try and make it. Just for an hour or two. The thing is . . . well, I won't actually know half the people there – it will be loads of Quinn's mates who I haven't met before.' She gave a nervous laugh. 'I'm sure we'll get on but . . . it would be nice to have a friendly face or two.'

'I get it. You want me on cheerleading duty.'

'No. *No.* Look, I realize I've been a bit crap lately. I know you think I've been taking our friendship for granted. But if you just give me a chance and come to the party, I'll prove to you this isn't true. I promise.'

Fran thought about it. 'Maybe I could show up for a while. But only if my parents get back in time.'

She had only just put the phone down when it started to ring again. This time it was Amira, calling to complain that the Stamping Butterflies had vetoed her plans to attend Firedog's gig in disguise because a) Quinn would spot her a mile off, and b) she couldn't be trusted not to make a scene – 'They reckon as soon as I hear what that pillock's done to my music I'll be storming off to grind his balls to mincemeat.' Fran laughed, but couldn't help thinking that the Butterflies were right, despite Amira's talk of GBH-free reprisals. She was already slightly regretting telling her about the after-gig party. To distract Amira from threats of violence, Fran steered the conversation to the gig on Sunday instead, and arrangements to run through the band's repertoire beforehand. 'I still have to try on my "Crap Idol" T-shirt, remember!'

As soon as she had said goodbye to Amira, Fran got ready to fetch out the ring and bring Ash up to speed on recent developments. And – might as well admit it – have an extended gloat about the 'Quintessential' performance. Then it occurred to her that perhaps she was becoming a little too reliant on Ash always being there. In fact, it was probably time that she started getting used to the idea of him moving on. And thinking of this, the grey empty feeling started creeping back.

On Saturday, the rest of the family left for her aunt's just before lunch and Fran had the house to herself for what felt like the first time in months. For a couple of hours she revelled in the peace and quiet, but by three o'clock the place was already feeling disconcertingly empty. By four o'clock she was bored, by five she was lonely and by six all she wanted to do was to get out of the house and find some people.

All the same, Fran continued to be in two minds about the night ahead. There was still no way she was going to show up at some grotty pub in support of a band she knew to be a rip-off outfit, and a poor one at that. As for the party, she wasn't going to fool herself into thinking that once she got there things between her and Francesca would be any different. Whatever Francesca had said about keeping her and Quinn's relationship under wraps, Fran was ready to bet that they would be all over each other by tonight – leaving Fran adrift in a crowd of older, cooler, scarier strangers. Why should she put herself through all that just because Francesca suddenly decided she needed her again? And yet . . . the two of them had been friends, *best* friends, for nearly ten years. However much things had changed, that still counted for something.

If only, thought Fran, I knew one, just one, person there who I could talk to. Ten to one, she'd end up hiding in the toilet, whinging to Ash. But at this thought, inspiration struck.

Ash could come to the party! She'd use a wish to give him temporary human form! It was obvious, really – she couldn't imagine why it hadn't occurred to her before. This way she'd have someone to gossip with in a corner while he could have a few hours off from his enslavement. It would be her way of saying thank you for being, well, such a good genie. She did briefly wonder if Ash could be trusted to behave, but decided that even if he did start being weird or insulting people or whatever it wouldn't be the end of the world. If Ash chose to make rude remarks about Quinn's hairdo again Fran, for one, wouldn't be complaining.

Feeling very pleased with herself, Fran bounced upstairs and began choosing her outfit for the party. She found she was humming the love song from the audition-she-never-did, but this time the tune didn't feel so melancholy; instead, it made her feel energized and a little reckless. There was a turquoise halter-neck top in her wardrobe that she'd bought ages ago but had never worn in case it made her look fat. Now she tried it on and smiled at her reflection. She undid her plait and let her hair fall in pale ripples over her shoulders. Maybe it wasn't as sun-shiny blonde as Sadie's, but at least it was natural . . . I'll tell everyone that Ash is a foreign-exchange student, she decided, giggling to herself, here to experience the joys of the English education system.

Suddenly Fran was brought up short as she remembered her resolve not to be so dependent on Ash being around. Now here she was about to spend one of her last three wishes so that the genie could keep her company for the evening! Wasn't that a touch . . . clingy? But no, she told herself, she was doing this for Ash's sake as much as for hers. The poor boy deserved to get out of that wretched ring once in a while.

Nonetheless, Fran was taken aback by Ash's reaction to the news that he had seven hours of human freedom at his disposal. He didn't seem to believe it at first, but stared at her, stammering slightly and asking her if she really meant it.

'Of course,' she said for the third time. 'It's no big deal. It's only because I won't know anyone at this party tonight and, well, I thought you'd like the chance to, um, get and out and about properly for a change . . .'

'No one's ever done this for me before,' said Ash emotionally. He fixed her with huge black eyes, then in one graceful movement got down on one knee and knelt before her. 'I thank you.'

It was very different from his usual bowing-and-scraping theatrics and Fran didn't quite know how to respond. She felt embarrassed and oddly guilty. 'I'm just sorry I can't make the wish, you know, permanent,' she muttered.

'Ah, but it's the thought that counts,' said Ash, unexpectedly cheerful again. 'You realize it's been hundreds of years since I've been to a party – do you think there'll be dancing girls?' He began to shimmy on the spot, swaying his hips and pouting over his shoulder at her. Fran hoped this was in imitation of the girls, rather than a demonstration of Ash's ancient Baghdad-style dance moves. Otherwise they could be in trouble.

'I think we'll need to do something about your clothes,' she said, eyeing the silk trousers doubtfully. Ash was now practising wavy arm movements, while hovering in mid-air in the lotus position. 'I'll go and have a look at Dad's stuff.'

'Don't forget the magic words—'

'Oh, how silly of me! I wish that you, Ash, would be human again,' she said quickly.

The fulfilment of the wish wasn't any more dramatic than any of the others, except that Ash came crashing down to the floor with a very solid bump. He swore loudly.

'God, are you all right—' Fran rushed to help him to his feet.

'Me? I'm fabulous! Fantastic! Wonderful! WHOOO-HOOOOO!' He scrambled to his feet, grinning, then caught her by the arms and began to dance round the room, crashing carelessly into the furniture and singing loudly in Arabic. Soon Fran was singing too. The warm pressure of his grip shouldn't have anything special about it and yet the touch of his skin, his *human* skin, on hers, gave her a jolt. It struck her that she hadn't ever touched him until now, but before she could work out why this sudden contact should feel strange, Ash had let go. He began to move from one object in the room to another, tracing the pattern in a photo frame, running his hands over the surface of the wall, caressing the handle on a drawer, smoothing the crease on her pillow.

'Everything feels so much more *real*,' he said at last. 'I'd forgotten there was such a difference.' There was a bruise on his arm from where he'd fallen, and he stroked it in a kind of wonderment. 'It's hard to explain, but everything about me, you, this room, even the air around us . . . it all seems more solid. More . . . alive.'

To Fran, Ash looked exactly the same as he always had. The only change was that the faint wisp of smoke that would occasionally curl from under his trousers was gone. That, and the feeling of shock when he had clasped her arm. 'I'll go and find you some clothes,' she said again. She felt she needed something practical to do.

'Clothes? What's wrong with the ones I'm wearing?' he asked suspiciously.

'Nothing, if you want to turn up to this party looking like an escapee from the circus.'

Fran had hoped that Ash would be too overcome with the thrill of humanhood to pay much attention to the whole What-Not-To-Wear issue, but in this she was mistaken. He was determined to attend his first party for centuries in the style to which he was accustomed, and flatly refused to consider the 'muddy' and 'shapeless' degradations of twenty-first-century British menswear. 'I'm an Arabian prince, not a potato farmer!' Eventually, after nearly half an hour of bickering, Fran persuaded him to ditch the floaty waistcoat for a black T-shirt of her father's. Since Ash was both taller and broader than Mr Roper, the T-shirt turned out to be quite a snug fit – at any rate, Ash spent an indecent amount of time admiring his new look in the bathroom mirror. With his top half looking fairly conventional, the silk trousers and embroidered slippers could just about pass for exotic rather than eccentric. She hoped.

As for Fran, she was more relaxed about her own appearance that she'd been for ages, but even so something still didn't look quite right. She was wondering whether she should try something different with her hair when Ash came into the bedroom and looked her over appraisingly. 'Loose the ring-and-chain combo,' he advised, 'it's spoiling the line of your top.' She took the ring off its chain and put it cautiously on her third finger. Although it slipped on easily, the fit was snug enough for her to feel fairly secure – and Ash was right, it *would* be a shame to spoil the halter-neck effect. In response he was waggling his eyebrows at her suggestively. 'Told you: now you're one hundred per cent delectable.'

The fuss over the clothes had taken longer than Fran had reckoned, and at half past seven she realized with a start that she had completely forgotten about Firedog's performance. Soon it would all be over and Francesca on her way home to make her final preparations for the party. Fran wondered how the Three Lions crowd were reacting and whether Zoë was able to get what she needed on tape. Her attitude to the night ahead had begun to change; she was even feeling a little guilty about pretending to celebrate the gig when she knew it could well be Firedog's last. Making the effort to arrive at the party in good time and to be as sociable as possible no longer seemed like such a sacrifice.

'Fran?'

'Mm?'

'Why didn't you tell me about your singing?'

They were in the kitchen getting something to eat before going out, while the radio burbled away in the background and the rain pattered against the window. It was very peaceful. Up until now Ash had been reminiscing about his days as a playboy prince: his prowess in camel racing, the time he double-crossed a cheating spice merchant and the proper marinade for a roast-quail kebab. This abrupt change of subject took Fran by surprise.

'You knew I was into music. I told you about wanting to be in the band and the audition and everything.'

'Yes, but I didn't realize you were any *good*,' Ash said bluntly. 'I thought the main reason you wanted to be a Firedog was to seduce the dung-beetle blond.'

'Not at all!' Fran reconsidered this. 'OK, I admit the dung-beetle blond was a part of it. Quite a big part, I suppose . . . The truth is, I've always been pretty unfocused about what I wanted to do. Sort of bumbling along, daydreaming, waiting for stuff to happen. But finding you, meeting the Butterflies, getting over Quinn – well, it's as if all the things in my life that were fuzzy have suddenly become clear.'

'Yes. When I was watching you sing with those girls, it was like you suddenly came into focus. Became that bit more . . . defined.'

'Like you getting out of the ring?'

'Exactly.'

It was with some reluctance that Fran prepared to leave the cosy kitchen and venture into the windswept streets. Ash, however, didn't seem to mind the bad weather and strode along in his thin

T-shirt and flimsy trousers, tilting his face to the sky. 'Ah, you can't imagine how good it is to feel rain on my face again . . . Tonight even your dirty English drizzle has its charms.' Under the glow of the street lamps the tiny water droplets in his hair shimmered like silver, and gave a sheen of moisture to his bare brown arms. Yes, thought Fran, there *was* something different about him in human form – a vibrancy, an intensity, that hadn't been there before. Or maybe it had and she just hadn't noticed.

Francesca opened the door wearing the same gracious smile her mother had used at the drinks party the week before.

'Fran! So glad you could make it!' She kissed her lightly on both cheeks. 'Today's been utterly *mad*, of course, but I think things are finally – oh.' Francesca had just seen Ash. She stared, gulped, and stared some more. 'Wow . . . er, hello, I mean.'

'This is Ash,' said Fran airily. 'I hope you don't mind me bringing him along. He's on a foreign-exchange trip – friend of a friend and all that.'

Ash bowed.

'Great.' Francesca had somewhat recovered. 'That's great. Glad you could come along, um, Ash. I hope you enjoy the party.'

'No doubt it will be a night to remember,' he said, charm oozing from every pore.

Francesca ushered them inside, shooting Fran an

incredulous look as soon as Ash's back was turned. Fran smiled blandly. She was beginning to have a good feeling about this evening.

Although it was only quarter to nine, noise levels indicated that the party was already well under way. The Goldsworthys' vast drawing room was almost unrecognizable as the setting for Richard and Marina's cocktail soirée: most of the furniture had been moved elsewhere or pushed against the walls, the ceiling was covered with black and silver helium balloons and the only lighting came from hundreds of tea lights dotted along the mantelpiece and in the now-empty bookshelves. The green glass bowl that stood on the coffee table was heaped with a glistening pile of jelly beans, and an extra table – draped in silver cloth – had been put by the window for drinks. Music was pounding from the stereo.

'Wow, Francesca – it looks fab. But don't your parents mind?'

'Oh, I told them to make themselves scarce for the night.'

Fran looked around the darkened room again and found that she recognized a few faces from the older years in school – and could that be *Wayne* over there by the window? 'Turn's out he's Liam's cousin,' Francesca explained. 'To be honest, I've lost track of who's invited who . . . but on the subject of surprise guests,' she added, lowering her voice, 'when are you going to dish the dirt on your Mystery Hottie?'

Fran found she resented the implication of the question, but was even more resentful of the way in which Francesca was eyeing up *her* genie. Francesca, she saw with a pang, was looking effortlessly chic in skinny jeans and a silk paisley top in purple and bronze. 'I told you: he's a friend of a friend.'

'That so? Well, I have a feeling he's going to be making a lot more friends tonight,' said Francesca sardonically as a girl in a lace dress sauntered over and presented Ash with a drink and a smile. Ash himself looked supremely relaxed and was surveying the room with an anticipatory gleam in his eye. 'Never mind – come and help me stock up the nibbles.'

Fran felt that she really ought to keep an eye on Ash, but it didn't look as if he was having any difficulty adjusting to the human social scene. At any rate, he and the girl in the lace dress were already chatting merrily away. Perhaps he was dazzling her with tales of camel racing. Fran pursed her lips and followed Francesca downstairs.

Once the two of them were alone in the kitchen however, the awkwardness of the last few days returned. After several minutes of silently putting food into bowls, Fran steeled herself to ask how the gig had gone. Francesca looked uncomfortable. 'Not great actually. There was a problem with the mikes and Rob forgot to . . . well, anyway, I think most of the people there thought we were just a bunch of kids messing around. Quinn was pretty upset about it.'

'That's a shame.'

'Yeah, but never mind all that. Let's get back to your exotic new friend—'

'Isn't that the doorbell?'

It was: heralding the arrival of the rest of the Firedogs, plus entourage. Fran took advantage of the distraction to go and check on Ash, who, she was relieved to find, had moved on from Lace Dress Girl and was talking to Wayne. Ash's face lit up when he saw her, but that may have been because she had a plate of brownies in one hand.

'Where did you –' he was beginning to ask, when the people around them began to whistle and cheer. Rob, Jez and Liam had just come into the room, proudly brandishing carrier bags full of beer. They were followed by Quinn and Francesca, who made their entrance with arms entwined around each other, to the sound of more cheering. Somebody began to croon the chorus of 'Looking-Glass Girl'. Quinn raised one arm – like a rock star acknowledging the acclaim of the crowd – before kissing Francesca with extravagant, prolonged and very public enthusiasm. Fran had to look away.

'How are you coping, hon?' asked Sadie, appearing at her elbow as if by magic. 'I mean, seeing your best friend snogging the face off your One True Love must be, like, totally gutting.'

Fran began to mumble something about being happy for Francesca, but Ash got there first. 'Rarely have two people deserved each other more,' he pronounced. 'Right, Fran?'

Zara had arrived to mix up something poisonous on the drinks table, stubbing her cigarette out on Wayne on the way over. At the sound of Ash's voice she turned around and gave him a long stare. 'I don't believe we've met,' she said huskily. She had acquired another eyebrow piercing since Fran saw her last, and was wearing her best sneer in combination with lashings of leopard print.

'Ash, Zara. Zara, Ash. Ash, Sadie. Sadie, Ash,' Fran muttered.

'*You* came with *him*?' Sadie looked from Ash to Fran and back again with disbelief. Then she pulled her glittery pink top a couple of notches lower and simpered, 'Pleased to meet you.'

Ash gave a slight bow to each. 'To make your acquaintance, Fair Ladies, a man would truly pay a price beyond compare.'

There was a bemused pause. 'I take it you're not from round here then,' said Zara through a cloud of cigarette smoke.

'Your perspicacity does you credit. I am, indeed, a citizen of Baghdad.'

'Cool,' said Sadie with a giggle, 'I've never met anyone from the Axis of Evil before.'

Now it was Ash's turn to look confused. 'Is she talking about my ex?' he whispered in Fran's ear.

'For God's sake, Sadie, don't be such a bimbo.' Zara tossed her head. 'All that Axis of Evil stuff is *so* two thousand and one. It's now a democracy over there.'

'Oh yeah, that's right,' said Sadie, beaming. 'You guys are practically Americans!'

Ash put on the sorrowful expression Fran knew so well. 'Alas, I have not been to my home city for many years. I was . . . exiled . . . a long time ago.'

'A rebel, huh?' said Zara, impressed.

'But how *romantic*!' cooed Sadie.

Fran decided to leave them to it.

By now the party was in full swing and Fran wandered around aimlessly for a while, drifting through a haze of pounding music, raucous laughter and flushed, unfamiliar faces. Even so, there was no escaping Francesca and Quinn, who seemed to be everywhere: lips locked and eyes aglow. So much for the hush-hush strategy.

So much, too, for her hopes of spending the night quietly gossiping with Ash. Last time she checked, the Zara 'n' Sadie fan fest had been joined by Lace Dress Girl and the Year Thirteen goth from the Firedog audition. Fran knew it was unfair of her to begrudge Ash's popularity, but she couldn't help thinking that all his complaints about enduring centuries-worth of neurotic females rang a bit hollow now. He didn't seem to have a problem with desperate women once there was none of that tedious Slave of the Ring stuff to cramp his style.

'Bride or groom?'

Fran was suddenly aware that someone was trying to talk to her and looked round, flustered. A boy she'd seen with Liam earlier was standing there grinning at her.

'Don't look so horrified. I was only wondering whether you were a friend of Francesca's or Quinn's.'

'Sorry,' she said, returning his smile. 'I'm a friend of—'

'There you are!' It was Ash, who had shouldered past in a really rather rude way. 'Why do you keep disappearing on me?' he demanded.

'I don't know what you're talking about,' said Fran irritably. The other boy started to say something, but, after a frosty stare from Ash, shrugged and moved on.

'Yes you do. One minute you're there, the next you're not. I saw you in the main room just now, but the moment you caught my eye you ran off again.'

'Did I? Well, perhaps I didn't want to get in the way of your whole Sultan of Smarm performance.'

'*Sultan of Smarm*?' Ash repeated in outraged tones, every inch of him a quiver with indignation. And although Fran was still cross with him, and even crosser with herself for being so, the situation suddenly struck her as being terribly funny. She began to giggle, in spite of herself, and a moment later Ash was laughing too. 'Come on,' he said at last. 'There must be somewhere in this place where we can find a bit of quiet.'

Fran wanted a glass of water and so the two of them began to make their way downstairs. Francesca was standing in the hallway talking to Rob; she gave them a little wave, which Rob followed up with a grade-A glower. Sadie had been ignoring him ever since they got to the party and it didn't take a genius to work out who was to blame. 'Ali Baba, I presume,' he said, moving to block Ash's path.

'Fallen among the Forty Thieves,' agreed Ash serenely. 'Which number are you?'

Rob's face turned angry red. Francesca, however, cut in before he could reply. 'Fran,' she exclaimed brightly, hoping to cause a distraction, 'that's a pretty ring! Have I seen it before?'

'It's just a bit of cheap tat,' Fran mumbled, trying to hide the offending finger behind her back. Too late: Francesca had caught her hand.

'Look, the purple stone matches my top – can I try it on?'

And somehow, before Fran had time to react, the treacherous ring had slipped off her finger and on to Francesca's.

'*Love* the bling. Hang on though, it seems to have got stuck . . . Funny, it felt so loose when I was putting it on . . .' She began to twist the ring back and forth.

'No, wait, you mustn't –' cried Ash and Fran together. But amid the dull roar of the party, the urgency of their plea was lost. Francesca, her attention wholly focused on getting free of the ring, barely heard. As for Rob, he was beginning to think that his fifth rum and coke of the evening had been a mistake, because there was a moment or two when the insufferable Ash actually seemed to flicker before his eyes. He shook his head blearily, only to find his vision was clouded with purple haze. Yeah, he was starting to feel well dodgy . . . Rob staggered off to find a toilet.

'Sorry, Fran,' said Francesca, 'looks like I'll have to go and run it under the tap. Just wait a sec.' Quinn was gesturing to her from the kitchen and, smiling, she turned to go.

'Oh my God,' said Fran, whose heart was thundering so hard she could barely breathe or move, 'we *have* to get that ring!' She gazed at Ash, horror-struck, then did a double take. 'Hold on: why are you still here? I mean, if you're a genie again, surely only Francesca is able to see you?'

'I don't know,' said Ash blankly. 'This situation has never happened to me before . . . I suppose just because the ring has changed owners doesn't cancel your wish. Or not entirely.'

'But what are we going to *do*?'

'There's not much I can do,' he said grimly. 'I'm in the ring's power now and that means I'm in hers, too.' He began to go after the new Commander of the Ring, Fran following helplessly. 'Listen, Francesca—'

But someone had turned up the music in the kitchen, making conversation temporarily impossible as blasts of drum 'n' bass battled it out with the hardcore techno emanating from upstairs. 'RING . . . SLAVE . . . WISH . . . SEVEN,' bawled Ash as Francesca smiled, nodded and obviously didn't hear a word. By the time the volume had returned to less deafening levels she was locked in yet another snog-fest with Quinn beside the fridge. 'Ah well, no one can say I didn't try,' said Ash, shrugging.

'She's not going to get away with this,' Fran snapped. Francesca already possessed the alpha-male boyfriend, the rock-chick glamour and the designer house, but Fran was damned if she was going to have her genie as well. It was time for brute force, not feebleness. She marched over to Francesca, ignoring the fact that she was still busily stuffing her tongue down Quinn's throat, and prepared to tear the ring off her finger herself.

Unfortunately, before she was got within grabbing distance, Sadie popped up between them.

'Hi, guys. Enjoying the party?'

'I've had better,' said Ash distractedly.

'Didn't realize you Middle Easterners were such party animals,' remarked Quinn. He was now playing with Francesca's hands, one thumb idly stroking her ring finger. 'Isn't against your religion?'

'Oh, but they have belly dancers and Turkish Delight and snake charmers and stuff,' Sadie enthused. 'Must be, like, awesome.'

'I wish we could see for ourselves,' Francesca said politely.

Brrrrring! went the doorbell.

The dancing girls were the first to arrive: a-flutter with rainbow silks, a-tinkle with silver bells and flashing more bling than a rappers' convention. They were trailed by Security – an immense man wearing an immense turban, immense moustache and with an even more immense scimitar stuck in his belt. A group of musicians in scarlet robes arrived next, followed by a procession of people laden down with silver and gold platters. Last to enter was a very fat woman carrying a tray of scented oils and rather sinister metal implements on her head.

Ash took charge. 'Caterers – into the kitchen.

Band and dance troop – upstairs. Masseuse – guest bathroom.'

The four girls sashayed up to the main room, blithely impervious to the dumbstruck expressions of those they passed. The scary scimitar man stumped after them. There was a momentary pause, then the techno beat was replaced by a medley of lutes, pipes and drums as the band struck up. Soon this was joined by the sound of stamping feet and raucous cheers.

'Er . . . um . . . did you arrange for all this?' Francesca asked Ash as she stood back to allow the masseuse's assistant to sprinkle rose water over the hall carpet.

'In a manner of speaking.'

'Very kind of you,' she said faintly.

Ash swept back to inspect the kitchen. 'Quails' eggs, larks' tongues, Osmanli quinces, Omani peaches, citron sorbet, honey tarts, candied figs . . .' he rattled off, checking the trays one by one. 'Not forgetting the peanut butter and jelly sandwiches of course . . . glass of iced sherbet, anyone?'

'Ohmigod!' shrieked Sadie. 'There's, like, a *camel* in the garden!'

After the initial shock, it wasn't long before Francesca's guests got into the spirit of things, considerably helped by the constant flow of sherbet 'n' champagne cocktails. Sure, the surprise Arabian

Nights theme was a bit full on for a house party but everyone knew the Goldsworthys were loaded. Or maybe it was down to Ashazra-whatsit – according to which rumour you believed, he was either a Bollywood film star or the son of a Saudi oil tycoon.

'I thought it best to cancel the snake charmer,' the man in question confided to Fran over a roast swan's leg. 'I shouldn't like to go overboard, after all.'

Fran was still trying, and failing, to get a grip on recent events. To calm her nerves she had downed three glasses of the fizzy sherbet drink, which tasted (not unpleasantly) of liquid Refreshers. As a result their situation felt slightly less urgent, but considerably more muddled.

'Oh, Ash,' she wailed, 'everything's in such a hideous mess. I don't know where Francesca's got to and any minute now she could figure out what the ring's for or – flippin' hell – make a wish for something *really* disastrous.'

'Don't get your turban in twist.' In the exhilaration of procuring a party after his own heart, Ash appeared to have got over his earlier anxieties. 'If she wishes for anything horrendous by accident you can always use the emergency-exit clause.'

Fran stared at him uncomprehendingly. 'What are you talking about?'

'The old "I wish I could wake up and find this was all a dream" trick,' he said airily. 'It's part of the

Sacred Seal Health and Safety Directive, I believe. Basically your brain is tricked into thinking whatever mess you've got yourself into was a simple matter of nodding off on the job. It's the only wish that overrides the seven-hour time limit. Didn't I mention this before?'

Fran was speechless. She thought of the agonies she'd endured over Boris and the Candid Camera Conjuring Tour . . . the stomach-churning guilt she'd felt about Mr Mayhew . . . and all the while, her git of a genie could have cancelled everything out in the blink of an eye!

'C'mon Fran, don't look like that; spending a wish to forget a wish is such a waste hardly anyone ever does it. And anyway, we should be making the most of an authentic Arabian Nights Entertainment – a much classier wish than anything *you've* come up with, I might add.'

'Since when were peanut butter sandwiches authentically Arabian?'

He waved the issue off impatiently. 'You know what? We should go and dance.'

'This is an *emergency*, Ash. We can't just—'

While she was still protesting, he took her by the wrist and marched her upstairs to the main room again. The dancing girls had taken centre stage, jiggling and wriggling with expert skill, while their scimitar-equipped minder cast a forbidding eye over would-be molesters. With the musicians perched around the sofa, this didn't leave a lot of space for everyone else, and the party had surged into the other rooms on the floor. Zara and Sadie were using Mr Goldsworthy's office desk – a monolith of finest Amazonian teak – as a DIY dance podium. Goth Girl was having a stuffed-date-eating contest with Wayne Roberts in the guest bedroom. Rob Crawford was in the bathroom having wax picked out of his ears by the fat masseuse. 'Isn't it fabulous?' exclaimed Ash with pride. But Fran was still hanging back.

'Ash,' she faltered, 'is the emergency exit thingy the wish you told me about before, the one more powerful than enchantment?'

He hadn't heard her, or not properly. 'Enchanting! That's exactly right! All this –' waving towards the dancers, the band, the trays of exotic canapés – 'is my chance, my one chance, to show you something from *my* life.' His eyes were shining and his cheeks flushed, everything about him glowed. 'I know we're in a fix, but sometimes with magic you have to go with the flow . . . leave things to fate, luck, whatever. In a few hours it will all be over anyway. Why not enjoy what we have? Please?'

Fran looked back at him, and felt a surge of dizziness. Delayed shock combined with one too many sherbet cocktails. The musicians had struck up a new tune, something with a maddeningly quick, bright beat, something it was impossible not to move your feet to. Champagne was sparkling in her head, there was a heady smell of rose perfume and smoke and strange spices in the air and the whole house seemed to throb with music and bodies and laughter. Magic. Fate. Luck. Whatever. Dazedly, she let herself be drawn into the crowd. 'Just one dance,' Ash murmured in her ear, 'and then we'll find your scary ginger friend, get our ring back and things will return to normal. I promise.' But what does normal mean any more, she wanted to ask. How can things be normal ever again? She leaned a little closer to him and closed her eyes.

'YOU BASTARD!'

Conversation faltered, heads turned.

'TWO-FACED CHEATING SCUM!'

The music paused, dancers halted.

'CRETINOUS, TALENTLESS, PLAGIARIST PIG!'
Smack.

And, to the sound of collective gasps, a room full of Quinn Adams's closest friends and admirers saw him being slapped around the face by a very angry girl nobody had ever seen before.

'WELL?' demanded Amira. 'WELL?' She fetched a crumpled poster from her pocket and jabbed her finger at the line announcing 'Tonight at the Three Lions – Firedog sings "Looking-Glass Girl"'. 'WHAT HAVE YOU GOT TO SAY FOR YOURSELF?'

But Quinn could only splutter witlessly, leaving Francesca to step into the breech. 'Look,' she said,

'I don't know who you are or what the hell this is about, but you can't barge into my house and start assaulting my boyfriend.'

'Too right,' chorused Rob and Liam and the rest of the Firedog entourage. They were joined by the Baghdad bouncer, who was clutching his scimitar in a menacing sort of way. Quinn took courage from it.

'The girl's a lunatic, or a crazed fan or some-thing,' he announced. 'I've never met her before in my life.'

Amira looked ready to explode. 'Why, you little sh—'

'Don't talk to Quinn that way,' said Zara.

'You are, like, *so* out of order,' said Sadie.

'SHUT UP.'

This time it was Francesca who was doing the shouting. She had her hands on her hips and was breathing hard. 'Right. Obviously, there is some sort of problem here, but this is hardly the time and place to sort it.' With a visible effort, she smoothed her hair and put on her hostess-with-the-mostest smile. 'I just wish we could leave off the dramatics and get on with enjoying the party . . . Candied fig, anyone?'

'Camel turd, more like,' said Ash, shooting a dis-gusted look at Quinn. Thanks to Francesca's wish, Amira's entrance hadn't disrupted the festivities for more than a minute or so, but for Fran, the dizzy, dreamy feeling of before had swiftly evaporated and she and Ash were now standing glumly in a corner. She couldn't help feeling that Quinn's reprieve – however short-lived – was a bad omen. It was clear that AWOL wishes caused nothing but trouble.

'Wait here,' she told the genie. 'I'm going to put a stop to this business once and for all.'

This time she found Francesca relatively quickly; even better, she was temporarily free of company. But before Fran could make her move, somebody else once again got in the way. Amira was slightly glassy-eyed, but her hug had lost none of its bone-crushing strength.

'Fran! Sorry for making a bit of scene back there – I think it was this recording, see, that Zoë played me and . . . well, I don't really remember why it got me so mad . . . but . . . isn't it a fab party?'

'Yes, yes it is,' said Fran distractedly. 'Hi, Francesca, you know the ring you borrowed? Have you managed to get it off yet?'

'Ring? What – oh, sorry, I forgot . . . yes, it's still stuck, I'm afraid.'

'Hey,' said Amira, plucking her arm, 'me and the girls—'

'This isn't really a good time, Amira. Look, Francesca, I *have* to get the ring back. *Right now*.'

'Well, there's no need to be aggressive about it. I thought it was just a bit of cheap tat anyhow?'

'Er, yeah, but it's got sentimental value—'

'All I wanted to say is that the Stamping Butterflies think it's so great—'

'What do you suggest then? Wrenching it off with pliers?'

'– now you've joined the band.'

'Band? What band?' frowned Francesca.

'*My* band,' said Amira. 'That Fran's going to sing in. Right, Fran?'

'Fran?'

There was a loud crash. Fran turned round to find one of the dancing girls sprawled on the floor, merrily entangled with a member of the school rugby team, while Francesca looked in horror at the green glass bowl now lying in about six different pieces around them. They must have fallen over it on the way down. 'Dad is going to *kill* me,' she moaned. 'Things are getting way out of hand.'

It was true that the evening was starting to deteriorate. A food fight had erupted in the hall and quite a few guests, as well as the wallpaper, were wearing a light smattering of squashed dates and citron sorbet. While the dancing girls were on a break, their minder was demonstrating his scimitar-thrusting technique on a thousand pounds-worth of damask curtains, while the masseuse was mixing up a batch of seaweed foot scrub in the toilet bowl. Several people had got bitten in the course of attempting to pet the camel, several more were beginning to realize that iced sherbet and vodka Redbull don't mix.

Ash surveyed the shambles and shook his head disapprovingly. 'You just can't get the staff these days.'

'Get rid of them then!' hissed Fran, who was crouched on the floor simultaneously trying to soothe Francesca, gather up the glass and get at the ring. 'Tell your, er, staff to go wait in the utility room and lock the door on them while we get things sorted.'

'And how do you suggest I do that?'

'You're a prince – you're meant to be good at ordering people around. Threaten to withhold their tip or something!'

'I'll help,' said Amira unexpectedly. 'I dunno about royalty and that, but bossing people is my speciality.'

Ash put on his haughtiest expression, stalked into the main room, clapped his hands and started shouting something in Old Arabic. Then he pushed his way downstairs and did some more bellowing in the direction of the kitchen. He got some dark looks and even darker mutterings from the 'staff', but they eventually tore themselves away from their various activities and allowed Amira to shepherd them into the utility room on the ground floor. There were some boos and jeers from the other guests, but by now most people were too far gone to care.

Meanwhile, Francesca was still hyperventilating about the bowl. 'It's a Venetian antique! Collectors' item!' she kept wailing. 'Dad bought in Murano for three grand!'

Fran decided that now was not the time to break the news about the scimitar-slashed curtains. 'There, there,' she soothed, patting Francesca's hand while attempting a surreptitious tug at the ring, 'I'm sure the insurance will cover it.'

'OW!' A boiled quail's egg had just bounced off Francesca's head as the food fight surged up the stairs and on to the landing. 'For God's sake,' she said crossly, 'I wish you'd all just *GROW UP*.'

Amira 'Triple Platinum' Patel pushed back the sleeve of her Armani suit to check her watch; she had a breakfast meeting with the boys from EMI tomorrow and couldn't afford to stay out late. In the meantime she suppressed a yawn and tried to show a passing interest in the conversation at hand.

'. . . So you're an estate agent, you say?'

'Sure am,' said Quinn Adams. 'Though as vocations go, I like to think it's more about the people than the property.' He treated her to the warm, soulful smile suburban housewives found impossible to resist when he was showing them double-glazed conservatories. 'And what do you do?'

'I'm in the music business.'

'Oh, you work for a record company?'

'I own one.'

'Impressive.' Quinn retousled his thinning locks in what he fondly imagined was a boyish manner. 'Y'know,' he said in his most chocolatey tones, 'I used to be in a rock band myself. Didn't ever come to much, but people seemed to think we showed a *lot* of promise.'

'Really.' Amira couldn't remember the last time she'd had a night out and hadn't been cornered by some middle-aged bore with a Mick Jagger complex. As Quinn launched into his reminiscences, she scanned the room in hope of rescue . . .

Rob and Sadie Crawford were huddled by the mantelpiece, bickering over whose turn it was to drink and whose to drive. Suddenly Sadie clutched Rob's arm. 'Ohmigosh, it's *him*!'

'Him who?'

'You know, the actor. The totally *hot* actor. He was in that film we saw, the one where he gave the kiss of life to what's-her-face. You know – that famous actress. With the French boyfriend?' Christ, her husband could be gormless at times. 'Never mind. I'm going over.'

As she pushed her way towards the window, Sadie reflected that if she'd known there was going to be a famous actor at the party she would at least have got her roots done. Five kids down the line, her cleavage wasn't what it used to be either . . . Just as well Robbie had promised her a new set of boobs for Christmas.

'Well hell*oo* there,' she gushed, 'I hope you don't mind me saying so, but I think you're, like, *majorly* talented.'

'Um, thank you,' mumbled Wayne, turning pink. Even after his BAFTA award, not to mention coming seventh place in *Cosmo*'s Fifty Most Fanciable list two years running, he wasn't much good at dealing with this kind of thing.

'I've always been *such* a fan. Like, *obsessed.*'

Wayne shuffled his feet uncomfortably and caught the eye of a dark-haired woman standing near by, who bared her teeth in a wolfish smile. There was something about the smile that sent a shudder down Wayne's spine. She was swathed in fur, had a diamond stud in her nose and was smoking a cigar. A thick-set man dressed in black was standing beside her, with a holster-shaped bulge under his jacket and a long scar running down his face. When any of the guests got too close, he moved his hand towards the bulge and glowered. On second thoughts, Wayne decided that a maybe a demented fan wasn't such bad company after all. 'And what do you do?' he was beginning to ask when he became aware of a commotion on the other side of the room. It looked as if some young girl had fainted.

*

'It's all right,' said Fran to the circle of concerned faces around her, 'I think the poor thing just needs a bit of air. If someone could help me get her out of here –'

'Allow me,' offered a rather charming young man in silk trousers. Between the two of them, they half-led, half-carried a very groggy Francesca out to the spare room, which was otherwise unoccupied. Although her eyes remained closed she was moaning slightly.

'Looks like she's had a bit too much to drink,' said Fran, hastening back from the bathroom with a glass of water. 'Oh good, she's coming round.'

But after one horror-stricken look at Fran, the girl promptly fainted on to the bed again.

'Do you know who she is?' asked the young man.

'I'm afraid not – though I suppose her parents must be around here somewhere. Mind you, she *does* look familiar . . . and so do you, actually.' She looked at him again with a slight frown. 'It's rather odd; everyone I've met tonight seems so familiar and yet I can't quite work out what we're all doing here. I mean, from the state of this house –' glancing around the room disapprovingly – 'it's the kind of student party I remember from music college.'

'Fran,' said the young man earnestly (he really was *very* charming!), 'I think it's time you realized what's going on. Look at the ring.'

Fran's eye fell on a piece of that ridiculously kitsch jewellery young people were so fond of. What they used to call 'bling' in her day. Nonetheless, there *was* something strangely compelling about that shiny purple jewel . . . before she knew it she had taken Francesca's limp hand to examine the ring better. As her own hand made contact with the gem, she felt a cold shock jolt through her body.

I wish you'd all just GROW UP . . .

Grow up

Grow up

'No,' she whispered disbelievingly, heart thundering, throat dry. 'No, I don't . . . I won't . . . this can't be happening.' As if in a dream, she brought her hands up to touch her curiously light head of hair. This neat, sleek bob couldn't be *hers*, could it? Where did this silk shirt come from, and what about this faint, expensively delicious perfume she could smell? 'It can't . . .'

'It already has,' said Ash impatiently. 'Now's your chance – grab the ring, quick, and do an emergency exit special before she comes round again.'

Too late. In a matter of seconds Francesca went from dead to the world to full blown hysterics. In the end, Ash had to hold her down while Francesca tugged at the ring with the ruthlessness of desperation – once, twice, three times. And then, at last, amid the screeches and wheezes and thrashing limbs, it was hers.

'I wish,' she quavered, 'for everyone to wake up from Francesca's wish for us to be grown-ups and find it was all a dream.'

'OW!' Francesca was slumped across the bed, sucking her bruised and swollen finger. 'Flippin' hell, Fran, I should sue you for assault. *And* battery.'

'Sorry,' gasped Fran, still trembling with shock. 'There wasn't any other way to get it off . . . are you going to be all right?'

'I'll live. Though I think the pain must have made me pass out for a moment; I had the weirdest feeling . . . dream or – or *something* back there.'

'I know what you mean,' said Fran, rubbing her eyes. She could remember Ash yelling at her to make the wish, she could remember saying the words, but up until that moment everything was hopelessly blurred. Like the memory of a memory of a dream. Elsewhere, the rest of the guests had all closed their eyes for a second or so, yawned hugely, then rubbed their faces in a bleary sort of way. It was, in any case, nearly one a.m. and they'd been partying hard. 'Do you know where Ash went? He was here a minute ago.'

'No, and I don't know where Quinn's got to either. Let's go find them.' They opened the bedroom door and stepped back into the hubbub of the party. 'Fran-flakes?'

'Mm?'

'You really like him, don't you?'

'I keep telling you, Quinn and I—'

'Not Quinn. Ash.' Francesca was paused at the entrance to the drawing room and smiling at her: not her new grown-up smile, nor the old Francesca grin, but something in between the two.

'*Ash?* No! No, I don't. We – I can't. No.' She was overcome by confusion, and a kind of helplessness.

'Oh for God's sake! The problem with you, Fran, is that you're so darned *wet*.' Then her face softened. 'I've seen the way he's been looking at you, girl. I . . . I haven't noticed much lately, I know, but I've noticed that. Maybe it's time you did something about it.'

Left behind on the landing, Fran was still trying to collect her thoughts when Ash reappeared, wearing a part-guilty, part-nervous expression to mirror hers. She gave herself a shake. Another crisis, no doubt. Other matters – other feelings – would just have to wait.

'What now?' she asked, going to join him at the head of the stairs. He didn't need to answer, however, since the noise coming from the utility room downstairs made the problem plain enough. The Arabian Nights staff were getting restless. And vocal. Very angry and very vocal.

'They're demanding to be paid immediately,' he explained, 'with compensation for false imprisonment and stress. The masseuse is saying that if we don't let her out this minute she'll set the Palace Guard on us.'

'But she can't do that . . . can she?'

They both flinched as a sickening crunch announced that the Baghdad bouncer had taken matters into his own hands and was attempting to break down the door with his scimitar. Yells and shrieks from the other end of the hallway indicated that someone had let the camel into the kitchen.

'The novelty of returning to flesh and blood is starting to lose its charm,' said Ash, who was turning a shade paler with each crunch of the scimitar. 'In truth, I was rather hoping to spend the rest of eternity with all my limbs intact. Perhaps, O Fair Mistress—'

'My last wish,' Fran said quietly. She heaved a sigh. 'But I don't have much choice, do I?' Right on cue, there was another crunch, followed by a blood-curdling roar. One more blow and the door would be down. 'So what should I ask for?'

'Another "and then they woke up to find it was all a horrible nightmare" sounds good to me.'

Fran frowned. Nerve-racking as the last few hours had been, she didn't want them wiped from her memory. The sight of the fat masseuse picking wax out of Rob Crawford's ear was something she'd always cherish. 'I don't know . . .'

'Then think of something else! Anything! Just get them out of here!'

'OK, fine, I, uh, wish that some nice people would come and collect all the Arabian, er, entertainments and they'd all disappear on a lovely trip far away from here.'

'Inarticulate but adequate,' said Ash. 'I'll book a coach.'

'Is this your friends' first trip to London?' enquired the twinkly blonde tour guide who had materialized on the doorstep. She came equipped with a clipboard, a perky smile and an even perkier red suit.

'Yes,' said Fran, 'and I'm afraid they don't speak much English.'

'Audio guides are available in fifteen different languages,' the woman informed her brightly. 'I thought we'd whip round the city's major landmarks, followed by a visit to West End club. Sound good?'

'Delightful,' said Ash, translating rapidly for the benefit of the assembled Baghdadians, who appeared to have got over their fury at the utility-room incarceration. The bouncer had his arm round the fat masseuse, who was pointing out things of interest on a map of London. The dancing girls were inspecting their collection of mobile telephone numbers – scrawled on arms, scribbled on napkins – with some bemusement. The caterers were handing round little packs of canapés for the journey. Meanwhile, one of the musicians was picking out something suspiciously like '(We're all going on a) Summer Holiday' on his lute.

'Okey-dokey, people, it's time to get this show on the road . . .' Without more ado, the guide began to shepherd her charges outside and on to the waiting bus, which bore the legend SESAME OPEN-TOP TOURS on its side. Parked behind it was a car with some kind of horsebox attached, into which a chauffeur was tenderly escorting the camel. 'Cool Britannia here we come!' A few minutes later, to the sound of cheers and popping corks, bus, car and camel drove off into the night.

The Arabian Nights Entertainment might have gone, but there was no chance of it being forgotten. There was the smashed-up door to the utility room for one thing. The seaweed-stuffed toilet, the shattered bowl and scimitar-slashed curtains for another. Not to mention the pounding headaches of those who had overindulged on the iced sherbet. Right now, Zara was examining the camel-bite on her upper arm and swearing loudly. Francesca was coming to terms with the fact that she was about to be grounded for the rest of her life.

'Such a shame,' the genie was saying. 'I mean, I

know things got out of hand, but everyone was having so much fun up till now.'

'So much fun,' Fran echoed faintly. She felt over-whelmed with exhaustion. She momentarily closed her eyes and, through a mist of purple haze, saw her and Ash, swaying, among perfume and heat and wild music. *Maybe it's time you did something about it* . . . But there was nothing she could do, nothing at all, because there were no more wishes. No more magic. No more heart's desire. No more Ash. Fran touched the ring again and felt how loose it had become on her finger, as if it was already impatient to move on. Who would the ring find next? Perhaps it would be a stranger in the street, perhaps it would be someone she knew.

'Ash,' she said, 'let's go and sit somewhere quiet for a bit.'

He looked at her sadly. 'We haven't got much time.'

'I know.'

'In fifteen minutes, it will be half one and my seven hours in human form will be over. I'll be back in the ring and I won't be your genie any more. We'll never—'

'I understand,' said Fran, and she took his hand.

So they went and sat side by side on the stairs, and quietly talked about the things that only the two of them could share. About vengeance and its permutations, wannabe rock stars and man-eating rocs, and whether peanut butter 'n' jelly was superior comfort food to chocolate spread. They reminisced about Boris and his squeaky trousers, Mr Mayhew and the purple blusher, Quinn and the Bad Hair Day.

To Fran it seemed impossible that in ten minutes or less the warmth and weight of Ash's body against hers would dissolve into memory. All around them, meanwhile, were the sights and sounds of a party on the wane. A few people were still stumbling around on the dance floor and a few more were hunched in corners, snogging in a desultory sort of way. Squashed dates and burst balloons littered the floor. Robbie Williams was crooning on the stereo, accompanied by a slurred chorus from the rugby lads. From the upstairs bathroom came the sound of somebody being violently sick.

'And that other wish, the one that turned into a dream?' Fran asked. 'The one where Francesca wanted us to grow up?'

'What do you want to know?'

'Was I – did I –' She paused. 'Did I look anything like Sabrina?'

'No.'

'Then . . . did – did I smell of burnt beans and have mascara down my face?'

'No.'

'Then what was I like?'

He looked at her and smiled. 'Like Fran. Like

apricots and honey. Like pale silk and skies of silver. You were like you.'

Fran looked back, right into his eyes. They were dark and glittering. She had a lot of things to say and only minutes – seconds – to say them. 'I wish . . .' she murmured as she leaned to kiss him, 'I wish . . .'

It seemed to happen of itself, like blinking against dust. She could feel him tremble against her, the warmth and weight of him, and a faint scent of smoke and spices. Tears stung her eyes and yet it didn't matter, nothing mattered any more, but this. Their final moment.

Well, slightly more than a moment. A good few minutes in fact. Nearly five. And counting.

'You know, I thought we'd run out of time –'

'Your watch must be fast –'

Every second could be their last. Once more they clutched at each other with shining eyes and stammering hearts. Then Fran abruptly disentangled herself. 'No, I mean it, you should be gone by now We're getting on for ten minutes past the end of the wish and *you're still here.*'

There was a breathless silence. Ash swallowed, tried to speak, and found that every muscle was frozen in disbelief. 'Oi, lovebirds,' said Cath Watson, shoving past, 'stop clogging up the stairs.'

'You're still here,' Fran whispered again. *Some wishes are more powerful than enchantment . . .* As if in a dream, she bent to pick up Ash's arm-bracelet, which was lying in two pieces on the stair below. It looked as if the metal had been snapped in half. Had her kiss done that, or the wish behind it, or both?

In turn, he took her hand and slipped the ring off her finger. It felt light in his palm, the only gleam in the jewel was the sheen of plastic. '"Employ Suitably for Hart Desiring",' said Ash, his voice shaking a little. 'But I never was much good at following instructions . . . Fran, I –' And then, to his eternal embarrassment, his voice choked up.

'Careful what you wish for,' said Fran, and grinned. She kissed him again. 'Welcome to London, Prince Ashazrahim.'

For a long while they had been aware of nothing except each other, but now, slowly, the sounds of the outside world began to filter through. The rugby lads were still singing along to Robbie Williams, somebody was still throwing up in the bathroom. And somebody else was shouting, shouting in a familiar sort of way . . . 'TWO-FACED CHEATING SCUM! CRETINOUS, TALENTLESS, PLA-GIARIST PIG! SLIMY, SWINDLING, TONE-DEAF –'

It seemed that the ring's power had been broken in more ways than one.

'Hey, everyone!' yelled Rob, charging out on to the landing. 'Some chick's gone mad and smacked Quinn in the eye!'

'Fran!' said Francesca, stumbling out after him.

'She's saying she's going to take the Firedogs to court! And you know all about it!'

'Don't answer her, Fran!' bellowed Amira behind her. 'You're a Stamping Butterfly now – that information's classified!'

Fran and Ash exchanged glances and sighed. 'What next?' asked Fran.

'Who knows?' Ash gave a broad, slow smile. 'Fate. Magic. Luck. Whatever. But as my good friend Scheherazade would say, *that* will be a story for another day . . .'

Acknowledgements

I don't have an enchanted ring, but I do know a lot of geniuses. So a big thank you to Sarah Davies, Harriet Wilson, Fliss Stevens and Lauren Buckland at Macmillan, and the magical Sarah Molloy at A. M. Heath.

A special – and long overdue – mention to Matt Symonds, Sultan of Sagacity, without whom this writing lark might never have started.

A selected list of titles available from Macmillan Children's Books

The prices shown below are correct at the time of going to press. However, Macmillan Publishers reserves the right to show new retail prices on covers, which may differ from those previously advertised.

Rose Wilkins

So Super Starry	978-0-330-42087-9	£5.99
So Super Stylish	978-0-330-43135-4	£5.99

Jaclyn Moriarty

Feeling Sorry for Celia	978-0-330-39725-7	£5.99
Finding Cassie Crazy	978-0-330-41803-0	£5.99
Becoming Bindy Mackenzie	978-0-330-43885-9	£5.99

All Pan Macmillan titles can be ordered from our website,
www.panmacmillan.com, or from your local bookshop
and are also available by post from:
Bookpost, PO Box 29, Douglas, Isle of Man IM99 1BQ
Credit cards accepted. For details:
Telephone: 01624 677237
Fax: 01624 670923
Email: bookshop@enterprise.net
www.bookpost.co.uk

Free postage and packing in the United Kingdom